M000167315

Stone Broke Heiress

Stone Broke Heiress

Danielle Owen-Jones

bookouture

Published by Bookouture in 2022

An imprint of Storyfire Ltd.
Carmelite House
50 Victoria Embankment
London EC4Y 0DZ

www.bookouture.com

Copyright © Danielle Owen-Jones, 2022

Danielle Owen-Jones has asserted her right to be identified as the author of this work.

All rights reserved. No part of this publication may be reproduced, stored in any retrieval system, or transmitted, in any form or by any means, electronic, mechanical, photocopying, recording or otherwise, without the prior written permission of the publishers.

ISBN: 978-1-80314-057-5
eBook ISBN: 978-1-80314-056-8

This book is a work of fiction. Names, characters, businesses, organizations, places and events other than those clearly in the public domain, are either the product of the author's imagination or are used fictitiously. Any resemblance to actual persons, living or dead, events or locales is entirely coincidental.

For Mum, Tom, and Poppy...
Thank you for always believing in me

ONE

It's hard to believe that six months ago, I was the heiress to a multimillion-pound soup empire. Now, I'm standing in a giant bin. A Super Saver supermarket bin, to be precise. My limited edition Hunter wellies, that once graced Glastonbury's VIP area and the idyllic fields of Cheshire for my horse riding lessons, are stained by rotting rubbish.

I'm manically rummaging around for any food worth saving. Packs of tomatoes emblazoned with today's expiry date? They'll do. Wonky celery sticks? Golden. A battered bag of potatoes? Jackpot.

A flashlight momentarily blinds me as I chuck the food over the side of the bin. 'Come on, Bella, we only have a few minutes left, hurry!' shouts my fellow dumpster diver, as he piles discarded fruit and vegetables into a huge bag.

'It's Sunday,' I whisper. 'You know they'll have thrown out the good stuff. I just need to dig a little deeper...'

I grab a bag and it splits, splattering everything, including myself, with a foul-smelling yellow sludge. I shudder. I'd rather not guess what it is. Then, I spy exactly what I'm looking for –

at the opposite end of the enormous dustbin, of course. Unde-terred, I hike my wellies up to cover my filthy Armani jeans and begin to make a run, or a slow traipse, towards it.

Never in my life did I imagine I would be looking at a bin bag with the same desire that I usually reserved for an Hermès Birkin.

'I found it!' I excitedly shout after peeking into the bag, heaving it out from the rest of the pile and clambering down from the ten-foot-tall bin. 'You'll be happy with this one.'

'I'm sure I will.' My scavenging partner smiles and picks a soggy lettuce leaf from my birds' nest hair. 'But we need to get out of here.'

I switch off the torch as we sprint across the supersized car park, each lugging four heavy bin liners fit to burst with our technically stolen goods.

We climb into the back of the bright yellow VW camper van to admire our handiwork. 'Wait until you see this.' I grin, grabbing the bag that is the holy grail of supermarket waste. I tip it upside down and out fall countless bags of healthy-looking fruit and vegetables, Hovis loaves, tins of baked beans, cartons of orange juice and packets of bashed biscuits, completely filling the floor space.

My partner's eyes light up as he studies the groceries. 'A perfect haul,' he says. Together, we shuffle the goods around the cramped boot of the van before crawling into the front seats, and he twists the key to breathe life into the knackered engine.

We wait patiently, side by side, as the twenty-year-old camper van slowly groans to a start. I catch my reflection in the battered mirror and smile as we sit, surrounded by bursting bin bags and discarded vegetables. The whiff of his aftershave, combined with a tinge of smelly bin juice, fills the air as we roll away into the night, like a budget Bonnie and Clyde.

Six months earlier

'To Arabella and Francis.' Clink.

The best bit about being newly engaged (aside from my gorgeous fiancé, of course) was the way my diamond ring would clink against my champagne glass, the sparkles dazzling against the dancing bubbles inside the crystal flute.

'The proposal was in Capri, wasn't it?'

'Mm-hmm.' I swooned at the memory of my now-fiancé (eek!) Francis's romantic proposal on our one-year anniversary. He'd hired a private gozzo boat to take us to the Grotta Azzurra – and I could feel myself grinning dreamily at the memory of the spectacular sea cave, one of the wonders of the world. He took my hand in his, and stretched his long legs into a wobbly kneel, thanks to the gently lapping waves underneath the boat. Then, he asked me to be his wife. I said yes, but only after a surreptitious glance at the huge rock nestled inside the blood-red Cartier ring box.

My daydream was interrupted by the popping of champagne bottles, which peppered the soundtrack of our engagement party. A band played softly in one corner, and guests dressed in their finery laughed and chatted on the rooftop terrace that showcased a spectacular view of the sun setting over Liverpool.

'Let's see the ring again,' my best friend, Tabby, said. I shimmied proudly as I held my hand out in the middle of the group and their heads lowered for a closer inspection. I'd never tire of showing off the stunning rock. It was perfect; a diamond-encrusted platinum band with a whopping princess-cut stone in the middle. It felt heavy on my ring finger as I admired it in the flicker of the candlelight.

'Did you want one that size?' Tabs asked, running a manicured nail over the sparkling diamond. 'I thought you'd go bigger, to be honest.'

'Bigger than a three-carat? I'd struggle lifting my finger.' I laughed.

'I guess,' she replied, nonchalantly. 'I mean, I'd want at least a five.'

I pulled my hand back and crossed my arms defensively. 'I think it's perfect,' I said. 'Francis designed it himself.'

'And I thought you wanted to get engaged in the Maldives anyway, not Italy.' Tabs raised an eyebrow as she sipped from her glass, which was obviously not her first one.

'I used to,' I replied, with a subtle glare. 'But then I met Francis.' I sighed dreamily. 'He could've proposed in a bin and I would've said yes.'

Tabs rolled her eyes and gulped her drink. I reassured myself that she was just jealous, and maybe a little drunk. Tabs had been off and on with Francis's best friend, Hugo, for years. They were off again for the millionth time, so celebrating my engagement probably wasn't how she wanted to spend her Saturday night – even if she was my supposed best friend.

'I haven't seen my family or fiancé all evening, I'd better go and say hello,' I said. I was in desperate need of a reprieve from her snippy attitude.

Sipping the final dregs of my glass, I looked around the crowded terrace – lit only by a sprinkle of flickering candles and rows of fairy lights, and covered in tables with abandoned, half-full glasses of bubbly. It was slowly getting darker, and the panoramic view was speckled with the lights of the city. As I scanned the faces of the crowds on the terrace that led to the opulent function room, I spotted a familiar one at the bar and I headed over.

'Hey, Dad,' I said, as I leant against the bar to give my feet a rest from my towering Louboutins.

'My Bell Bell.' He leapt from his stool and kissed me gently on the cheek. 'Here, have my seat.' He helped me onto the ridiculously high stool – which I managed in a semi-ladylike manner – before grabbing two fresh champagne flutes.

'Thanks,' I said, as he passed one to me. I swished the satin of my short purple dress around my lap to make sure I was decent as I perched. I felt like a child again, with my feet swinging underneath the chair. I'd inherited my height from my dad rather than my former-model mum, and was struggling to reach the stool's footrest, despite my vertiginous heels.

'I can't believe my baby is engaged.' Dad's warm smile pushed his dark eyebrows upwards and deepened the wrinkles in his forehead. 'Are you having a good night?'

'I am.' I took a sip from the glass. 'Even if I've drunk my bodyweight in champagne over the last week.'

'If you can't celebrate when you're getting married, when can you?' He clinked his glass against mine.

'True.' I nodded while I took a sip. 'Although I think I only know about thirty per cent of the people here.' I looked around the crowded room, bustling with chit-chat. It seemed the whole of Merseyside had been invited to our engagement party.

'Me too.' Dad grinned. 'Blame your mother. She *had* to invite her closest friends, of course, all two hundred of them,' he chuckled.

'You can't talk, you invited everyone from work,' I said.

'Everyone at work is practically family to us, you know that,' he replied, trying to hide his hurt. 'I thought you didn't mind?'

'I don't mind, it's OK.' I patted the arm of his suit jacket. 'There are just some of our lovely colleagues that I prefer over others.'

'You can't leave anyone out though, can you?' Dad was too diplomatic for his own good.

'Technically you could.' I hiccupped. 'It's your company, after all.'

'That wouldn't be very "inclusive" of me, would it?' He

ruffled his salt and pepper hair as he emphasised his new favourite buzzword, discovered on our most recent team-building holiday to Cannes.

The problem with being who I was, Arabella Whittington of Whittington Soup, meant that certain people in the company made it their everyday mission to make me feel like I was only the PR manager because my last name was Whittington and my dad, Wilfred, was the chairman.

Our soup company was truly a family affair. My great-grandfather, Ernie Whittington, had built it from nothing, working from his tiny kitchen in Liverpool during World War Two. He wanted to help feed his neighbours when food was scarce and available only through rations. After the war, his customer base grew and grew as word spread about Ernie Whittington's incredible soup recipes.

Ernie always said blood doesn't run through our veins, soup does. Which, when you think about it, is kind of gross, but that was how much Whittington Soup meant to my family. It was in our blood. And now, it was going to be an even bigger family affair, as my dad's business partner was Francis's father, Jonathan. Dad credited Jonathan with helping him to save Whittington Soup when it ran into trouble a few years ago. Since Jonathan came on board, they've built it into what it is now – a multimillion-pound business and the most successful soup brand in the UK.

'Anyway, enough office talk.' Dad nudged me playfully. 'Let's talk about anything except work. Like how much the wedding of the decade is going to cost me. Where is my future son-in-law, anyway?'

'He was here before,' I said, as I swivelled the seat of the bar stool and looked around. Chandeliers softly lit the glamorous crowds, as musicians played a gentle backdrop of Vivaldi's *Four Seasons* to the echoing sounds of chatter and laughter. I only recognised a handful of family, friends and colleagues amongst the sea of men in identical black-tie suits and women wrapped in the swooshing fabrics of their evening dresses.

I turned back towards Dad, who'd managed to claim the next available stool at the busy bar and pulled it next to mine.

'I still can't get my head around how it's all worked out.' He tilted his head back to gulp the final sip from his glass. 'You and Francis. My precious daughter and my wonderful soon-to-be son-in-law, who also happens to be the son of my business partner.' He gestured around, beaming. 'You couldn't write it. It's perfect. The next generation of Whittington Soup. If you can persuade Francis to leave the thrill of the stock market and work at the family business, that is.'

'Maybe one day.' I smiled weakly. 'Let's hope Jonathan is as pleased about our engagement as you are.'

'You haven't spoken to him?' Dad asked, his brow furrowed.

'I've hardly seen him since we announced it, and I don't think he's shown up tonight.' I rolled my eyes. 'Haven't you bumped into him in work?'

Dad shook his head. 'I left a voicemail to say congratulations and that we need to go for a celebratory drink, but I haven't seen him much, he's been busy.'

I nodded. It was the busiest period for the family business, with contract renewals, new business pitches and product launches.

'*And* it's the Soup Convention in a few weeks,' Dad said. 'Which means he's been locking himself away in his office all day and night. You know how he gets this time of year.'

'If he's been pulling all-nighters, that means you've been busy too, right?' I eyed Dad.

He straightened his tie. 'Of course.'

'No visits to the golf course this week?' I eyed him again.

'You know I do my best networking on the golf course.' He

winked. 'Ah, there you are!' Dad exclaimed, looking over my shoulder. 'The man himself.'

I felt a warm hand on the bare shoulder of my asymmetric dress and turned so I was facing my handsome fiancé. 'Oh, hello,' I said. 'Where have you been? I've hardly seen you tonight.'

Francis rubbed the back of his neck, his face pinched. 'Can we escape and go home yet?' He glanced around the room.

'What's the matter?' I held his slightly clammy hands in mine.

'Nothing, it's nothing,' he said, his jaw clenched. He hesitated, before loosening the black dickie bow perched at the top of his crisp white shirt.

'I'm sorry.' He planted a lingering kiss on my left hand, the huge diamond on my ring almost touching his nose. His pained expression marked the unspoken end of any further conversation.

'How about we go and find your mother, hey?' Dad said. 'We'll see if we can convince her to have a dance.' He pushed himself down from the leather bar stool and held his hands out for me.

The brief respite had given me enough time off my feet to semi-forget just how much my poor toes were suffering in my new shoes. But they were as eye-wateringly painful as they were expensive (and fabulous), so I forced myself to suck it up. All in the name of beauty. And a lifelong commitment to Mr Christian Louboutin that I would take (almost) as seriously as my wedding vows.

Francis's stiff posture relaxed a little after the removal of the dickie bow and loosening of tight buttons. I tried to shake off his weird mood as I spotted Mum at the far end of the room, and led Francis and Dad through the crowd.

As predicted, Mum was in the French-manicured clutches of her clique – a group of women whose facial expressions were practically impossible to read, yet alarmingly similar, given they all opted for the same aestheticians. The same went for their identical boob jobs and full-body liposuction.

'I just don't know how we're going to replace her,' one whined, overlined pink lips pursed. 'She's the best nanny we've ever had.'

'It's simply *impossible* to find the right help these days,' another clone nodded in sympathy.

'The girls loved her, they really did,' she said, as she discarded the bread and cheese from the canapé and ate only the tiny tomato.

'Honestly, Bella, this group...' Dad whispered to me. 'Who needs a live-in nanny for their *cats*?'

I fought to stifle a giggle – nothing surprised me about that clique. The only reason Mum hung around with them was to have an ear in the scandalous gossip and to debate the effectiveness of the latest anti-ageing treatments in their combined quest for endless youth.

'Hello, darling,' Mum greeted me tipsily. 'Rosalind is just telling us about her dear nanny. I don't suppose you know any experts in feline psychology who are also Michelin-starred personal chefs, do you?'

'Err, can't say I do.'

'Hmph,' Mum mumbled and gulped her bubbly. 'Well, if you're here to ask me to dance,' she said sternly, 'I shan't tell you again, Arabella Allegra—'

'I'm not,' I said.

She nodded dramatically in relief.

'Shall we have a dance?' Dad unknowingly said to Mum, as he stood at her side after escaping the gaggle of gossiping women.

'I can't dance tonight, Wilfred, you know I can't!' Mum cried.

'Why? What's actually the matter?' I asked.

'You know what the matter is,' Mum said earnestly.

'Don't worry, Ms Whittington, I've told all my guests here not to mention that time you were on *Strictly*,' Francis said, tapping his nose reassuringly.

'Thanks, Francis,' Mum said through gritted teeth. It was an unwritten rule that nobody could bring up Mum's appearance on *Strictly Come Dancing* and her premature departure, after she tumbled head first into the live orchestra during a particularly enthusiastic paso doble, making her the first contestant to be stretchered out on live TV.

'But no, it's not that, my dear Francis. It's nothing to do with *that show*.' Mum shuddered theatrically. 'It's actually a rather long and difficult story.'

Dad caught my eye and rolled his.

'If you must know' – Mum cleared her throat – 'recently, it came to my attention that I appear to have acquired' – she coughed again – 'a different, rather unusual *texture* of *skin* on my feet and around my ankles.'

'You mean *wrinkles*,' I said, stifling a laugh.

Mum's eyes widened with fury, before she quickly composed herself. 'It is not a laughing matter, Arabella,' she stuttered, with a menacing glare. 'You don't understand what I've been through. The hardship. The judgemental stares. I haven't been able to wear peep toes for *years*,' she said with a sniff. 'But I've *finally* found a solution.'

Francis glanced apprehensively at Dad and back at me.

'I've had Botox!' Mum grinned with the same level of pride that she had at my graduation.

'In your... face?' Francis asked, bewildered.

'No, *mon chéri*, no. Oh gosh, of course not. Just how old do you think I am?' Mum cackled, her eyes wide and nostrils flaring. 'I'd never touch my face. *Non*, never. *Non*. In fact, dermatologists won't allow it,' she rambled. 'They all say my skin is much too young for Botox, or any facial aesthetics. In fact, I've seen several leading experts in the UK and back home in France, and they've all said it would be a travesty for someone as young-looking as me to have any work on my face. In fact, they practically frog-marched me out of the clinic!'

Dad and I exchanged knowing looks. She was sticking to that story until her dying day.

'I've had Botox in my *feet*,' Mum announced with a flourish, before lifting her floor-length tulle evening gown that was embellished with tiny beads. 'Look, I can wear peep toes again!' Mum exclaimed proudly, as she nimbly lifted a leg up higher so we could have a closer look.

'Ah,' Francis nodded politely. 'Well, your feet look great, Mrs Whittington. Like a... like a twenty-year-old's feet,' he said, to Mum's delighted shimmy.

'Why don't we have a dance to celebrate your youthful feet then?' Dad asked.

'Well, I can't *dance* because I've lost all sensation in my toes, and in my lower legs entirely,' Mum said breezily. 'But I can *shuffle*.'

'A shuffle it is.' Dad smiled. The man had the patience of a saint. 'Come on, before our song is over.' He took Mum's hand and led her to the dance floor, where the band was playing Ella Fitzgerald's 'Dream a Little Dream of Me'.

Francis and I followed them and held each other closely as we moved to the music, his broad body pushed up against mine.

Growing up, all I had ever wanted was to find my Prince Charming and have a marriage like my parents'. I still couldn't wrap my head around the fact that now Francis and I were engaged, my dream was finally going to come true. He was my first love *and* he would be my last love.

Francis drew me in close and kissed me as I counted my lucky stars. What did I do to deserve my life? How was it possible for everything to be so perfect? As we kissed, I tapped the wooden floor with the tip of my perfectly pedicured toe. I've never been superstitious, but it's better to be safe than sorry, right?

TWO

Thanks to my timesaving, twice-weekly, bouncy blow dry yesterday (you can't beat a 'curly blow' by a hairdresser with a Liverpool postcode), I was dressed and ready, second coffee in hand, by 7 a.m.

It was my first day back at the office after a two-week holiday; a magical week in Capri, followed by a week of engagement celebrations and catch-ups with friends. But now, work desperately needed my undivided attention. The most important date in the Whittington Soup corporate calendar was looming – the Soup Convention, held every year on the last Friday of March.

All the big players in the food industry were invited to the annual conference at the Royal Liver Building. It was pretty much the Met Gala of the food world, minus any form of glitz or glamour, of course. But over the years, I'd learnt how important it was for the family business. It was the number one opportunity to land lucrative contracts, scope out competitors and impress potential new buyers, suppliers and clients.

'Good morning, Hannah,' I said to the friendly receptionist after pushing the heavy rotating doors open – no mean feat with

a full coffee in one hand and a briefcase bulging with paper-
work in the other.

The morning sunshine illuminated the already bright white
reception of the company headquarters on Old Hall Street in
the city's bustling commercial district.

My heels echoed across the sharp edges of the gleaming
room. I stepped into the open lift and pressed the button
signalling the sixth floor. With a subtle ping, the doors started
closing. Until a bear-like hand prised them open at the very last
minute.

I recognised those hands. I held my breath as Jonathan
forced the doors open. His instinctual reaction was discomfort
as he realised that I was already standing inside the lift, but he
quickly masked it with two polite kisses on either cheek.

'Bella,' he said. 'How are you doing?'

'Great, thank you,' I said, as airily as I could manage.

'Congratulations, by the way,' he said. 'You and Francis. I
guess we'll be in-laws soon then.' He grinned, but with a hint of
a grimace. I knew Jonathan thought I wasn't good enough for his
precious son.

'Yes, we will,' I smiled back, hiding my panic at the
painfully slow rate at which the buttons that showed the
climbing floors illuminated. The conversation felt more like
forced small talk with a distant relative than a chat with my
soon-to-be father-in-law.

'I'm sorry I couldn't make the party, I had an urgent work
issue,' he said, fiddling with the enormous Hublot Big Bang on
his wrist.

'It's fine,' I replied.

The doors opened and I breathed a sigh of relief when he
stepped out of the lift and marched to his corner office. The
floors and walls vibrated as he shut the big, wooden door that
read 'Jonathan Burton, Managing Director' behind him.

I planted my briefcase next to my desk, opposite Polly –

Jonathan's assistant and my work bestie. She was balancing the phone between her shoulder and neck, and gave me a look as if to say, 'I bet that'll convince you to take the stairs now.'

My laptop flickered to life, and I smiled as I caught a glimpse of my screensaver displaying my favourite picture of Francis and me, on a yacht in Antibes.

'How was your weekend?' Polly said as she pushed the phone back onto the receiver. 'Sore head after the party?' she asked mischievously.

'I was fine, surprisingly. I think I did more mingling than drinking.'

'Wish I could say the same.' Polly rubbed her temples. 'I can't handle hangovers any more; it's been two days and I still feel hung-over.'

'I'm not surprised – weren't you doing Jägerbombs with my mum?'

She shuddered. 'Tequila shots, actually. But yes, blame your terrible influence of a mother.'

'Never let Aurelia Whittington talk you into doing shots,' I said, speaking from personal experience. 'She says her alcohol tolerance comes from her days on The Rolling Stones tour bus.'

'That explains a lot,' Polly said, an eyebrow raised.

I opened my favourite Smythson notebook and tried not to hyperventilate at the sight of my to-do list. I'd written it out before we went on holiday in the hope of being organised the minute I got back.

My head start on the day and getting into the office early meant I had a solid ninety minutes before the day's calls, meetings, and back-and-forth emails began. The first daily task, as always, was media monitoring. I checked the Google alerts that had popped up over the weekend for Whittington Soup.

'Oh, bloody hell,' I mumbled, feeling my heart sink as I scanned the headlines and photo after photo documenting mine and Francis's relationship.

A mountainous pile of newspapers and gossip magazines slammed onto the desk, making me jump in my seat. The silhouette of our marketing director and Jonathan's right-hand man, Dave, hovered in the space next to me.

'I take it you've seen these?' he said roughly.

'Not the print versions, I'm just looking through the online stories now,' I replied.

'The online stories are worse – at least the print stories aren't littered with comments about how lavish your engagement party was and how much your ring cost.' He rubbed his face dramatically.

'I haven't read the comments online yet,' I said timidly. I made the mistake of looking at the comments about myself on a gossip site once and wouldn't be doing it again. I didn't need to hear about how I was ugly/fat/spoilt from enthusiastic keyboard warriors.

'Sorry, I thought you were the PR manager now?' Dave didn't attempt to hide his distaste. He liked to belittle me as much as he could get away with, especially since I'd taken over his role when he was promoted to marketing director last year. Still, Dave's dislike of me was better than my previous job, working in fashion PR in London. I shuddered as I remembered it – juggling the egos of the designers and the flakiness of the models, while essentially being a glorified coffee runner.

Dad had encouraged me to spend a few years in London and enjoy life in the capital. But I always knew what I wanted to do and where I wanted to go with my career – I wanted to prove myself at Whittington Soup. So, I jumped at the chance to move back home last year when Dad and Jonathan offered me the role as PR manager. My plan was to put the hours in and prove everyone who thought I was just 'The Boss's Daughter' wrong. I'd establish myself in the corporate world and lay the foundations for an amazing career. Then I also met Francis, fell in love, and everything slotted perfectly into place.

'Don't worry, I'm on it,' I said, attempting to radiate confidence and reaching deep down for that special Whittington inner grit.

'Good.' He picked off non-existent fluff from the arm of his tailored suit. 'We can't have any distractions from the Soup Convention this year. Not a whiff of any negative press if we want our contracts renewed.'

'I know,' I said. 'I'll deal with it.'

He huffed away as Polly raised her eyebrows at me across the desk.

'Cup of coffee?' I offered.

'Have you ever known me to say no to coffee?' Polly replied. 'But I'll get them,' she said, grabbing my favourite Royal Copenhagen mug. 'You have enough work to do.' She gestured towards the stack of newspapers.

As lunchtime loomed and my stomach rumbled, the office door swung open and Dad wandered in. A chorus of 'Good morning, Wilf' and animated chatter rang throughout the room. He nattered with every employee he passed, asking what they'd got up to over the weekend and beaming about how hopeful he was that the balmy spring weather was going to last. 'I play my best golf in the sunshine,' he insisted to all the golf fanatics in the office (of which there were not many).

But the lively atmosphere ground to a halt the second Jonathan's office door opened. It instantly felt as though the room temperature dropped from the scorching spring day that it was to a freezing winter night. The friendly chatting and laughter was swiftly replaced by the sound of frantic typing, and everyone quickly veered their eyes back to the computer monitors in front of them.

'Wilfred, can I talk to you, please,' Jonathan stated sternly, in the same tone as a headteacher summoning a naughty pupil to their office.

'I hope I'm not in trouble.' Dad smiled, pushing his sunglasses on top of his thick hair. He walked across the floor space, gently touching my shoulder as he passed my desk. Jonathan shut the door firmly behind the two of them, eradicating any possibility of me being able to listen in.

'What's that about?' Polly gestured towards the office.

'No idea,' I said. 'He's probably had the bill through for our team-building holiday.'

'Your dad *did* insist on upgrading everyone's suites.'

'Wilf,' I corrected her. I always referred to him as Wilf in work. 'And not *everyone's* suites,' I said defensively. 'Only the team that won the rounders match.'

'All I'm saying is that it was already a five-star hotel in Cannes. *And* an all-expenses-paid work holiday. The final bill probably made Jonathan cry into his whisky, especially given the fact he wasn't even there.'

I shrugged. 'His choice. We did try and persuade him to come. And Wilf likes to spoil his staff, he always has.'

'I know.' Polly grinned. 'I'm excited to see what I get for my one-year work anniversary.'

Another of Dad's insistences, together with team holidays, optional casual dress code, home-working, performance-based bonuses and a generous profit share scheme, was work anniversary presents. Even when the company was struggling a few years ago, he'd dipped into his own pocket to motivate his employees by rewarding them with milestone gifts.

'Don't get your hopes up too much,' I said. 'It's only your first anniversary.' Polly liked to think I had an influence on what was bought (I didn't; in fact, I steered clear), and she'd been admiring my Celine briefcase an awful lot over the last few weeks.

'Alan in accounts got a pair of Yeezys for his first anniversary,' Polly sulked.

'I have to admit, I thought Wilf was being ironic with that one. Somehow, I couldn't see Alan in a pair of Yeezys.'

Polly shrugged. 'He said they "jazz up" his suit.'

'He does weirdly pull them off.' I giggled.

A bleep from my phone distracted me from thoughts of Alan, very much a stereotypical corporate accountant, wearing brand new Yeezys with his standard uniform of pinstripe suits.

Meeting is running over. Won't make lunch. Sorry. See you back at home x F

I glanced through my never-ending list and quickly concluded that I probably would've struggled fitting in a proper lunch break, anyway. I'd be working into the night to finish everything. Francis would likely be fast asleep by the time I got home; it was non-negotiable that he clocked up at least eight hours of sleep every night to ensure he had enough energy for daily 5.30 a.m. workouts with his personal trainer.

One of the main projects I'd been working on was my presentation for the Soup Convention. It was my chance to prove myself, and my first time presenting as the newly appointed PR manager. I knew how important this presentation was – both for the company and for my career. But my plans were finally coming together; I had a decent idea of what our competitors would be focusing on, and I knew we needed to be better than ever.

The heavy door behind me opened and closed quickly. 'Wilf,' I said, as he shuffled past my desk, away from Jonathan's office. 'Wilf!' I shouted.

'Oh, sorry, Bell.' He turned around. 'In a world of my own,' he said, shaking his head.

'Everything OK?' I nodded towards Jonathan's office.

'Of course, everything's fine,' he said, before biting his lip.

'Are you sure?'

'Jonathan's just been telling me about all this press coverage, Bella.'

'I know, I'm dealing with it,' I said firmly. I was still trying to prove myself in this job; I didn't want to just be 'The Boss's Daughter'.

'Honestly, the press will move on to something else soon,' I said, to Dad's concerned expression. 'You know the saying, "today's news is tomorrow's fish and chip paper".'

'It's just that we've never experienced anything like this before.' He shook his head. 'I guess I've been a little bit naive in the past, but I always thought the press were on our side. They usually have nothing but good things to say about us and the company. A few of the reporters writing the stories are the ones who have been away on press trips with us.'

'They love to build you up and then tear you down.' I shrugged. 'It's how it works. Everyone loves gossip, even if it isn't true.'

'I suppose.' He shook his head again. 'It's such a shame too – the timing of all this overshadowing your engagement.'

'Don't worry about that, it can't be helped.' I forced a small smile. 'Work has to come first. I knew what I was getting myself into when I took on the PR manager role.'

'I'll always be grateful to Jonathan for spearheading the idea of you joining the company when the job came up.' The wrinkles around his eyes deepened as he smiled. 'Anyway, I must dash.' He slipped his hands into his pockets. 'Your mother wants to go shopping, and you need to get back to your Soup Convention presentation.'

'Don't remind me,' I groaned.

'You'll be great,' he said. 'I have every faith in you. You can do anything you put your mind to, Bella.' A quick kiss on the cheek and he was out of the door.

The feeling of dread and immediate sweaty palms at the thought of standing up in front of thousands of people, combined with a weird nagging feeling about Dad and Jonathan's chat, were thoughts I was desperately trying to push to the back of my mind.

THREE

The Liver Birds slowly came into view as the car rolled through the gridlocked traffic, inching closer to the Liverpool waterfront. The pair of fabled guardians observed the city from their perch at the top of the Royal Liver Building, as my chauffeur, Jeff, steered towards the crowds that were already beginning to gather for the Soup Convention. Legend had it that if the two birds were to fly away, then the city would cease to exist. But I wished I was the one in a position to spread their wings and fly away; my stomach was in knots. I'd recently learnt that the famous quote 'all publicity is good publicity' is undoubtedly one of the biggest misconceptions about public relations.

We were in the middle of a PR 'domino effect', and I was fighting fires that were only burning brighter since mine and Francis's engagement had made the headlines. The news, coupled with anonymous reader comments online, had piqued the media's interest and a relentless news campaign focusing on the family behind Whittington Soup had erupted, causing a seismic shift in public scrutiny that was getting more intense every day.

Mum had refused to leave the house ever since the papers

insinuated that she used to be an escort. They'd printed old topless photos next to a shot of her leaving a private jet in Las Vegas with a Russian oligarch who'd been rumoured to pay for the pleasure of young ladies' company. Mum had insisted that the photos were supposed to be tasteful and were taken in her early modelling days when she was young and naive. She also said the Russian billionaire was in fact gay, and he'd persuaded her to accompany him to the Dreamboys' first Vegas residency – in her words, it was an offer she couldn't refuse. Despite her insistence that she was now living her life as a recluse, I noticed her imminent monthly Botox appointment marked on the kitchen calendar, so the real test was yet to come.

Next on the chopping block was a story about me and my apparent diva antics at work. An anonymous source was quoted saying that I 'go in late, leave early, mess around on Instagram, and the only reason she has her job is thanks to her surname'. The journalist ran the story and chopped off ninety per cent of my statement, which confirmed my sixty-hour average working week.

Even Dad hadn't escaped the wrath of the media. They'd had a field day with a list of extravagant purchases he'd made over the years, especially when it came to the Whittington Soup office parties. There was great debate over how much he'd paid Gary Barlow to perform, though Dad insisted Mr Barlow had given him 'mates rates' after losing a golfing competition between him and Jürgen Klopp. Then there were the Christmas parties, when Dad once hired two hundred reindeer and turned the office into a winter wonderland that would rival The Plaza in New York (coincidentally, that was where the 'Christmas Consultant' he'd flown in for the weekend worked).

Every day marked a fresh flurry of emails and phone calls from reporters asking for quotes, or confirmation of facts and absurd stories in equal measure. Jonathan had insisted that a simple 'no comment' would suffice. But I wasn't prepared to let my family's reputation be torn to shreds without a chance for us to defend ourselves, so I'd spent what felt like all my waking hours battling with journalists over statements I'd issued.

I tried to push the PR crisis to the back of my mind as the Mercedes swooped around and joined the queue of chauffeur-driven cars, emblazoned with various logos. Each one hovered as they dropped their guests off at the magnificent building. The white faces of the clocks high in the blue Liverpool sky served as a reminder to me that in just a few hours, I'd be standing in front of the people who were crucial to the future success of my family's business.

We edged closer while time ticked along, and I rubbed my clammy hands together to try and calm myself. But as we crept nearer to the drop-off point, I noticed the flash of colours weren't just crowds of people. Placards on wooden handles danced above the heads of the waiting mob, the signs multi-coloured and illustrated with disturbing pictures. I squinted through the blacked-out window but was struggling to decipher exactly what the posters displayed, and after seeing the furious faces of the people holding them, I felt too scared to roll the window down and get a better look.

The chanting became louder as the car rolled along, but the heated message was muted by the cheering crowds who clapped at every word spoken by a man yelling animatedly through a megaphone.

'Is this protest why there's a hold-up?' I put my hand on my knee to stop my twitching leg. My nerves wouldn't calm no matter what I tried. I knew I shouldn't have deleted the Headspace app from my phone; perhaps meditation really was the calming influence I needed.

'I think so,' Jeff said, leaning closer to the window and clocking the number of cars ahead of us in the queue. 'Shouldn't be too long now.' He winked at me through the rear-view window reassuringly.

I wished my dad was with me; he and Jonathan were already in their first meeting of at least twenty scheduled throughout the busy day. There was a gap in the agenda so they could watch the Whittington Soup presentation, but I wished he'd had time to give me another reassuring pep-talk beforehand if I was to get up on that stage and not pass out. Or perhaps passing out was a good enough excuse not to do it?

A woman with multicoloured hair, almost entirely covered by a hat with bunny ears, stalked the waiting cars in the line-up. She was holding a placard with one hand and pointing it towards the passengers while chanting, 'Animal rights! Join our fight!' and waving the other fist in the air. I flinched as she flashed a horrifically graphic photograph showing a poor animal in a terrible state. It broke my heart. Animal welfare was something we prided ourselves on at Whittington Soup; we only ever worked with high-quality farms and suppliers.

'They must be protesting against one of the companies here,' I said to Jeff as the furious campaigner moved on to the next car. We trundled past the barriers and the handful of police officers that were blocking the protestors from the entrance to the building. Good job Mum wasn't here; she often regaled us with the shuddering memory of having red paint thrown on her (faux, she insisted) fur coat after watching a show at Paris Fashion Week.

'Do you want me to come in with you?' Jeff asked, his kind eyes watching me with concern through the rear-view mirror. 'I can do the valet parking instead and escort you inside?'

'No, don't worry, Jeff. I'll be fine,' I promised, smoothing down my hair and wiping my sweating hands on my skirt. 'Wish me luck,' I said, clicking open the back door and shimmying across the leather seat with my matching blush-pink Celine handbag and briefcase in tow.

'Good luck, have a soup-er day.' Jeff grinned through the open window. 'In all seriousness, Bella, you know nothing bad can happen when the Liver Birds are watching over you.' He pointed upwards at the city's guardians, offered an encouraging smile and then pulled away with a wave.

The fresh air and cool breeze from the nearby River Mersey revitalised my foggy head and momentarily subsided my worried thoughts as I walked from the car into the building, under the watchful eyes of the protestors to one side and the Liver Birds above. Despite the negative press, everything was solvable. Everything was going to be fine. Nothing bad was going to happen.

Well, the Liver Birds were obviously sunbathing with a piña bloody colada when they were supposed to be making sure nothing bad happened.

Let's start at the beginning. The USB stick with my entire presentation on it had broken, which wasn't the best start to the day, but it was still manageable. I thought I was going to be OK; I knew every word on that USB, and who enjoys looking at PowerPoint slides, anyway? But the lights, the *lights*. Gosh, they were so hot and bright. I felt like I was in a production of *Hamilton* on Broadway – only with less rapping, although I was talking so fast that I might as well have been. And all the staring faces – I'd never seen so many pairs of eyes in my life. It might also come as a surprise that the Soup Convention crowd don't have the best sense of humour, so my attempts at soup jokes and (excellent, might I add) puns fell rather flat.

Then there was the grilling from the journalists. The way they carried on, you'd think it was an official government inquiry into a leak of state secrets, not a presentation to reveal that powdered quinoa was the next big thing in soup! Of course, the negative stories about my family came up too. And some-how, the press had also got hold of internal figures, and in a true 'gotcha' moment asked me to explain how the total cost of the

Whittington Soup team-building holidays over the last two years added up to more than £750,000. Even by my *enthusiastic* spending standards, I could agree that perhaps it was a little excessive, but I could hardly admit that publicly, as I watched Dad squirm in his seat next to Jonathan. At least that explained what their angry office meeting had been about – it wasn't the casual disagreement about the negative press coverage of my engagement that Dad had painted it as when I'd asked him about it.

But the media grilling wasn't even the worst thing that happened. No, not even close. I still can't quite *comprehend* the worst thing that happened. But you know when you go to the toilet, and you double-check that your dress isn't tucked into the back of your knickers? And then you breathe that *humongous* sigh of relief because it was, but you've caught it before venturing out in public again? Well, let's just say it might've been related to that. On stage. In front of three thousand people. But not just any people: *everyone* related to Whittington Soup – clients, competitors and suppliers, to name just a few who giggled away at the sight of my bare bottom as I turned to leave the stage after my already disastrous presentation.

So, I might've run away. Well, not *run* away, exactly – I got an Uber Executive to my favourite spa, where Tabs and I had spent the last five nights. Francis and I had hardly spoken, except a few WhatsApp messages that weren't much longer than a few words at a time. There was no doubt he was acting distant, and I tried to push it to the back of my mind. He could be a little image-obsessed sometimes, and was probably mortified about all the negative publicity.

My doomed presentation – now officially known as 'The Presentation That Shall Not Be Named' – was enough to make me want to hibernate for the rest of the year. But the break to the sacred grounds of our favourite spa had done Tabby and me the world of good, especially Tabby, who was still a bit subdued after her recent break-up with Hugo. We'd originally planned on filling our days with sunrise yoga, organic smoothies and quiet afternoons curled up with good books – literary classics to nourish our souls and challenge our minds. Instead, we spent it guzzling Veuve Clicquot, eating our combined body weight in ice cream, and rereading our favourite Jilly Cooper bonkbusters.

I'd turned off my emails (not the most responsible act, I admit, but what was I supposed to do? I'd flashed my bare, tan-lined and slightly sunburnt bottom to *thousands* of people!). Dad had told me exactly what I suspected as he dealt with the aftermath: our clients thought Whittington Soup was dropping the ball, and our competitors were ready to swoop in and steal the ball – or the bouillabaisse, our most popular flavour.

But the most shocking part of it all was the discovery on my return of who had leaked the stories to the media that led to the bad publicity. It almost knocked me off my Jimmy Choos when I heard. It was Polly. *Polly.* I'd been betrayed by someone I thought was my good friend outside work, and best friend at work – and one of the few people who took me seriously in the office.

It came down to money, so I'd been told. Word around the office was that she was skint, and the journalists were paying her for story tips. A tidal wave of memories hit me when I heard: downplaying selling her clothes on eBay, saying she was saving for a holiday. Always bringing her own lunch to work instead of buying takeaway like everyone else. Skipping work drinks whenever the invitation landed a week before payday. Her upcoming work anniversary present – was she excited about it because she wanted to pawn it for money?

Despite my initial refusal to believe it, they'd found the emails and her computer history. She'd sabotaged the USB stick with my presentation on it and had leaked the figures about the team-building holidays as well. Apparently, Jonathan was quite brutal and fired her in front of everyone. He said he wanted to make an example of her because what she'd done to the company and to my family was so abhorrent. It was a bit of a scene; she was in tears and ended up being escorted out by security, which I thought was a little unnecessary.

Every time I tried to call her for an explanation, it went straight to voicemail. Given that she hadn't bothered to get in touch with me either, I guessed she'd blocked my number. But despite everything she'd done, I still missed her, and work wasn't the same without her. The messy desk opposite mine looked exactly as it had when she sat there every day. The remaining belongings scattered around spoke volumes about how she'd left in a hurry. She'd even forgotten her Fleetwood Cat mug – one of her most prized possessions, a tribute to her favourite band and animal. Feeling a pang for the loss of our friendship, I'd surreptitiously slipped it into my bag.

Setting foot in the office again had taken some desperate persuasion from my dad. He reassured me that my accidental nudity and disastrous presentation was old news and practically forgotten after Polly's scandalous firing. On my first sheepish day back, it seemed there had been an internal memo about not mentioning the words 'Soup Convention' or 'presentation' in my presence, although I knew it must've been the talk of the office afterwards.

Suddenly, as I sat at my desk, a red box flashed across my laptop screen with a ping.

Notice: Urgent staff meeting

All senior staff members must go to the boardroom imme-diately.

Strange. Dad hadn't mentioned any big company news, and he was usually quite transparent with me. As well as being PR manager, I was a non-executive director of the company, which basically meant I could attend the board meetings but couldn't make any decisions. I had a plush leather seat at the table, but it held no power or influence.

I grabbed my handbag, shoving my phone into it, and headed to the boardroom on the next floor up. The second I pushed open the mahogany door, I knew I'd interrupted something. My dad, usually the world's happiest man, looked totally broken. His kind eyes were filled with sadness.

'What's going on?' I asked.

Jonathan was leaning forward against the back of one of many leather chairs around the huge table. Neither of them said anything.

'Seriously, what's going on?' I asked again. Before they had a chance to answer, the rest of the senior staff and board members poured into the room. I tried to catch Dad's eye, but he was staring ahead in shock. I noticed him quickly hide his shaky hands in his pockets as the room filled with people.

I pulled the nearest chair out and sat down on it, with Dad next to me, and Jonathan standing at the head of the table. The gossiping whispers fell silent the minute Jonathan cleared his throat. He always knew how to silence a room.

'Thank you everyone for coming to this meeting at short notice. I know you're all very busy,' Jonathan began. 'There has been a development at management level, and we thought you should all know about it before any rumours start to spread.' He cleared his throat again.

'Recent events that have come to light, and the loss of some of Whittington Soup's biggest clients to competitors, has attracted the attention of the board,' he stuttered. 'There's really no easy way to say this. The board members have called an emergency meeting to vote on whether or not Wilfred Whittington should remain as acting chairman of Whittington Soup.'

FOUR

Dad and I waited impatiently outside the boardroom. I alternated between frantic pacing up and down the corridor, and leaning against the wall like a dead weight. We didn't utter a word to each other; neither of us knew what to say while we waited to learn our fate.

I pictured the twelve members of the board. They were the people who would decide my dad's future. I couldn't take part in the vote as I was a non-executive director. But Jonathan could vote, and there were several others who'd been with Dad since the beginning, so I knew we definitely had a few votes secured at least – but we needed seven to win a majority. Did we have seven votes?

Dad was surprisingly composed, given the circumstances. He always managed to keep calm under pressure. I wished I'd inherited that gene and not Mum's hysterical nature. Inside, I was screaming. The family business meant everything to me, and to Dad. This couldn't be the end – how could it be? Our name literally *was* the business: Whittington Soup couldn't exist without the Whittingtons.

Every now and again, Dad and I would hear Jonathan's

distinctive cough, likely exacerbated by his favourite pastime, a night spent smoking his stash of beloved Cuban cigars.

The boardroom door opened and my heart leapt to my throat.

'Come in, please,' Jonathan gestured.

The faces in the room looked pale and haunted.

'I'm afraid it's bad news,' Jonathan said, rubbing a hand over his flushed face. 'Wilfred Whittington has been voted out of the company. He is no longer chairman of Whittington Soup.'

Everything began to move in slow motion. Every person in the room was staring at us and I gazed around at the blurry figures. Who had voted against him? Who had betrayed my dad, their boss? Who had used their vote to kick my dad out of the business our family had started from nothing?

I stared straight ahead, through the window that overlooked the city. Dad didn't move an inch. I tried to breathe in and out, slowly and calmly, until a wave of anger came flooding through me. It replaced the feeling of nausea and my whole body started to shake.

I knew I had to get out of there.

'You can take this as my resignation too,' I stammered, unable to meet anyone's eyes. I wobbled away and pulled open the heavy boardroom door, stumbled along the corridor and down the stairs to Dad's office. Pushing the door open, I fell inside and collapsed against the back of the door, before slowly slipping down to the floor.

What had just happened? All I could do was stare at Dad's desk in front of me. The desk that my great-grandfather had sat at every day for years before entrusting the family business to his only son. It was the desk I'd learnt to read on. The desk where I did my homework at half-term. The desk where Dad and Jonathan had popped countless bottles of champagne whenever they'd landed big contracts.

Tears rolled slowly down my cheeks, before pouring uncontrollably all over my red face, stinging my eyes and landing on my lips. A quiet knock at the door shook me back to the present moment. I knew it was Dad, and all I wanted to do was hug him and tell him it would be OK, that we would figure it out. I leapt to my feet and flung the door open.

'Are you all right?' I asked, attempting to rub the mascara stains off my cheeks.

He nodded sombrely. I felt like the entire situation was my fault in so many ways. If it wasn't for the negative press attention, my disastrous presentation and my friendship with Polly (a.k.a. Judas), we wouldn't have just lost our family business we both loved so much – the business his own grandfather had started from a tiny kitchen in Liverpool more than eighty years ago.

Dad knew what I was thinking. He gave me a big bear hug.

'Don't you worry, my little lamb,' he soothed, stroking my hair. 'Everything will be OK. We're Whittingtons. We started this business in the middle of a world war. We can get through anything.'

I nodded and he held his arm out for me to link with him. 'Come on, let's go home, we need to tell your mother about all this.'

'What about Jonathan? Can't he do anything?'

'He did everything he could, Bell, but a vote is a vote.' Dad forced a smile, but his sad, puppy-dog eyes revealed his true feelings of devastation. 'I'll ask our family lawyers what they think. There might be some sort of legal loophole that means we can appeal it.'

'Let's hope so,' I said, steadying myself on his arm.

As we stepped outside together, I glanced at Dad, who wiped a single tear from his eye as he looked back up at the Whittington Soup headquarters.

'Well, that's that then,' he said, his shaky voice breaking.

FIVE

After the vote, Dad and I went back to Southport to break the news about what had happened. Mum was less hysterical than Dad and I had expected. Instead, she started mumbling furiously, half in French, about going on a date with a mafia boss once and that she might still have his number lying around. She disappeared to her dressing room for a while, then reappeared to stomp downstairs in her feather-trimmed pyjamas and heeled slippers. 'When he told me that he was big in "the maff", naturally I assumed it was the abbreviation of mafia,' Mum sighed. 'But no, it seems he was actually a senior accountant in the Ministry of Agriculture, Fisheries and Food.' She groaned defeatedly before swigging a gulp of Grey Goose from the bottle.

After a brief break, she then proceeded to unpack suitcases filled with the 'healing crystals' she'd used for a holistic therapy-themed ladies' luncheon – one of many annual luncheons she held to raise money for charity (although they mostly consisted of getting her friends drunk so they'd offer ludicrously large bids on ridiculous auction items).

Mum placed the crystals around the house, before deciding

that burning sage was a better option to 'rid us of negative energy' – only she didn't have any sage, so she burnt the leaves of a basil plant instead. After a minor meltdown because neither Dad nor I were joining in and 'our healing process is a family effort' (according to the American self-help guru she was manically texting for advice), she stalked around the house and made us chant affirmations from her *Little Book of Spirituality* that was in an old Fortnum & Mason Christmas cracker.

Eventually, Dad escaped to the quiet of his study, while Mum got steadily drunker on vodka martinis as she binge-watched *Killing Eve* and decided she would channel her inner Villanelle to track down anyone who voted against Dad. But she quickly forgot her plans when she was distracted by Jodie Comer's *fabulous* wardrobe.

All I wanted was to slip away and leave them to it, so I called a taxi and headed back to Liverpool. I needed a very hot bath and a very large glass of wine, followed by an impressive amount of carbohydrates, preferably smothered in cheese. My hands were still trembling from the shock of the day as I turned the key in the lock. Never had I been so happy to get home.

The muted sounds of music in the kitchen greeted me as I pushed open the door. Francis must've left the radio on before he left for work, and I was grateful for the melodies cutting through the silence and distracting me from the thoughts swarming around my mind. Francis wasn't due home from work for another couple of hours, but I wanted to tell him what had happened before he heard it from Jonathan.

I grabbed a wine glass from the cupboard and headed straight for the fridge. To my surprise, there was already an open bottle of white wine on the shelf inside. It wasn't like Francis to drink on a weekday, but I was grateful for his uncharacteristic craving as I poured the rest of the chilled Chablis into the glass. I took a gulp and scoured the 'treats cupboard' (a location I frequented much more often than Francis) in search of my favourite Charbonnel et Walker white chocolate truffles as a pre-dinner snack. It was never a good idea to drink on an empty stomach.

Clutching my survival kit for the day from hell and kicking off my shoes, I padded along the soft carpets, up the stairs to the master suite, while debating which Jo Malone bath oil I was in the mood for; one that would calm my mind and soothe my body, which was drained from the floods of adrenaline, while also offering the answers to what had happened in the board-room. That wasn't too much to ask of a bath oil, was it?

As I neared the bedroom, I heard grunting. Strange. Francis must've been home after all. He'd probably left work early and launched himself straight into a workout – he just couldn't give those online Les Mills classes a break. Getting closer, I could hear music over the groans. It was Marvin Gaye, his soulful voice suggesting we 'get it on' – not Francis's usual choice for an intense workout.

I pushed open the bedroom door and froze in shock at the scene. The soundtrack of music and moans assaulting my ears fitted the appropriately seductive setting: the dim room, lit only by the flicker of Diptyque candles scattered around every surface, and two glasses of wine on the bedside table.

There were two naked bodies entwined on the bed; they were contorted, mid-grind. My body and mind were both momentarily numb with disbelief, and the first thought that struck me was how impressed I was with their flexibility. Until it quickly dawned on me who the panting man on his knees was, and then whose long legs were wrapped around his neck. The naked figures' expressions transformed from climactic ecstasy to sheer horror as all three pairs of our eyes met.

'Oh, fuck,' Francis gasped, his cheeks flushed.

'Shit,' gulped my best friend, Tabs, pulling up the sheet to cover her bare breasts.

I could feel the colour drain from me as I stood in the doorway, in front of the bed. I clutched my wine glass and choco-lates so hard that my knuckles were as white as the sheets that my fiancé and my best friend were wrapped up in. My heart thumped beneath my shirt. The three of us stared at each other, frozen in the moment.

'I... I came home early,' I stammered.

'I can explain,' Francis pleaded. He was still inside my best friend, so it'd have to have been a *very* good explanation.

My grip on the wine glass loosened. I heard the gentle thud of it landing on the fluffy rug, splattering its faux fur with the grand cru wine that also filled the pair of glasses beside the bed. I looked down and noticed the floor was covered in a scattering of belongings that were not mine: a silk dress, a pair of high heels, and ruby-red French knickers with a matching bra of deli-cate lace. Each item was a stepping stone to the king-size bed where my fiancé and best friend lay together.

I looked up at Francis again, beads of sweat clinging to the hair on his chest. Tabs's delicate collarbones moved up and down with every panicked breath. It felt like the thumps of my heartbeat were spreading across my whole body, until I could feel my pulse in my cheeks.

'Let's talk about this.' Francis awkwardly unwound himself from Tabs's grip and their twisty, vigorous position. Clearly, the two of them had been getting more use out of the Kama Sutra book he'd bought as a Valentine's Day present than we had. Francis launched himself from the bed, covering his flailing willy with a pillow. *Don't look at it.* I averted my eyes, feeling suddenly embarrassed and self-conscious even though he was my fiancé. *Don't look at him. Cheating Francis with his cheating penis.*

I'd watched scenes like this unfold in movies. I always thought I'd lose my mind with anger if it happened to me, but I was numb. My whole body was stunned to silence. Everything fogged over into a blur. Francis was talking to me, but I couldn't hear a word. Tabs rubbed her eyes, smudged with black mascara that stained the white sheets, and refused to meet my stare as I bit my lip and fought back tears.

The realisations peppered my mind, forming thick and fast, while my brain processed the reality of what was happening slowly, as if I was trying to sprint through treacle. His gym sessions, working late at the office, acting distant, and even how strangely both he and Tabs were behaving at our engagement party. It was the ultimate cliché of an affair; a checklist with a tick in each box of warning signs. The clues were there: how had I missed them?

My head was thick and cloudy. My arms trembled and my legs wobbled as another surge of adrenaline coursed through my body for the second time that day. Without a word, I turned around, slammed the door, and ran out of the apartment into the fresh air.

SIX

One month later

The longest month of my life had passed since I discovered my fiancé and best friend in bed together, on the same day that the Whittington Soup board members betrayed me and my family by voting my dad out as chairman of the company my great-grandfather had built from nothing.

My parents had spent the last few weeks working with our solicitors, who battled to challenge the decision made by the board, but with no success. It transpired that Dad had accidentally given the green light to rewrite the company by-laws a year ago, and he'd signed them off without reading them closely. Thanks to Dad's signature, we were powerless to reverse the boardroom vote. Jonathan was now the managing director *and* chairman of Whittington Soup. Dad had been beating himself up about how he hadn't seen the signs of how bad things were with the shareholders, but we tried to reassure him that everything was clearer with the beauty of hindsight.

Life had done a complete turnaround on me since the boardroom vote. Not only was I adjusting to being jobless and single again, after thinking my career was on track and I'd found the man I was going to spend the rest of my life with, but I'd lost my social life too. I hadn't heard from any of my so-called friends since the news about losing the business went public, and I assumed they'd also taken Francis and Tabs's side when news of the affair got out. Who loses their family business, job, fiancé *and* their friends all in one go?

I was about to add losing my home to the list too, as Francis and I finally had the conversation about moving out. Via text, no less, and probably while he was in Tabs's bed. The apartment was his, so despite everything he'd done, I didn't have a leg to stand on. I was moving out and I'd bet money that Tabs would soon be moving in.

But I didn't want to stay in that apartment anyway; it held too many memories. I couldn't get the image of Francis and Tabs out of my mind. Clearly, I did *not* do enough yoga or Pilates to achieve that level of flexibility. How on earth did she get her leg— *Don't think about it, Bella.* I shook myself back to reality, away from how impressed I was by their nimbleness, and reminded myself that it was my fiancé and my best friend who betrayed me. Impressive agility or not, they were terrible, terrible people.

The usually pristine penthouse apartment Francis and I shared was unrecognisable, with endless boxes stacked everywhere. But most importantly, I had almost finished packing. The contents of my make-up bag were rolling around the kitchen floor as I desperately tried to track down my favourite Bobbi Brown eyeliner. Recent events had taught me that eyeliners were like men; good ones, the ones with staying power, were rare. And the bad ones left a smudgy, tear-stained mess. An eyeliner pencil slowly spun along the marble floor, hitting a bag of Francis's beloved overpriced protein powder.

A thought came to mind.

No. No, Arabella Whittington, you can't *do that*, I admonished myself.

But... could I? Pushing myself to my feet, I grabbed the Le Creuset salt mill filled with pink Himalayan salt.

Surely Francis deserved some sort of punishment for sleeping with my best friend?

Before I could stop myself, I was aggressively twisting the top of the salt mill. 'Oops,' I said, as I poured the mountain of rose-coloured granules into the pricey powder. I brushed the remaining residue from my hands and tightened the lid back on the tub of soiled protein powder.

My act of revenge made me feel momentarily better, but I was still utterly deflated as I walked up the stairs to the bedroom to finish getting ready. For a fleeting moment, as I pushed open the double doors, I forgot about the fact that I was in the room where I'd discovered Francis in bed with my best friend.

My side of our his-and-hers walk-in wardrobes was completely empty. There were marks all over the walls where my pictures used to hang – the memories caught on camera, of Francis and me together, my parents, Tabs and my friends.

What the hell was happening to me? To my life? It still felt surreal. I should've been spending the weekend planning my wedding – touring venues, pencilling in dates, trying on dresses and pinning colour schemes on Pinterest.

I sank down next to my pile of evening gowns. They looked so glamorous – the chiffon, the silk, the vibrant colours and the intricate detailing. I wondered when (or if) I would wear one again, now that I wouldn't be moving in the same social circles. Why hadn't I ever appreciated the beauty of dresses like this before? I'd just buy one, wear it, have it dry-cleaned, and then put it away in my wardrobe, never to be worn again. God forbid I would be caught repeating an outfit. Stroking the pile of dresses with a new-found affection, I felt a tear sting my eye. I knew I wasn't just mourning the breakdown of mine and Francis's relationship, but my previous life too, before everything went wrong.

My phone beeped with a text from Dad telling me he was outside, ready to help me pack my belongings before the removal vans arrived. Until I found a new apartment, I was staying in a hotel. Mum was always redecorating and renovating the house, so it came as no surprise when she told me a long and rambling story about how she was refurbishing the third floor to create a huge walk-in wardrobe, and the house would be terribly dusty and noisy during the work. To be honest, I was happy having my own space; I needed time to think and work out my next steps. If I was at home, Mum would've been dragging me out with her personal trainer at 6 a.m., and then for various happy hours from 6 p.m.

Every step I took echoed loudly throughout the apartment, which felt so empty but so full at the same time. I pulled open the front door and turned back to look around, knowing it would be one of the last times I'd walk out of the door of the place that Francis and I had called home.

SEVEN

Renting a luxury flat was expensive. Who knew? I certainly couldn't afford the extravagance of the Albert Dock any more – not now that I was unemployed, and Dad had put me on a new, modest allowance while my parents figured out their finances and legal fees. So far, the rent on all the apartments I'd found was more than my monthly shopping bills and that was saying something.

For the first time in my twenty-four years of existence, I was looking at prices and saying things like, 'Fifteen pounds for avocado toast? That's daylight robbery!' And I was learning a lot about everyday life without the endless funds of my dad's credit card to fall back on.

Out of pride, I lied to my parents and told them I'd landed a job at a top PR agency in the city centre. They knew how much my career meant to me, and I couldn't bear any more of Dad's sympathetic glances and Mum's constant comments about 'joining the LinkedIn' (which she thought was some sort of ladies' luncheon group).

But in reality, I was jobless, with no prospects. So far, I'd heard zilch from the countless companies and recruitment agencies I'd sent my CV to. I'd previously listened half-heartedly to friends moaning about how competitive the job market was, but I'd never given it a second thought. Of course, that was when I thought I'd prove myself in the corporate world and forge an impressive career leading the PR department at Whittington Soup and work there until I was a little old lady.

I tried to focus on the good things and look on the bright side. Things were bound to improve soon – they couldn't get any worse, anyway. And I was looking forward to a nice catch-up dinner with my parents that evening. Usually, we'd make a reservation at somewhere fabulous, but for some reason, my parents had opted for an Italian I'd never heard of outside the city centre. I assumed Mum was in the midst of some sort of crisis and was in desperate need of comfort food to cheer herself up – you always knew Mum was under stress when she ate simple carbohydrates.

While my parents were renovating their house in Birkdale, and until I found a new apartment, a tiny room in a bed and breakfast called 'Sleepz Eazy' somewhere between Southport and Liverpool was my temporary home. My new shoestring budget (ironically named, given I couldn't afford my favourite shoes) didn't allow for the luxury hotels that I was used to. And most of my belongings were back in storage after Dad admonished me for trying to sneak nineteen suitcases in. Then we got into a *very minor* disagreement about how many pairs of shoes were 'essential' (in my defence, it was less than a hundred).

This will do for now, I assured myself with wobbly optimism, as I shut the door of the musty room and the dodgy lock clicked into place. Surely it wouldn't be *too* difficult to find a nice three-bedroom apartment with city views, a dressing room and an outdoor terrace on my budget. I'd even sacrifice the third bedroom and go for a two-bed if push came to shove. Something was bound to come up soon, I nodded confidently as I crossed the road.

Besides, today was a big day. I was going to experience public transport for the first time! I'd never actually used it before and was already fighting the urge to call Dad and beg him to pick me up.

I tried to ignore those nervous feelings from fear of the unknown – all I knew was that public transport was just so *public*. But at least I looked good, which gave me a confidence boost. I wasn't sure what the dress code was for the restaurant, as it didn't appear to have a website. So, I'd opted for a classic combination of a cute silk Chloé skirt and matching top, my favourite Balenciaga bag, and some gorgeous Giuseppe Zanotti heels that I'd been waiting for the right occasion to wear ever since I bought them – and now I hoped that my first bus journey was worthy enough. If there was anywhere in the world that a bus journey would warrant a fabulous outfit, it'd be Liverpool. One of my favourite things about the city was that you could always rely on Scouse girls when it came to glamour.

I smoothed my skirt down nervously and adjusted my top as I tottered over to the large map and timetable of bus services. I hoped the poster lived up to its helpful-sounding name of 'Journey Planner' – I'd plan my journey and arrive at the restaurant to the 'ooh's and 'aah's of my parents, who would be in awe of their wonder child – probably the first person in the family to conquer public transport!

Leaning in to get a closer look at the map, I traced the different lines with my fingernail. *Wow*. So many options, so many routes, so many buses! Liverpool was bigger than I'd thought. Typically, I stuck to where I knew – my home in the Albert Dock, the Whittington Soup headquarters in the commercial district, shopping in The Metquarter, and then the usual haunts for brunches, dinner and cocktails. What an adventure this was! I felt silly about how worried I'd been as I took in my surroundings while sitting on the hard yellow seat in the shelter. Although my bum was already getting numb –

were buttery leather cushions too much to ask? Perhaps I'd suggest it to the bus driver, or see if Dad knew the CEO of Arriva.

Taxis pulled up along the barriers on the other side of the bus lanes, but I was smugly relishing my new feeling of independence. Who needed a chauffeur when you could enjoy the delights of the bus? I beamed at the woman rocking her pram next to me and she smiled politely back. Then, right on time (how *efficient!*), the aquamarine double-decker bus rolled around the corner. The number 47 glowed orange, with Liverpool City Centre emblazoned as its destination.

My heart raced at what felt like two hundred beats per minute, a pace usually only reserved for Barry's Bootcamp. Well, that one time when Francis dragged me along with the promise of pancakes afterwards. *Never again,* I shuddered.

The bus pulled up and I noticed the huge queue of people suddenly winding behind me. My plan was to copy what the new mum next to me did, but she expertly collapsed her pram, jumped on and flashed a bus pass with expert ease. Then it was my turn.

'Good evening,' I greeted the bus driver, who tipped his glasses to the end of his nose and smiled pleasantly at me. His white shirt was lovely and smart, with the Arriva logo stitched onto the pocket. This was already much more civilised than I imagined. 'I need to get to Toxteth, and I'm aware I need to get two buses, so is it possible to purchase both tickets from your kind self?' I fluttered my eyelashes, hoping he'd forgive my ignorance.

'Single?' he said.

I jerked my head back in astonishment. 'I beg your pardon,' I said, not attempting to hide my horrified expression.

'Single?' he repeated with a tired sigh.

I ran my hand over the spot where my engagement ring once sat. 'Not that it's any of your business, and I think it's very inappropriate for you to ask, but I was engaged, yes, although it didn't work out and now—'

'Single ticket, love,' the bus driver clarified. 'Single or return ticket. Are you travelling one way or both ways? I'm happily married, I'll 'ave you know,' he chuckled.

'Oh,' I mumbled, my cheeks flushing pink with embarrass-ment. 'Erm, yes, a single ticket, please,' I said sheepishly, pained from embarrassment, and also reminded of my new relationship status. I popped the £10 note on the tray below the dividing glass window, and he exchanged it for a small ticket and the coins that made up my change.

'Thank you,' I stammered, dropping the loose change into my handbag. I wobbled precariously along the empty rows of aqua-blue seats, gripping the bright yellow poles fixed between the floor and the roof. I jumped as a high-pitched ding filled the bus every time I touched one of the poles. I hesitated, before touching the next one and it happened again.

'Bloody 'ell, love, you a musician now an' all?' the bus driver chortled, watching me through the mirror next to his seat.

'I'm sorry...' I stuttered. 'I think these things are faulty.' I gestured to the pole next to me, eyeing it suspiciously.

'Love, there's a little red "stop" button on the other side,' he replied. 'That's what the noise is. If you press it, it'll ding, and the bus will stop.'

It sounded dangerous, the bus just stopping like that. What if it was on a busy road? Should the passengers really be allowed that much control?

'Oh,' I said. 'My fault, sorry.'

He shook his head, his lips shaped into an amused grin, and continued counting out the next passenger's change.

The middle rows seemed the safest bet, so I took a seat next to the window. At least I'd be able to watch the world go by and hopefully regain some of the confidence I'd already lost on my first bus adventure. I hugged my handbag into my lap and watched the queue. Person after person paid their fare, or waved their pass, and took their seats. Some headed up the stairs and I wondered what was up there. Gosh, it'd be fabulous if it was a refreshment bar like on the Emirates A380.

Eventually, the entire bus vibrated and the engine rattled to life. We were off! I looked around excitedly at the other passengers, but none matched my enthusiasm as they gazed out of the windows. We rolled through the streets, stopping to pick up the passengers who were waiting at bus stops with an arm in the air, and dropping others off at the designated stops (after they rang the bell).

I daydreamed as we zigzagged around the outskirts of Liverpool, in an area I'd never seen before. A mural of The Beatles decorated the wall of a derelict gym where an overflowing skip marked the entrance, and a group of kids on bikes gathered outside a corner shop, staring menacingly at every car that drove past.

Hugging my arms around my handbag, I cursed myself for wearing five-inch platforms. Three-inch heels would have been the sensible option. I'd get through this in three inches, but five? What if I had to run from the scary youths on bikes?

I breathed a sigh of relief when the Radio City Tower crept into sight, knowing I was getting closer to the city centre. I was practically light-headed with the relief that I'd survived the first half of my journey, and it hadn't been too traumatic. But then the bus slowed and swerved into the next bus shelter where a sea of football shirt-wearing men gathered. They couldn't possibly be getting on, could they? Surely there was no room for them. I looked around at the unconcerned faces around me, hoping perhaps we'd all rally together in bus passenger solidarity.

The doors opened and a flurry of noise and energy filled the bus. The men were chanting in perfect synchronisation, only pausing for friendly banter with the driver. The smell of beer wafted under my nose gradually, until it was so strong that I was forced to breathe through my mouth. Just when I thought the last person had stepped onto the bus, another one jumped on, and another! They took every spare seat from the back to the front, and gathered in the aisles, swaying from side to side.

The bus croaked to a start again as one man clumsily plonked himself down next to me. My eyes widened with horror as I felt him sitting on my skirt. The beautiful silky fabric was almost making contact with the crack of his hairy bottom peeping over the waistband of his jeans. I stared straight ahead. *Don't say anything. Don't make a fuss.* The chanting began again, quietly at first until the volume grew so loud that I couldn't hear myself think.

'I'm terribly sorry.' I turned to the man next to me. 'But do you mind?' I waved my half-covered skirt next to him.

'Sorry, love,' he slurred, shifting his weight over slightly. His half-closed eyes widened as he looked at my skirt and then my shoes. 'Ey, look at your clobber, girl.' He squinted at me. 'You're a proper prin you are, like.'

'Thank you,' I said nervously, unsure if he was complimenting or insulting me. What on earth was a 'prin'?

'Whaddya doin', all on yer tod?' He swigged the final dregs from the can of beer in his hand, before pulling another from his jacket pocket, tapping the tab and then clicking it open to the sound of an effervescent fizz, which he slurped noisily.

'I'm going for dinner with my parents.'

'Ahh, I could do with a good scran, me. Celebratin' the match, we are!' he garbled, before turning around, raising his arms up and joining in with the thunderous chorus again. In his excitement at a particularly passionate line, he stood and waved the full can around, drowning me in a shower of beer.

'Argh!' I squealed, brushing the foamy bubbles off myself. The drink had already stained my immaculate top and left dark circles all over my skirt. I felt my feet squelch inside my high heels as the liquid formed a pool around my toes.

'Aw, love, I'm sorry.' He lifted his hands to help. 'It's chocka block in 'ere.' He gestured around him.

'It's fine,' I huffed through gritted teeth.

'Aw, I am sorry though, love,' he repeated.

'It's fine,' I sighed, hugging my bag to myself protectively, and turning my attention towards the window instead. We were pulling up to what I assumed was the next bus station. I needed to get off the bus, breathe in air that didn't smell like a brewery, and find the next bus that would take me to Toxteth and to my parents.

I made a silent vow that I'd never, ever get the bus again. A lifetime of taxis would cost less than all the clothes I'd have to replace if this was what happened on public transport.

EIGHT

Hurrah! I'd made it to the restaurant, even though I was covered in the murky brown splodges from the spilt beer can, and I smelt like I'd rolled around the ale-covered floor of a pub. But at least I had dinner to look forward to. I salivated as I thought about what I fancied; maybe scallops and a chilled glass of champagne to start, followed by a fillet steak with all the sides and a full-bodied glass of red. Then dessert, even if Mum gave me a hard time about it. Dessert – and alcohol, plenty of alcohol – were probably the only things that could calm me down from the stress of the journey.

I followed the instructions that the second bus driver gave me for the Italian restaurant where Dad had booked the table. I took the driver's chortling at my never having heard of the 'legendary' Papa Jack's Pizza in good humour. After clip-clopping on my heels along the pavement like a pony, I looked around as I stood outside. Dad must've made a mistake and booked a table at the wrong place, or maybe it was one of those secret bars that look neglected from the outside, but on the inside they're all plush leather, flattering lighting and creative cocktails – there were a few of those in Liverpool.

The neon light on the sign outside the restaurant was broken, but the random letters that were lit up flickered ominously in the wind. If it was a secret bar, it was *very* well disguised. I tottered warily forwards and pushed open the creaky old door. Mum and Dad were the only people inside; they were sipping wine at the back of the empty restaurant that definitely didn't double up as a luxury venue. Mum had her sunglasses on, despite it being 7 p.m., and the fact that they were in a questionable restaurant in Merseyside, not soaking up the sun along the Grand Canal in Venice.

'Oh, hello, sweetheart!' Dad jumped to his feet as soon as he saw me.

'Hello, *mon petit chou*,' Mum whispered, without looking up from the table.

'What on earth...?' I said, placing my Balenciaga bag in its own seat.

Mum was almost unrecognisable in her oversized dark lens sunglasses, a headscarf and deep plum lipstick; she was even wearing leather driving gloves. It reminded me of the time when she tried dermal fillers in her wrists because her friend Cordelia had convinced her they 'gave away her age'.

'I wouldn't have recognised you.'

'Good,' she hissed. 'That's the idea. I cannot believe your father has brought me here. I wouldn't be caught dead...' She tilted her shades and looked me up and down, her feathery eyelash extensions framing her wide eyes. 'Goodness gracious me, Arabella Allegra. What on earth happened to you? You look like you've been dragged through a hedge backwards – and not in a hobo chic, Alexander McQueen collection, circa 2001, Milan Fashion Week way!'

I caught a glimpse of myself in the window as I worked through the knots in my hair with my fingers. My bouncy curls from my DIY blow dry had already turned to frizz without my beloved Olaplex No.3 Hair Perfector treatment I could no longer afford, and my eye make-up was smudged around my eyelids.

'I got the bus!' I proudly declared, ignoring my bedraggled appearance.

Mum's jaw dropped, as if I'd just confessed to her that my favourite pastime was killing puppies. Or shopping in the sales. Both would've had the same effect.

'You did *what*?' She held her head in her hands and shook it dramatically. 'You took *public* transport? How? Why? Oh *mon Dieu*. Wilfred, this is all *your* fault. I told you we should've picked her up. Oh, my darling girl. My little pain au chocolat...' She put her glove-covered hands over mine.

'It was fine,' I said as breezily as I could muster, straightening my posture. 'I'm an independent woman now. I'm standing on my own two feet.' Ouch, my feet hurt. I kicked my shoes off under the table. My skin was raw with blisters.

'Wilfred!' Mum roared, slapping her hands on the table suddenly and making me and Dad jump. 'Clearly Arabella is working through some sort of...' She motioned with her hands. 'Issue. An early mid-life crisis, perhaps.' She took her sunglasses off and stared intensely into my eyes. 'Do you want me to see if I can get you into The Priory? I still have a friend there, I could pull some strings...'

'Don't be ridiculous, Aurelia,' Dad said, 'we're not shipping her off to rehab.' He turned his attention towards me. 'Although, Bella, sweetheart. Are you *sure* you're OK?' He flashed Mum a concerned glance.

'It's only the bus,' I half laughed, while simultaneously shuddering at the memory of the man's bum crack on my beloved skirt that I'd now have to throw out because I didn't know how to wash silk. But I wouldn't admit defeat to my parents. 'It was fine – it was jolly good fun, actually! There was singing and everything. There might've been a refreshment bar on the upper level too.'

'Can I get you anything?' The bored-looking teenage waitress thankfully interrupted the tense moment, as she sulked at the side of the table. 'Any more drinks?'

'A bottle of champagne, please,' Mum said on autopilot.

'Oh, OK, erm...' The waitress bit her lip. 'I'll have to check if we have any.'

Mum turned to face me, eyes wide with horror. 'What kind of establishment—'

'We need to speak to you about something, Bella,' Dad interrupted.

'Is this about Mum's anti-cellulite Turkish massage again?' I rolled my eyes and tapped the table with my nails.

'Sweetie muffin,' Mum mouthed, reaching across the table to hold my hand. 'All I'm saying is that you might've felt better about the presentation "incident" if you'd been to my bottom masseuse specialist. It's very important to keep your blood circulation going. I should know, I was—'

'Yes, yes, you were the poster girl for it, we all know,' I said as Dad rubbed his temples.

'I was *huge* in Istanbul,' Mum said proudly. 'Literally, there were *huge* billboards of me *everywhere*, darling. My posterior and I are utterly legendary.'

'Aurelia,' Dad said, gently but firmly, to Mum's mutterings that her fame was totally unappreciated in this family. 'We really do need to talk to you, my Bell Bell.'

Mum put her dark shades on again and nervously pulled her fringe back behind her ear, only for it to fall upon her heavily made-up face again. She brushed some non-existent crumbs off her lap and drank her entire glass of rosé, seemingly in one giant gulp.

'There's no easy way to say this, but your mother and I...' Dad took Mum's hand. 'We've decided to move to France.'

I felt my mouth drop open. 'France? As in, France? France in Europe?' I said, studying their nervous faces.

Dad nodded as he stroked Mum's hand with his thumb. 'We've been through so much lately. Not only the whole situation with Whittington Soup...' I looked away at the very mention of our beloved family business. I still blamed myself for everything that went wrong – my friendship with Polly, the disastrous presentation and the negative press.

'Everything that was in the papers about your mother and our family,' Dad continued, as Mum shuddered theatrically. 'You know your mother's friends will never forget a juicy scandal. We've had a wonderful time here in the UK, but we're both ready for a new chapter in our lives.' They smiled at each other.

'OK, but why France? Yes, it's where you're from, Mum...'

'*Oui*,' Mum shrugged nonchalantly.

'But why go back now? I thought you started modelling so you could get away from there?'

'I grew up in a very small town, *mon amour*,' Mum said softly, taking her sunglasses off again. 'I left because I wanted to see the world. I've lived in the bright lights of the city – London, Paris, Milan, New York.' She sighed with nostalgia. 'I fought off a polar bear in Alaska with my bare hands when a modelling shoot went wrong. I survived being lost in the Peruvian rainforest when Richard Branson's plane crashed. I've trekked through the Sahara Desert with only a camel for company when the Sheikh and I split up, and I called the wilderness of the Tianzi Mountain my home for two months when Madonna's hen party got out of hand.' Mum shook herself back to reality. 'But I digress, my darling. My point is that I've seen the world, I've had my adventures, and sometimes, you don't realise what you want until it isn't there any more. I'm craving a simple life again.' Mum turned to Dad and kissed him on the cheek. 'A simple, low-maintenance life.'

'I'm dead sorry,' the waitress said as she skipped to our table. 'We haven't got any champagne. We've got some fizzy stuff from the Spar though, that's basically the same thing, isn't it?'

Mum inhaled deeply, closed her eyes and took three audible breaths.

'Not to worry,' Dad said calmly, clocking Mum's impending meltdown and first test of 'a simple, low-maintenance life'. 'We'll have three margherita pizzas, please, and three glasses of Chardonnay.'

As I clocked the plastic, food-stained menu, Mum opened one eye and pointed to the menu and then to her gloves. 'Swimming. In. Bacteria,' she mouthed to me across the table, nodding knowingly.

'*Large* glasses,' Dad emphasised to the waitress as he passed the menus to her.

'Make it a bottle,' Mum interrupted. 'In fact, make it two. No, three!'

The waitress nodded at Mum and scurried away.

'Have you thought about where you're going to live in France?' I asked, before nibbling a breadstick and swiftly putting it down again as its stale flavour filled my mouth.

'Do you remember when your mother's aunt Hélène died?' Dad said.

'God rest her soul,' Mum declared dramatically as she made the sign of the cross, despite not being remotely religious and referring to her favourite Garrus rosé as her 'holy water'.

'We hadn't really considered it seriously before now,' Dad said, 'but she left us a run-down cottage in the Loire Valley.'

'A *run-down cottage*?' Mum exclaimed. 'It's a *maison de campagne*, Wilfred.' She turned back to face me after admonishing Dad. 'A country house,' she clarified. 'Though it's *practically* a château,' she murmured.

'Anyway,' Dad said, widening his eyes at me in mock despair. 'It's a *country house*,' he said cautiously. 'Practically a château,' he repeated slowly. 'But it needs *a bit* of work doing to it,' he said, to Mum's satisfied nod. 'Our plan is to do it up and run a bed and breakfast.'

'That's great,' I said. 'I'm happy for you both.' I felt my bottom lip wobble as Dad squeezed my hand. I'd had enough of crying over the last few weeks, but I couldn't believe my parents were moving away – something else to add to the long list of things I was losing in my life.

'At least you'll still have your house in Southport,' I affirmed. 'Gosh, those renovations you're doing at the moment sound incredible too. Maybe I'll move in for a few months while I search for a new apartment? I don't mind house-sitting.' I smiled at them.

Mum and Dad looked at each other, before they both shuffled uncomfortably in their seats. I could sense the tension immediately.

'What?'

'That's the thing,' Dad said, looking down at the table. 'The house in France, the work that needs to be done...' He cleared his throat. 'Well, it's all very expensive, petal. It's going to cost a lot.' He loosened his top button.

'Right...' I answered. I stared at them both, knowing there was more to come.

Dad laid his hands down on the table and inhaled deeply. 'We've sold the house.'

'You've what?' My mouth dropped again.

Dad tried to fill the silence by babbling on, but I only heard segments of what he was saying. My mind was working overtime. I was trying to digest the fact that the house I'd grown up in, the only house I'd ever truly called home, wasn't going to be my parents' any more.

'It's not as if we had a choice, really,' Dad reasoned. 'We had a look at our finances. They took a serious bashing with all the legal fees and obviously I didn't get any sort of payout from the company when I left...' He corrected himself. 'When I was forced out. But after selling the house and a few other assets, we'll have enough money to pay for the renovations to our new house.'

'So, you lied to me about why I couldn't move in for now? You're not turning the third floor into a huge walk-in wardrobe?' I looked open-mouthed at Mum, who sheepishly turned away. 'Why didn't you tell me?'

'It all happened so fast, my little lamb.' Dad held his palms out. 'It sold within twenty-four hours. It helped that we lived next door to a Liverpool FC player and a two-minute walk from the golf course.'

'But what do you mean about your finances?' I asked desperately; I assumed my new, reduced allowance was temporary.

My head was spinning. I thought about the five figures on my monthly credit card bills that I would hand over to Dad with a shrug. They were always my rewards for working so hard, for burning the midnight fuel at the office: my *enthusiastic* shopping habits. My luxury spa days. My penchant for vintage champagne and overpriced yet extremely photogenic cocktails. How could I afford everything I loved most in life?

'You must have, like, savings or something? What's that thing called... a pension?' My voice was getting more and more shrill.

'We're not *pensioners*, Arabella Allegra,' Mum said, aghast. 'Exactly how old do you think we are?'

'We're not exactly "cash rich", my little lamb.' Dad squirmed in his seat. 'Of course, we'll give you some money from the house sale – it might not be much, after everything. But we'll make sure you have enough money to get by, and we're so proud that you have a job lined up so quickly.'

My cheeks flushed with the guilt of my little white lie. Why did I have to tell them I had a job? They might've given me more money if they thought I was unemployed, and I desperately wanted to go on a spending spree. Just a few treats to cheer myself up – a pair of Manolo Blahniks, maybe. Or a new Cartier watch. Or a Chanel bag. Something classic that would be an *investment*. Dad was always telling me to invest, after all.

'As for us,' Dad said, 'we're relying on the new B&B to see us through our old age.'

'Speak for yourself, Wilfred,' Mum shrieked.

'Our old*er* age, I should say,' Dad quickly added.

'Well, I'm so pleased you have everything figured out for yourselves,' I said, a little sarcastically, as I folded my arms over my chest. My stomach was churning, my heart was throbbing. Losing them, and the house, was the nail in the coffin of these hellish months.

'You could come with us, if you wanted to,' Mum pouted.

'You know I'm trying to rebuild my life and my career, don't you?' I said, biting my lip so I wouldn't let slip the white lie that I didn't have a job yet. 'I don't want to leave Liverpool. I want to make a life here. I can't just run away and pretend I'm on *Escape to the Chateau*.'

'Oh, that reminds me, I *must* phone the producer back,' Mum said, before stopping herself when she sensed my glare and Dad tapped her leg under the table.

'I know it's a lot to take in,' Dad whispered.

'And Mum.' I looked at her. 'You do know that running a B&B means doing housework, right?'

Mum opened her mouth and closed it again like a goldfish; we both knew she hadn't so much as glanced at a cleaning device since she accidentally hoovered up my pet gerbil, Roger. RIP.

'Hang on. Is this news anything to do with why we're here?' I asked suspiciously, while looking around the dim and dingy restaurant.

'Yes, petal. We thought it would be fun!' Dad clapped his hands together. 'A change of scenery! You know, a bit different from the usual places we go.'

'Wilfred,' Mum grunted. 'You might as well tell her.'

'Tell me what? What now?' I tried to sound calm as the waitress placed three glasses and three bottles of wee-coloured Chardonnay in front of us.

'Nothing, my little lamb, it just makes a change.' Dad poured the wine and it glugged messily into our glasses, which Mum had surreptitiously wiped approximately twelve times with a tissue from her handbag. 'You know, new surroundings, new places, it's all very exciting!' He took a sip from his wine and grimaced before forcing a smile. 'Excellent Chardy. Scrumptious.'

'Welcome to your new neighbourhood, darling,' Mum said, before sipping the wine and wincing as if she was in physical pain.

'I'm sorry, what?' The familiar feeling of panic I'd recently grown so accustomed to was rising inside me again. 'My new... neighbourhood?'

'We found a flat for you.' Dad smiled nervously.

'We?' Mum cried. 'No, no, no. *Non!* I had *nothing* to do with this.' She waved her hands furiously. '*Rien,*' she wailed.

'You've found one... here?'

'A friend of mine, Hector from golf. He owed me a favour,' Dad said. 'I mentioned we were looking for an apartment for you and he said he was investing in this area. You don't want to live at the Albert Dock anyway, do you, sweetheart? You don't want to risk bumping into Francis again.'

'Maybe not the Albert Dock,' I said. 'But you think that here would be the perfect place for me? *Here?* Really?' I took a cautious sip of the warm, vibrantly coloured, pungent-smelling wine.

'It's only ten minutes from the city centre,' Dad said optimistically. 'We met up with Hector before dinner, to sign the contracts and finalise it all for you. We thought it'd be a nice surprise.'

'It's all been decided for me then, thanks,' I said sulkily.

Dad nodded – either not detecting, or ignoring, my sarcasm. 'It's a lovely little studio flat, Bella. It's the perfect starter home. Plus, he said you can live in it rent-free for a few months while you get on your feet and settle in at your new job. Then afterwards, he's giving you a huge discount, so the rent is a steal!'

'Everything is probably stolen around here,' Mum muttered under her breath.

'It's an up-and-coming neighbourhood,' Dad pleaded to me and Mum. 'He said it's really popular with young couples.'

'Pregnant high school drop-outs,' Mum snorted.

'And young professionals,' Dad said.

'Drug dealers, he means!' Mum chipped in again.

'Aurelia, will you just... stop it, please.' Dad held his hands up impatiently and Mum gestured that her lips were sealed, though we all knew it wouldn't last very long.

'Where is this flat, then?' I asked.

'It's just around the corner, we can go as soon as we've finished our pizza,' Dad beamed.

With that, the pizza arrived at our table.

'Delicious!' Dad said as he picked up a slice – a long and stringy piece of cheese followed the chunky, stiff wedge of pizza to his plate. 'See, the crust is nice and thick – it's authentic pizza alla Siciliana – just like the pizza we had during that summer in Sicily!'

Mum and I watched him in silence as he chewed on the mountainous pile of cheese and thick dough for at least three minutes.

'Delicious,' he repeated, still mid-chew, as he avoided our stares and took a hasty glug of wine after an audible swallow.

Mum whimpered, began mumbling in French, and poured the rest of the wine bottle into her glass. An overhead light flickered on above us and I noticed properly for the first time that the dark sunglasses and the heavy make-up were hiding her bloodshot and swollen eyes.

'Are you OK, Mum?' I asked her. 'Your eyes look... You haven't been trying those experimental anti-ageing injections again, have you?'

'No, no, no,' she said. 'I've learnt my lesson, *mon amour*. Besides, I can't have them any more. *And* I'm banned from entering China because of them – remember?' Mum huffed impatiently. She brushed her clothes down before staring at me intently. 'No, my little blueberry muffin. I'm working through something right now. Something much more serious than the quest for eternal youth through untested and unapproved injections from the Far East.'

'What? What now?' I didn't think I could handle any more huge life developments over the course of one dinner.

'I've had to...' Mum's overly plumped lips began to tremble. 'No, I can't. It's too traumatic to talk about.'

'Would you like me to explain, Aurelia?' Dad said patiently.

'Mm-hmm,' Mum murmured, holding her head in her hands.

'Your mother has sold some of her belongings,' Dad said, choosing his words carefully.

'*Some* of them?' Mum wailed. 'I'm an empty nester, Wilfred!'

Mum lifted her head from her hands and wiped away the tears in her eyes. 'Darling Arabella, you should've seen my dressing room. Totally empty. Bare. Barren! An abandoned wasteland where my beloved collections once lived,' she sniffed.

'Aurelia, my love,' Dad said calmly. 'Remember, your wardrobes would be empty anyway, given that we've sold the house and we're moving to France.'

'You should've seen them, Arabella,' Mum barked, ignoring Dad. 'Cordelia and her cronies, all *dying* to get their hands on my vintage Chanel bags, my couture evening gowns,' she sniffed. 'They were like magpies to diamonds – *my Chopard diamonds!*'

'Aurelia.' Dad patted Mum's hand gently. 'We couldn't have taken everything with us anyway, you know that, my love. And we have more money for the renovations now, at least.'

Mum dotted her eyes with a paper napkin, then dramatically threw it down in despair.

'Perhaps you should think about selling some of your expensive handbags too, petal?' Dad said to me, before casually picking up another slice of pizza. He was the only one eating it. 'You do have quite the collection.'

'Wilfred, shh!' Mum cried, her jaw slackening, aghast. 'She'll hear you.' She glared furiously at my dad before lovingly cooing at my Balenciaga handbag and holding it in her arms like a baby. 'Let's not subject Arabella and her divine collection to the same grotesque fate my most prized possessions were forced to endure.' She scowled at Dad again.

'Everything all right, like?' the waitress asked, before flashing a double take at Mum's stilettos. 'Oh my *God*! Your shoes are *gorgeous*! They Louboutins? They blag?'

'*Black?* Yes, they're *black*,' Mum said bewilderedly, surveying her shoes under the table.

'No, I mean, are they blag? Or are they *real*?'

'Well, of course they're *real*. I'm wearing them, aren't I?' Mum looked to me and Dad for support, totally perplexed.

'I'd *love* a pair of them, me,' the waitress beamed. 'Proper prin shoes, them.'

Mum slowly lifted the glass of wine to her pursed lips. It was so full that it was almost overspilling. She took two big gulps.

'Would you...' she said quietly. She took another two mouthfuls, polishing off the glass entirely. 'Would you like to buy them?' she said, barely audible.

'Y'what? Really?' the waitress said, to Mum's gentle nod.

She looked excitedly at the shoes again. 'You look about the same size as me, an' all. You a six?'

Mum nodded silently again.

'How much do you want for them, like?'

Mum tipped her head back, lifted her chest and held her shoulders back defiantly. 'I'll take a hundred pounds for them.'

'Aw ey, really?! Bargain! I'll nip to the cashpoint and be back in a min. Aw, you've made me day, you have!' The waitress skipped happily away from our table.

'You know, you probably could've got a bit more for them,' I whispered to Mum.

'I don't want to discuss the matter any further,' she said, holding her hand up. 'This' – she gestured around our table in a circular motion – 'this never happened. We don't discuss this *ever* again.' She copied mine and Dad's nods of understanding and topped up her wine glass, filling it to the brim again, before slipping off her shoes under the table.

NINE

'What in the world...'

I took the first step into my new home. Gone were the floor-to-ceiling windows with panoramic views over the Liverpool waterfront and the buzzing nightlife of the Albert Dock. Gone were the Calacatta marble floors and cushy cream carpets. The mezzanine master bedroom, the walk-in dressing room, and the roll-top bath in the luxurious bathroom all felt like a distant dream. One single room – which would be my bedroom, kitchen and living space – was my new reality.

Mum hadn't taken her hand away from her mouth from the moment we walked up the stairs in the communal hallway. Well, Dad and I walked. Mum insisted on Dad giving her a piggyback from the restaurant, as she was now shoe-less and had refused the waitress's offer of her trainers when she handed over her heels.

'You've seen the flat before, Aurelia, I don't know why you're being so overdramatic,' Dad hissed.

'I'm not being dramatic, Wilfred.' She scowled and wrinkled her nose. 'I'm trying not to breathe in that revolting stench.'

'What *is* that smell?' I asked, before following Mum's lead and covering my mouth with my hand. My initial shock at the size of the apartment, if you could call it that, meant I hadn't even noticed the smell – which could only be described as rotting vegetables, topped with dog food and a smidgen of old fish. *Fragrant.*

'Don't be such wimps, you two, it's just a bit of new-flat smell,' Dad reasoned, as he tried, but quickly failed, to open the crumbling wooden window. 'I'm sure there'll be a handyman or a concierge around to help with things like that.' He brushed his hands together and a thick layer of dust fell from them to the carpet, landing on a sprawling red stain which I hoped and prayed was red wine.

Mum yelped. 'We can't leave our baby girl here, Wilfred. We just can't.'

Dad's face fell into a frown. 'I know, I know. We can't. I'm sorry, it was a silly idea. I don't know what I was thinking...'

'It's fine.' I sighed. Mum and Dad both turned to look at me. I assumed Mum was shocked, but her expressions were harder to read after her final round of Botox and fillers with her favourite Rodney Street dermatologist.

'Having a little bit more than usual to keep me going in France,' she'd reasoned after her appointment, unable to move her mouth or raise her microbladed eyebrows.

'What?' Dad said, his expression of disbelief much easier to interpret.

'Look, it's fine,' I repeated. 'I've been flat hunting for a little while now and I know there isn't much choice for my budget, especially not this close to the city centre. This... this is fine. Honestly.'

I smiled at the family of spiders in the corner, hoping they were friendly, like those animals in Disney films that sing and hang your washing out. 'I need to get out of that B&B anyway,' I reassured them, though I wasn't sure which was the worse option out of the two.

'We can carry on looking?' Dad offered.

'While you're renovating your French cottage?' I said jokingly. 'Honestly, it's OK, you've spent your entire lives looking after me. As you said, it's your time now.'

'But we simply cannot leave you in this godforsaken place!' Mum howled dramatically. 'Who knows who lives next door? There could be criminals, murderers—'

'Actually,' Dad interrupted, 'Hector mentioned a woman called Susie, who lives in the flat opposite. She's about your age, an artist, apparently.'

'Maybe I could go and have a chat with her tomorrow?' I looked at Mum, whose swollen lips were trembling. 'Susie doesn't really sound like a murderer's name, does it, Mum?'

'This place could be really nice.' Dad nodded, diverting his gaze from ninety per cent of the room. 'It has potential; it just needs a bit of TLC. And as you're not paying anything for the first few months, that should free up some cash for you to spend on it. Buy some nice cushions and curtains. You know, all those things you like.'

'They're called soft furnishings, Wilfred,' Mum said impatiently, as she tiptoed around. 'Darling Arabella, I think I still have some Diptyque candles left over from the last charity luncheon. They were only burnt for an hour, so it *does* seem a waste to simply throw them away...'

'Thanks, Mum, that would be lovely.' I held her hand in mine, and Dad's hand in the other. 'Thank you, both of you,' I said, genuinely grateful to them. 'This is great. It's all going to be great.'

Mum squeezed my right cheek between her perfectly manicured fingernails. 'My darling Arabella, all grown up. Living without a cleaner, or a gardener, or—' Her voice began to break as Dad gently motioned her away from me.

He stroked my hair and pulled me in closely for one of his distinctive bear hugs. 'I'm so proud of you,' he whispered.

'You've been so strong. Remember what we Whittingtons always say...'

'Roll up your sleeves and keep going.' We repeated our family motto together.

Dad kissed me gently on the forehead, his newly grown stubble brushing my skin. 'This could be the start of a new adventure.'

I smiled weakly at Dad. Out of the corner of my eye, I spotted the spider family creeping warily together a little further down the wall. I hoped I wasn't being deliriously paranoid, but the mummy spider certainly looked as though she was sizing up her new tenant.

I deserve this, I told myself, while popping open the second miniature bottle of prosecco Mum left for me and ripping off the note apologising that it wasn't champagne.

I'd spent the day moving everything from Sleepz Eazy into my new flat in Toxteth. I'd packed, unpacked and packed up again – due to a lack of space for eighty per cent of my belongings, which were now going into storage. All under the watchful and (many) eyes of my new, definitely-not-scary, pet spiders.

Cleaning was something I'd never done before and didn't fancy ever doing again. I wasn't even sure if I was doing it right, but I had a new-found respect for the cleaners I'd grown up with, as well as an appreciation for cleaning as a cardio workout.

I poured the prosecco into a mug the size of a bowl and took a couple of gulps, noticing the sky outside was getting darker. I felt drunk already, having not stopped to eat all day. My stomach rumbled and my mouth watered at the thought of food.

Dialling the number of the Italian restaurant where my parents and I had eaten a few days earlier, I felt a brave combination of too tipsy and too tired to care about the not-great pizza. I had fifteen minutes to spare before picking up my order, so I headed out to explore my new neighbourhood.

The streets were lit only with eerie yellow street lights and flickering fluorescent shop signs. Turning a corner, I headed down an alley that I was sure would lead me through a shortcut to pick up my impending feast. The narrow passage was almost pitch-black, with foul-smelling dustbins lining the graffiti-covered walls. There were puddles along the floor, with cigarette butts floating in the dark water, and the strong smell of ammonia made me wince.

A little further ahead, I could see black outlines of what I assumed were rubbish bags ready for the tip. But as I got closer, I saw that some bags had tufts of grey hair peeping out of the top, while others had old trainers and skinny ankles sticking out of the bottom. The sound of deep snoring filled the air, the kind of snore you only hear when there's a bottle of whisky involved.

I realised the dark shapes were not rubbish bags – they were people. People who were fast asleep in the shadows of the dingy alleyway.

There were a few elderly men with thick beards and pale skin. There was a boy who couldn't have been older than sixteen, hugging a battered guitar to his body as if it was a fluffy pillow, and a group of women with a small, scruffy dog snoozing in the middle of their makeshift sleeping bags. It was an entire community, hidden away under a blanket of darkness.

Tiptoeing quietly and carefully past them, I couldn't believe what I was seeing. Of course, I recognised that I had grown up with a privileged life and obviously I was aware there were homeless people in the world. But I guess I just hadn't ever noticed them. *Really* noticed them – not just shuffled past, pretending not to hear their pleas for spare change, or hurriedly passing over a crumpled banknote with a polite nod. What was worse, and what I hated admitting to myself the most, was that I didn't think I had ever really *thought* about them, and what it was really like to live your life on the streets.

It dawned on me at that moment just how selfish and super-ficial my twenty-four years of existence had been. The thought spinning around my mind was that the biggest problem in my old life, outside work, was what colour nail polish I'd choose during my manicure, and whether it would clash with the designer dresses I'd wear for parties and social events over the coming days. All the while, there were people out there – *real* people – who, each night, would rest their heads on a section of urine-soaked pavement they called home.

I picked up my takeaway pizza, took it back to the alley and placed it in the middle of the group. Then I ran back to my flat, lay on the sofa, and sipped my prosecco until the room started spinning and everything went dark.

TEN

A ferocious throbbing thundered between my ears. Rubbing my eyelids and slowly trying to prise them open, my day-old mascara stuck my lashes together like glue. Everything was blurry, but extremely colourful. Too colourful. The walls around me were spinning with bursts of every shade of the rainbow.

I jolted forward and sat up quickly, in a flash of panic.

I was on a bright purple sofa, covered in a multicoloured patchwork quilt. It was the same layout as my new flat, but it wasn't my flat. Where the hell was I? I had a sick feeling in my stomach – a combination of excessive amounts of prosecco on an empty stomach and that deep-rooted panic when you wake from an alcohol-induced blackout, a.k.a. Beer Fear.

The room was still spinning as I pushed myself up and stood, swaying. The floor was covered with wrinkled newspapers, pots of paints, easels and canvases. I edged forward and knocked over a tin of pale pink water, which made a loud clang as it hit the paint-stained wooden floor. I shuddered and held my forehead as the noise hit the exact spot of my horrific headache.

'Goooood morning!' a woman's voice sang from behind a beaded curtain covering the archway in the lounge area. Through my blurry vision, I could see a small kitchen behind the fluorescent pink fabric and the multicoloured beads. I froze in sheer panic. That wasn't a voice I recognised. The room wasn't a place I recognised.

'How's the head?'

The mystery woman pushed the curtain aside and stepped out from the kitchen into the lounge. She was carrying a tray and expertly dodging the various tins, paints and brushes that were spread out across the newspapers on the floor. She set the tray down on the table in front of me – it was stacked with coffee, tea, fresh orange juice, thickly sliced toast, Marmite and strawberry jam – and it smelt like heaven. Hangover heaven.

The woman smiled at me. I swore I'd never seen her before in my life – and she was the type of person you'd remember if you met her. Her wild hair was wrapped in a jade-green scarf and piled messily on top of her head. She wore bright lipstick, as red as her hair, teamed with teal eyeshadow, and her mismatched outfit looked like she'd woken up and decided to wear every piece of clothing in her wardrobe.

I tried to talk but my mouth was too dry, so all that came out was a pathetic high-pitched squeak, which vaguely sounded like 'help'.

'You were pretty wasted last night,' the Hangover Angel explained, sitting back on a squishy, lemon-coloured armchair opposite me. 'I say pretty... it wasn't exactly a pretty sight.' She giggled mischievously, before taking a big bite from a slice of toast slathered thickly with jam.

'What... what happened?' I garbled sheepishly, while reaching for a steaming mug of coffee and lowering myself back onto the sofa.

'You mumbled something about wanting to say hello to your

new neighbour,' she said, her mouth full of toast. 'And you had to reassure your mum that I wasn't a criminal or a murderer?'

I nodded, unable to form words or full sentences just yet.

'I came home from work at about 10 p.m. and you were pretty much comatose, leaning against my door with an empty prosecco bottle in your hand,' she said.

'Eugh,' was all I could manage in response, the memory hazy but slowly forming in my head. I nibbled a tiny bit of a crust, hoping my stomach would soon decide that it was an eat-all-the-food hangover – not a head-in-the-toilet hangover.

'Don't worry,' she said, brushing the crumbs off her denim pinafore, which was embroidered with butterflies and flowers. 'I tried to take you back to your own place, but you kept giving me an address in London, then Southport, and then one over at the Albert Dock, so I figured you'd reached the wine-mania, batshit-crazy stage of drunk and thought you'd be better on my sofa for the night.'

'Ha!' I shrieked, overly loudly, given my hangover from hell. 'Yes, probably. Damn wine-mania. How strange,' I mumbled, burning my lip on the coffee.

My new friend eyed me curiously, then began swiftly buttering another thick slice of toast.

'I'm Susie.' She smiled, holding out her crumb-covered hand.

'Thanks, Susie,' I said, shaking it timidly. My skin scratched against the rows of chunky jewelled rings that decorated her fingers. 'Thanks for looking after me in that state. My name is—'

'Yep, I know, you're Bella,' she interrupted, chuckling. 'We were actually talking for a good hour last night before you passed out again on the sofa.'

'We were? Huh.' I shook my head, then instantly regretted it as the action reinvigorated the throbbing. 'I'm sorry, every-thing's a little hazy.'

'Don't worry,' Susie said, mouth full of toast again. 'You

didn't make a tit out of yourself or anything. You were mainly talking about everything going wrong lately – something about your job and your horrible ex?'

I shuffled uncomfortably in my seat at the thought of Francis.

'It's OK,' she said softly, touching my knee with her big toe. 'You don't need to go into details, I get the feeling you've been through enough recently.'

I nodded, hugging the hot mug between my hands. I realised that, thankfully, she didn't know who I was – probably because if I looked in the mirror, I'd struggle to recognise who I was too. Feeling relieved, I tried my luck at the home-made breakfast buffet again.

'That's it then!' Susie exclaimed, making me jump and drop the toast from my mouth right at the point when I felt safe to take a normal-sized bite. *Argh.* Soon I'd be hangry as well as hung-over.

'I'm going to help you settle in. I think you could do with a friend around here. Am I right?'

'You could be right.' I smiled, before we demolished another half a loaf of bread and endless cups of coffee between us.

'So, what exactly is there to do in Toxteth?' I yawned, still suffering from last night's spontaneously heavy session, but hiding it fairly well thanks to my trusty pair of giant Chanel shades that were so big they made me look like a fly (according to my dad). It was a dull afternoon, but the faint glimmer of sunshine was still too bright for me.

'It's a funny old place, is Toxteth,' Susie said, pulling her pink bike along the pavement next to us. 'It's an area that's been seriously screwed over. Everyone just associated Toxteth – or Liverpool 8 – with the riots; there was an invisible red line around the area, and we were forgotten about. But things are changing now. Toxteth is kind of like Marmite, I guess, although more people love it than hate it.'

'*Love* it?' I repeated. I pushed my sunglasses further up my nose and tightened the ponytail that I'd quickly tied in the rush to get ready.

'Don't look so surprised,' Susie replied. 'Toxteth isn't what you think it is – not any more. Granby Four Streets won the Turner Prize, for God's sake,' she chuckled proudly.

'Who's Granby Four Streets? A local artist, like Liverpool's answer to Banksy?' I asked.

'It's an art project, I'll show you some time. They used art to regenerate the derelict properties around the area, it's amazing.' Susie surveyed her surroundings proudly. 'Toxteth is a close-knit community. Everyone knows everyone, which can be good or bad, depending on how you look at it. We do have our fair share of problems, of course, but where doesn't?'

She had a point. Back in mine and Francis's building, we had a terrible issue with the landlord a couple of years ago about guest parking permits. Nightmare.

I was starting to feel relieved that I'd kept some casual outfits handy, and had never been more grateful for sandals, jeans and a plain T-shirt. Granted, they were all designer, but you could hardly tell.

''Ey girl, giz a blowie,' a scrawny teen shouted while he whizzed past us on his BMX.

'Sure thing,' Susie retorted, as he nearly fell off his bike in surprise. 'Find me again when you grow some pubes,' she said, before he gave us the finger behind his back in response.

The more time I spent with Susie, the more I was learning that she played by her own rules – both fashion and otherwise. Her fuchsia bike (her 'baby') matched her bubblegum-pink fluffy jacket, which she'd teamed with a paint-splattered denim pinafore, magenta tights and mustard Doc Martens that looked at least three sizes too big.

'Is homelessness a problem here?' I asked, to Susie's silence. 'I saw homeless people last night,' I whispered, as we skirted around a particularly smelly stretch of discarded takeaway boxes on the ground.

'And?' Susie replied, nonchalantly.

'Is that normal?'

'Normal for Toxteth? Or normal for Liverpool?'

'Just generally, normal?' I asked.

'Do you mean to say you've never seen a homeless person before?' Susie suddenly stopped walking and looked at me as if I'd just said something unbelievable. 'Hun, where *are* you from?' She nudged me playfully as we carried on down the street.

'I mean, I have *seen* homeless people,' I said defensively. 'Obviously I have. I just, I don't know... I guess I haven't ever noticed them properly before,' I murmured guiltily.

'That's the problem.' Susie sighed, fiddling with the plastic flowers stuck to the wicker basket on the front of her bike. 'People don't notice them. They don't see them as human beings. Not always, anyway.' She looked at me. 'Last night, do you remember I told you what I do for a living?'

I turned to her, and despite wearing sunglasses that covered my face almost as effectively as a balaclava, I was sure she knew what my hidden expression meant. 'I don't think I even knew my own name last night,' I said.

'Funny you should say that actually. You kept telling me your name was Ms Arabella Allegra of Royal Birkdale, and that you were some sort of multi-millionaire heiress.' Susie burst out laughing. 'You were absolutely crackers. Funny, but crackers. Maybe stay away from the vino for a while.'

I laughed nervously. 'Definitely, ha. Bloody hell, how embarrassing.'

'Don't worry about it, it was entertaining,' Susie continued. 'Well, I help to run a soup kitchen for the homeless.'

'No. Way.' I grabbed the sleeve of her pink jacket, a handful of fluff coming off it. 'Are you serious?' I squealed, sneakily trying to pat the pink fluff back onto her jacket sleeve before she noticed.

'Err, yeah?' Susie raised a thick eyebrow that looked like it had never seen tweezers. 'Why the excitement?'

'I just really like soup,' I said, gleefully. 'I really, really like soup.'

'Are you still drunk?' Susie looked at me quizzically.

'Probably,' I declared, ninety-nine per cent certain that I was still drunk. 'Will you show me the soup kitchen?'

'Sure.' Susie grinned.

We retraced our steps down the street again, back towards our apartment block. Taking in the sights of the neighbourhood in the daytime, we made our way past a bright and colourful playground for children, a section of lush green allotments and a row of derelict, boarded-up buildings.

Susie was dragging her bike along to keep up with me, as I appeared to have discovered a spring in my step and was practically skipping along the road. I was excited at the prospect of discovering something familiar in this alien place. Soup had always been a huge part of my life and now, here it was again. Something I knew, something I loved, something that would always be familiar, stable and comforting.

But then I saw the building ahead that Susie pointed to and informed me was the soup kitchen.

It wasn't very familiar, with its cracked windows and paint peeling off the walls. It wasn't very stable – literally, as the building looked to be on the verge of collapse. And the only way in which it was comforting was for the comatose person who was leaning up against the wall, as if it was the headboard of a king-size bed.

'This is it?' I asked Susie, internally praying that she'd burst out laughing and ask if I was joking.

'This is it!' Susie exclaimed, as she chained her bike to a broken bollard in front of the building and said good morning to the person having a snooze.

I looked at the front of the red-brick building with the dark green door. 'What does that say up there?' I pointed to a faded wooden sign.

'Dan's Kitchen,' Susie nodded proudly. 'This is Dan's baby – Dan Rigby – he runs the place.' Susie beamed, as though he was the head chef at the best Michelin-starred restaurant in Merseyside.

'You'll have to excuse it at the moment,' she said apologetically, while picking up a small pile of Special Brew cans that were scattered at the entrance. 'We're waiting for a grant from the council and it's, well, it's a long story. But we're hoping we'll get it soon.'

She stood back on the pavement beside me and looked up at the building proudly. 'We'll get it fixed up in no time, just needs a bit of money, is all.' She pulled a piece of peeling paint from the doorway. 'I keep trying to paint it, but it bloody well keeps coming off, it's like the walls don't want to be painted!'

Susie detected my hesitance. 'Don't look at it like that. You mysterious snob, you. Come on, come in, it's much better inside. I'll show you around.'

She pushed open the door and we stepped into the huge hallway. She was right, the interior was a vast improvement from the exterior of the building. The walls were like rainbows, painted in the brightest array of colours. I realised at that point where Susie had got her inspiration for her flat. There were several rooms off the hallway, each one with an old TV, big bouncy chairs and sofas. There were cosy reading snugs, and there was a children's play area at the end of the hall.

'Do children come here?' I asked, clocking the tatty old pieces of Lego and the broken train set scattered on the floor.

'Yeah, they do,' Susie said quietly. 'It isn't just homeless people, you see. Some people don't have the money to feed themselves or their families, so we run a food bank to try and give them a little something to get by.'

Tears stung my eyes. How much did a Lego set cost? Fifty pounds? That was a bottle of champagne and a bowl of olives at my favourite bar – a standard Friday evening for me. How much was a food shop for a family, I wondered. Perhaps a hundred pounds? I'd spent at least ten times that amount on a handbag without so much as batting an eye.

Susie led me down the magnificently colourful hall and through a small, dark corridor. The only noise was the sound of a dog barking loudly towards the back of the building, and I hoped it wasn't one of those big, scary guard dogs.

When we reached the end of the narrow passageway, Susie pushed the huge door, which seemed far too heavy for her dainty hands. 'Hello, boy!' she exclaimed as a blur of fur came bounding towards us. 'You like dogs, don't you? I mean, who doesn't like dogs?'

'I love them,' I replied. If this excited bundle of fluff was the soup kitchen's guard dog then he wouldn't do much to deter anybody, except showering them with slobbering affection. The dog's tail whipped my legs as he rubbed his furry body against Susie and me. 'My ex didn't, he hated them.'

'Another good reason he's an ex then.' Susie smiled. 'This is Herbie.' She stroked the wiry curls on the dog's head.

Herbie sat down in front of me, and his blue collar jingled as he gazed up at me with big brown eyes that looked like they were lined with black kohl eyeliner. His bushy eyebrows and salt and pepper hair reminded me of my dad and I couldn't help but smile.

'Hello, Herbie,' I said, and he wagged his tail again at the sound of his name.

'He's our soup kitchen mascot.' Susie laughed. 'Even if all

he does here is eat the leftovers and steal the scraps that fall on the floor. Where's your dad, hey, Herb?'

Herbie trotted confidently around the industrial-sized kitchen.

'Daaan!' Susie bellowed. 'Dan! Where are you? We have a visitor!'

The echoes of her shouting forced my hangover headache back with a vengeance.

'You'll like Dan.' She turned around and winked at me. 'Everyone does.'

What on earth did she mean by that? I suddenly felt self-conscious in my creased clothes, combined with alcohol-induced dehydrated skin and greasy hair. I peered at my reflection in the door of an old-fashioned microwave to check I didn't have anything in my teeth, and fiddled with my messy ponytail, hoping Susie wouldn't notice. She did.

'I'm out here!' a distant voice shouted.

'Ah, he must be in the garden.' Susie gestured further down into the sparkling clean, but ancient, kitchen.

We squeezed between the small spaces among the floor-to-ceiling units. Every surface was covered in pots and pans of all sizes. Boxes and bin bags bursting with a kaleidoscope of colourful fruits and vegetables filled the floor.

Herbie led the way as if he owned the place, and I didn't tell on him when I saw him surreptitiously swipe a stray carrot baton. We followed the gentle padding of his paws on the tiled floor, ahead of Susie's walloping steps in her gargantuan Doc Martens.

The rusty hinges of the half-open door creaked as Susie pulled it open to the approving bark of Herbie, who licked his lips after crunching the final mouthful of stolen carrot. He darted through the door and into the wild and overrun outdoor space, which was enclosed by red brick walls covered in graffiti.

Herbie shot towards a figure leaning down in front of a neat row of planter boxes. The hem of his jeans was frayed and scuffed, and the back of his T-shirt displayed Guns N' Roses UK tour dates; the white print was faded from at least one decade of washing.

''Ey, boy!' the deep voice said with a Scouse accent, turning his attention towards Herbie, who circled around him, his entire body practically vibrating with joy. Herbie only left the man's side when he pushed himself to his feet and threw a stick into the yard, which was overgrown with wiry weeds and dense shrubs. Herbie disappeared into it as he searched for his prize.

'Hi, Dan.' Susie waved.

'Oh, hiya Suze,' he said when he turned around to face us. He lifted an arm covered entirely with tattoos and shielded his dark, velvety eyes from the low sun. 'I didn't realise you had company.' He nodded towards me.

'This is Bella.' Susie patted my back so hard I thought last night's prosecco was going to come up and say hello. 'My new neighbour,' she added. I swallowed the nausea back down again.

'Hi,' Dan said neutrally. He lifted his arm up higher, so his T-shirt revealed another display of artistic ink that illustrated his toned stomach.

I averted my eyes as I clocked that I was staring (so many tattoos – how rebellious!). 'Hello,' I said, flustered, hoping he hadn't noticed my gaze darting south of his face that was peppered with stubble, emphasising his chiselled cheekbones and adorable dimples. Now I could see why Susie said everyone loved him with a mischievous glint in her eye – he was Liverpool's own Regé-Jean Page lookalike.

'Nice to meet you, Dan.' I stepped forward and held out my hand to shake his. At least my nails looked immaculate, even if I didn't. I silently thanked the beauty gods for gifting the world with the phenomenon that is non-chip gel manicures; I had at least another week left in them.

Dan wiped his free hand on the soil-covered jeans that

clung to his muscular thighs. His nails were black with dirt and I winced as he shook my hand brusquely; his calluses brushed my fingers and his skin was as rough as sandpaper. This was a man in desperate need of an appointment with the same manicurist that Francis booked in with after his weekly cut-throat shave. Or at least some Elizabeth Arden Eight Hour Cream.

'Good to meet you too,' he said with a forced tone. 'Bella...?'

'Bella Whit—' I stopped instinctively, not wanting to say who I really was. 'Whitson. Bella Whitson.'

'You actually look a bit familiar. Do I know you?' His thick eyebrows knitted together as he squinted at me.

Panic rose up inside me like the hangover vomit I'd swallowed moments earlier. Did he recognise me? I couldn't reveal my last name, this was my fresh start. I took a closer look at him, pursed my lips and shook my head. 'No, I don't think so,' I said resolutely.

He nodded in acceptance, before swiftly turning back to the wooden planter which was bushy with vibrant green leaves. 'I was just cutting some herbs for tonight,' he said in Susie's direction.

I shuffled awkwardly back to my safe space next to Susie.

'What's on the menu?' she said breezily.

Herbie stormed victoriously through the bushes with the stick hanging out of his mouth. I knelt down to stroke him, relieved of the distraction that cut through the stilted atmosphere.

'Roasted red pepper, tomato and basil soup,' Dan replied, while hacking at the herbs with a big pair of shears.

'Ooh, my favourite!' I clapped my hands together excitedly.

Dan turned and glanced at me with a perplexed expression.

'I can help you make it, if you need a hand?' I said – partly as a peace offering, but also because I was already feeling hangover-hungry despite mine and Susie's breakfast feast. And although I had a somewhat limited cooking repertoire, at least

I'd always know how to make amazing soup – as my great-grandfather always said, soup was in my veins.

But Dan turned away again, ignoring my offer of help. 'What brings you here then, Bella Whitson?'

'Susie said she'd show me around—'

'Not to the soup kitchen,' he interrupted, and piled each of the cut leaves into a small wicker basket on the floor next to his knee. 'To Toxteth.'

'I just told you, she's my new neighbour.' Susie rolled her eyes at me behind Dan's back. 'Honestly, Daniel Rigby, you never listen.'

Dan shrugged and Susie gently pulled my arm. 'Anyway, I can see you're busy, we'll get out of your hair. Speaking of which, you *really* need a haircut, Dan. You're starting to look like Hagrid.' She patted Herbie's head and we walked back towards the door we came from. 'Bye, Herbie! Bye, beloved Hogwarts groundskeeper!'

'Bye, Dan, it was nice to meet you,' I said, to his hurried wave and his mumble of 'see you later' as he continued chopping the herbs without a glance in my direction.

Susie closed the door behind her as soon as we were back in the kitchen. 'Sorry, he's usually much more sociable than that.'

'It's OK,' I said, trying to shake it off and wondering why she'd said that everyone apparently loved this standoffish guy who was actually a little rude. And he did *not* look like the Duke in *Bridgerton*, I tried to convince myself; only, maybe, if the Duke was thrown out of high society, then lived in the wilderness for years and knew *nothing* about personal grooming.

'He has a lot on his mind,' Susie said apologetically.

'Don't we all.' I forced a smile and followed her through the building and out into the streets of my new neighbourhood. I hoped that the other residents who called Toxteth home were friendlier than Dan Rigby.

ELEVEN

I'd been shuffling round and round in circles for what felt like hours. It turned out using a paper map was a lot more difficult than Google Maps.

My mind took me back to memories of playful arguments about directions with Dad, and the times he'd drive me blindly around without any idea of the route, but stubbornly insisted that you should never rely on technology to get you from A to B in life. Well, I certainly wasn't getting from A to B in life any time soon. I was probably closer to Z than B.

The reason why I'd decided to finally heed my dad's advice and navigate a paper map in place of the digital alternative? I was on a self-imposed phone detox after spending far too much time on Instagram stalking Francis, Tabs and my former friends. I couldn't bear to see another photo of champagne bottles in ice buckets, picture-perfect plates of food in Michelin-starred restaurants, endless designer carrier bags from shopping sprees, or countdowns to exotic holidays. The fact that the expensive phone contract dug into my tight allowance might've also been somewhat of a factor.

So, there I was, walking in circles, gradually wearing down

the heels of my patent Louboutins, the soles turning from vivid crimson to dirty brown. They were my lucky shoes, and I needed some good luck. The last time I wore them was back in London, when I was accidentally caught in a paparazzi shot and named as Harry Styles's latest squeeze when I just happened to be walking into Sexy Fish for dinner at the same time, and gentlemanly Harry held the door open for me.

I forced my thoughts back to reality; I wasn't in London, and I wasn't going for dinner at Sexy Fish any more. I was lost. However, being lost had its good points, I reassured myself. I was getting to know the area that was now my home.

But when I realised that I was passing the same street for the fourth time in my lap of wrong turns, I decided to call it a day. I'd head back to my flat, put my pyjamas on again and continue my *Queer Eye* marathon; if only I could somehow convince Bobby Berk to work his magic on my new home. Though I would probably qualify for a total life makeover and pep talks from the Fab Five. An image of Dan Rigby popped into my mind – he could do with some grooming tips from Jonathan Van Ness when it came to facial hair upkeep. A little beard oil would not go amiss on that man.

'Whoops a daisy!' a tiny, silver-haired woman cried as I turned a little too quickly, almost bumping into her petite frame. 'Watch yourself there, lovey.'

'Oh gosh, I'm so sorry,' I bumbled, shoving the map into my oversized handbag. 'I wasn't looking where I was going.'

'Not to worry. I'm not surprised you nearly stumbled, look at the size of your heels!' She pointed to my five-inch platforms with a look of awe on her face. 'How on earth do you walk in them?' She pushed her delicate glasses up her nose and bent down slowly to take a closer look. 'They're impressive, even by Scouse girls' standards,' she whispered, with the same fascination as David Attenborough documenting an exotic species.

'I don't know why I bothered wearing them to be honest,' I

sulked, stomping my foot like a petulant toddler and feeling well and truly defeated by my day, despite it only being 10.30 a.m.

'What's the matter, queen?' the woman, dressed completely head-to-toe in purple, like the human version of a Liverpool wheelie bin, said as she reached out and held my hand in hers.

'I've been trying to find the job centre for hours,' I said, pulling the crumpled map from my handbag again. 'Maybe not hours, exactly, but most of the morning. And one minute in these heels feels like an hour.'

She took the map from me and held it in her petite hands. Vivid violet nails matched her glasses, dress, silk scarf and ballet pumps. 'The job centre is what you're looking for?' She narrowed her eyes and the wrinkles lining her skin deepened.

'Yes, that's it.' I nodded. 'I can't find it anywhere. I've walked up and down, going around in circles in these ridiculous shoes.'

She looked again at my Louboutins and then back to me. 'It's right here, my love.' She pointed at the betting shop. 'You have to go up the stairs round the back, you see.' She gestured towards the side alley.

'Oh,' I said, feeling embarrassed when I realised the name of the alleyway was the one right in front of me on the map.

'Don't worry, queen. You're not the only one. Kids today don't seem to look at anything except their phones – at least you're giving it a good go,' she said warmly. 'I can't get my head around these Goggle Maps or The Face Book. I prefer things the old-fashioned way, if I'm honest.'

'I know what you mean.' I smiled, remembering my dad.

'I'm Elsie.' She held out her hand and I shook it gently. Her skin felt as thin as tracing paper.

'I'm Bella. It's nice to meet you, Elsie.'

'Bella, what a lovely name, how exotic. Is it Italian?'

'Kind of,' I replied, hesitant about whether to give my full name.

Elsie pinched her fingers together and started gesticulating animatedly like a real Italian nonna. 'Well-a, as they say-a in Italia, ciao Bella,' she said, and I stifled my giggle.

'It really was lovely to meet you,' Elsie said, as she tightened the floral-patterned headscarf around her perfectly cylindrical curls – Scouse women always have great hair at any age. 'Good luck at the job centre!'

I watched Elsie wander elegantly along the promenade of shops, waving to each and every one of the various men and women perched on the chairs outside; some were drinking coffee or smoking cigarettes, others patiently waited for their bacon butty takeaways, and a few either celebrated or sulked after checking their bets from the bookie's.

Peering down the side alley of the betting shop, I tiptoed towards the rusty staircase that led up to the job centre, where Elsie had confidently directed me. As I reached the top of the spiral stairs, I found the row of offices, and a shabby sign informed me I had reached my destination.

The sharp sound of a bell chimed to inform the receptionist that someone was visiting. The room was dimly lit and cramped, with a small reception desk and a few individual offices. Rows of filing cabinets lined the walls where the paint was peeling.

The receptionist looked up from her desk, where she was avidly filing a bright yellow thumbnail. She raised a severely angled, jet-black eyebrow. 'Can I help you?'

'Yes!' I beamed over-enthusiastically, pleased that I'd finally found the place I'd spent my Saturday morning searching for. 'Yes, you can. I'm here for a job.' I proudly pulled my matching Celine handbag and briefcase in front of me and brushed my hair back behind my shoulders, all the while grinning like a maniac.

'Riiight.' She eyed me suspiciously. 'Let me get Ged, wait here a min.'

'Righto,' I replied, as she looked at me quizzically again. Righto? Where the heck did that come from? Interviews always made me nervous, even though I'd only had a couple in my life. But this wasn't even an interview, it was 'an informal chat to discuss options with our expert advisors' – according to the website.

Scattered across the room were various framed motivational quotes:

'Work hard in silence, let your success be your noise.'

'The expert in anything was once a beginner.'

'It always seems impossible until it's done.'

'Every day may not be good, but there's good in every day.'

'Everything happens for a reason.'

Despite my glass-half-empty attitude towards the day, I smiled at the last one. One of my favourite life quotes, even though it had worn a little thin recently. It's easy to believe that everything happens for a reason when you get a last-minute cancellation appointment at the hairdresser's, or a VIP invite to shop Mulberry's new season collection; much harder when your life as you know it comes crashing down.

'You can go through now.' The receptionist sighed as she took her seat back at the reception desk/manicure station and continued filing her sharp, fluorescent nails.

'This way?' I reconfirmed, making my way towards the door she'd just walked through.

'Mm-hmm,' she mumbled, without looking up.

I carefully nudged the fragile door open.

'That's right. Sweet and sour chicken. Egg fried rice.' The man sitting at the desk clutched a landline phone in his hands and gestured for me to sit in the chair in front of him.

'Yeah. And chips. And spring rolls. And don't forget the

prawn crackers,' he asserted, in a tone that introduced himself as a man who did not mess around when it came to prawn crackers.

I lowered myself slowly into the scruffy chair and rummaged around my briefcase in search of my CV. He hung up the phone after repeating his order and reaffirming the importance of prawn crackers.

'All right, I'm Ged.' He offered a big-knuckled hand and a vice-like grip that almost made me yelp.

'Bella,' I whimpered.

I rubbed my hand under the table as Ged hastily talked me through his role as an advisor, clearly hoping it would be a quick appointment before his early lunch was delivered.

'Sorry love, bit hung-over today, like. Was out on the bevvies with the lads last night, things got messaaay.' He pulled a tissue from his creased shirt and wiped his sweaty forehead.

'It's fine,' I said, unconvincingly. It totally wasn't fine, I could still smell the stale Jägermeister.

Ged continued to reel off a well-rehearsed script about the different job schemes they offered to give back to the community, before he gagged dramatically and swallowed hard. 'Sorry, think that was last night's doner. It's coming up to say hello, I can feel it—'

'I'm looking for something a little more... senior,' I interrupted, meeting Ged's bloodshot eyes and trying desperately not to sound as patronising as I did in my head. 'With a little more pay,' I added, slightly sheepishly.

'Right.' Ged sat back in his seat, his broad and heavy torso far too big for the small swivel chair. 'Something senior with lots of money?' he confirmed, brushing his sausage fingers through his short red hair.

I nodded and straightened my posture.

'Shall we take a look at your CV, in that case?' Ged reached forward and picked up my one-page CV that I'd printed in a local internet café.

He continued to pat his moist skin and flatten his crimson mane as he read through the details of my jobs, most recently as PR manager and non-executive director of Whittington Soup, and as a fashion PR assistant in London before I packed up my life and moved back home to work at the family business.

'Non-executive director, hey?' he mocked, leaning back in his chair and putting his hands up behind his head, my CV resting on his chest. 'Now, being totally honest with you here, love. A "PR manager slash non-executive director" role for a job that you don't even have a reference for smells a little bullshitty.'

I glared at him and he held his hands up defensively. 'Hey, I'm not saying it *is* bullshit. But I know what the job market is like these days.' He placed my CV on the table in front of him and rubbed his thick fingers up and down his pinstriped tie. 'If you don't have a specific trade, it ain't easy, even at the best of times.'

'But I *do* have a specific trade,' I barked, a little louder than intended.

I pushed my CV towards him again. 'See,' I said, pointing at the paper. 'I was PR manager, which was a demanding job in itself. But before that, when I was a graduate, I worked in every department of the company – marketing, customer service, sales, recipe production... I've done everything.'

'Look,' he said, with a hint of sympathy and a desperate need to get me out of the door before his Chinese takeaway arrived. 'I'm just saying, you don't have anything specific you can offer. Most of the higher paying jobs round here are trades – they're looking for mechanics, plumbers, electricians... I'm guessing you don't have any experience in those areas?'

I sank back into my seat.

'OK, well let's have a look at these job descriptions for director roles.' He clicked through the open tabs on his computer that listed job vacancies. 'Do you have five years' experience working with not-for-profits?'

'No.'

'Not that one then. Do you have a degree in business management?'

'No, my degree was in public relations.'

'That one won't do either. Or that one,' he grunted. 'How about "a proven track record of achieving challenging sales-led targets"?' Ged said, with a comical RP accent. 'Or "overseeing the development of key policies and procedures while maintaining relationships with stakeholders"?'

'No, I guess not.' I sighed and turned away, trying desperately to keep it together and not let my emotions get the better of me.

'I still don't understand why you don't have a reference for your last job, love.' Ged eyed me suspiciously.

I sighed. Where would I begin?

'Hang on...' Ged said, as he peered down at my CV and back at me again. 'I'm a bit slow today. Booze brain an' all, but I know who you are! Bloody hell. You're Arabella Whittington, of Whittington Soup.'

I straightened my posture. I was about to proudly state that yes, yes I was – before Ged boomed, interrupting me: 'Jeez, all that was a scandal and a half, wasn't it? Read all about it on the *Daily Mail* – the "sidebar of shame",' he air-quoted, chuckling. 'Not usually my cuppa tea, but it's good for a bit of gossip. Plus, it's got decent footie coverage! You a blue or a red?'

Was that to do with the football, or did he mean do I prefer Tiffany or Cartier? I opened my mouth to tell him I loved both. I mean, diamonds are diamonds, after all.

'I see,' Ged said before I could answer. He sat back in his

seat again, his hands propped on the back of his head. 'I see, I see, I see,' he said slowly, piecing the clues together like a detective in a cheesy crime drama. 'That explains why you don't have a reference then. Ah, I'm sorry though, love, you're going to struggle getting in at one of the top PR agencies in the city now. Not with all that hoo-ha at Whittington Soup under your watch.'

I bit my lip. I was right to keep my identity a secret, if Ged's reaction was anything to go by. I knew that who I really was and the well-known decadence of my previous life wouldn't go down well with Susie and Dan.

'But surely somewhere might give me a chance,' I whispered. 'It wasn't my fault, what happened there, not entirely. Maybe, if you could just get me an interview, then I could explain to them what happened. I have a lot to offer, I really do. I'm enthusiastic, I'm a fast learner, I work hard...'

Ged could smell the desperation as strongly as my Jo Malone perfume. I felt his tough exterior soften as he picked up on my defeat, but we were interrupted by the ringing bell at the office door.

'Hang on, my Chinese is here,' Ged said. 'Let me show you the list of job schemes we have locally.' I opened my mouth to insist again that it wasn't what I was looking for, but he held his chunky hands up. 'Just have a look, OK? I know it's not ideal, but it's better than nothing.'

He clicked open another list on the computer, before grabbing his wallet and shuffling out of the door to pick up his lunch. I leant over the desk and scrolled through the long list of vacancies for local job schemes. The money was minimal, but the jobs were all either in Toxteth or within walking distance.

Then, among a section of adverts for cleaners (certainly not a skill that the local community would thank me for offering), I saw it. A full-time helper and cook at Dan's Kitchen – the soup kitchen!

'Seen anything you like?' Ged said, bounding through the office, the smell of greasy takeaway filling the room.

'I think I have.' I smiled, shoving my CV into my briefcase.

'Good!' Ged scoffed, his mouth full of at least three prawn crackers. 'See, ye of little faith. I knew we'd find something – they don't call us expert advisors for nothing!'

TWELVE

'You'll have to work hard,' Susie said sternly. 'I know you've said you can cook, but you'll have to learn how to clean too.'

I ran as fast as my Louboutins would carry me (not very fast, I discovered) from the job centre to Susie's flat as soon as I saw the notice for the soup kitchen job. She'd put the idea to Dan, and we were waiting for his answer.

'Cleaning? But the ad said the role was for a helper and cook, nothing to do with cleaning.' I shuddered as I remembered my not-so successful attempts at cleaning my flat when I first moved in.

'Cleaning *is* helping.' She rolled her eyes.

'Why didn't you mention it, anyway? You knew I was looking for a job.'

'Something – just something – told me that getting down on your hands and knees and scrubbing the floors of the soup kitchen might not be your cup of tea,' Susie said jokingly, as she moved a newly finished canvas from the wooden tripod across her cramped lounge.

'What gave you that impression?' I crossed my arms defensively while I leant across the breakfast bar, which was scattered with piles of paintbrushes and mugs filled with murky water.

'Probably because I walked in on you trying to clean your toilet by filling it with washing-up liquid?'

I blushed. 'I've learnt my lesson, OK? Besides, the label was very misleading. I *was* technically *washing* the toilet.'

Susie raised her eyebrows and tried to stifle a giggle at the memory. 'Thank your lucky stars that the bubbles didn't seep into the flat downstairs. Plus, you were talking about getting a high-flying job with a big fat pay cheque. That doesn't exactly scream "cook and helper at the soup kitchen", does it?' Susie carefully positioned the painting directly in front of the open window in the hope that it would dry quicker.

'Yeah, I mean, a couple of those jobs *did* call me in for an interview,' I lied. 'But, you know, with the cost of travel and everything, I thought I'd rather work somewhere a bit closer to home.'

Susie wrinkled her nose.

'*And* I'd get to work with you and Dan! How fun would that be?' I clapped excitedly. 'Yay!'

'Is that "yay" for working with me? Or with Dan?' Susie smirked.

'You, obviously. I don't think Dan likes me very much.' I shuddered as I remembered our first meeting and the way he looked at me with a mix of suspicion and indifference. In fact, I wasn't sure I liked him all that much either.

'You just caught him on a bad day, that's all,' Susie said reassuringly. 'You'll grow to like him, I'm sure.'

'I don't know about that,' I scoffed. 'Dan is *so* not my type. He couldn't be further from the opposite of my ex.'

'I meant like him in a platonic way,' Susie said.

'Oh.' I blushed.

'Anyway, isn't that a good thing?' Susie said. 'If he's the opposite of your ex, who's obviously an ex for a reason?' She fiddled with the window latch to try and force open its wooden frame further.

'Good point,' I acknowledged, remembering Number One Scumbag, Francis. And how his scumbag ways should outweigh his bulging wallet and abs you could grate cheese on.

'What's Dan's deal, anyway?' I picked up one of the paint-brushes and started swirling it around the dirty water. 'Why does *everyone* love him?' I asked, remembering Susie's intro-duction.

'Dan's a pretty special guy,' she said, matter-of-factly. 'And there aren't many of those around.'

'Tell me about it,' I mumbled.

'It's hard, isn't it? I don't know about your parents, but mine are desperate for me to "settle down".' She rolled her eyes.

'I know what you mean.' I sighed, feeling a sudden surge of sadness at the thought of my parents. Thanks to my phone detox, I hadn't spoken to them anywhere near as often as I usually would. Our conversations were now restricted to Zoom calls on my laptop, but the Wi-Fi at my flat was so tempera-mental that most of our stories went unfinished. Even so, I gath-ered they were loving life under a blanket of sunshine and wine in France.

'Speaking of parents, you don't really talk about yours much,' Susie said tentatively, as she gathered the mountains of brushes and placed them in the paint-splattered sink, ready to be cleaned. 'Are you close to them?'

'I am,' I said sheepishly. 'But they live abroad. It's a long story.'

I wanted to shut the conversation down as quickly as possi-ble. I *knew* I should've told Susie who I really was by now. But I also knew she wouldn't be impressed with my previous over-indulged life of luxury. Not when she and Dan both committed their lives to helping people in need and living more frugally than I could ever have imagined. Heck, their monthly outgoings pretty much matched my previous *daily* outgoings. I'd keep quiet, I decided, and keep my identity a temporary secret. I was really trying to embrace my fresh start in my new life, and I couldn't run the risk of alienating my new friends – my only friends. Especially after Ged's reaction to my name. I still felt like a laughing stock.

'Say no more,' Susie insisted, as she pottered around with various painting paraphernalia, expertly dodging each paint tray lining the floor. 'I'm the queen of family issues. I see mine once or twice a year and that's more than enough for me.'

She clutched her pocket as her phone vibrated. 'Here we go, the moment of truth...'

'Is it from Dan?' I asked, hopelessly optimistic.

'Mm-hmm,' she mumbled as her eyes darted around the screen.

'Go on then, put me out of my misery, what does it say?'

'He said yes.'

'Yay!' I jumped up and down and clapped my hands together.

'Hold your horses.' Susie lifted a ring-covered finger. 'He said it's a trial, and you need to start tomorrow because he's short-staffed as it is.'

'Wow, no hanging around there then.' I grinned. 'That's fine. It isn't like I have much to do anyway.'

Susie picked up another paintbrush. 'Try not to mess it up, Bella. Dan can be difficult, I know, but the soup kitchen really does mean the world to him, and he's been looking for the right person to help out for ages.'

'I wish you'd have a bit more faith in me!' I stretched my arms out. It had been a long day, but one with a wonderful ending – I had a job! 'I'd best be off,' I said to Susie.

'Any plans for your last night of freedom?' she asked, picking up another paintbrush.

'I'm going to have a relaxing, pampering night before *my*

first day at work tomorrow,' I beamed. 'I'm thinking the works: hair mask, face mask, nails, toes, body scrub, fake tan... the whole shebang!' I clapped my hands together excitedly again before my blissful dream of indulgence was shattered. I couldn't book in for a last-minute spa session. This was going to have to be a DIY job.

'Do you happen to know what I can use for home-made hair and face masks?' I asked as I twiddled a lock of hair around my finger.

'Sure,' Susie mumbled, her eyes squinting in concentration while she painted. 'Coconut oil for your hair, works a treat. Then you can use most household things for a face mask... avocado, Greek yoghurt, honey, oats, turmeric, cinnamon. I never understand why people spend twenty pounds on a face mask when everyone has most of the ingredients in the cupboard.' She shook her head disapprovingly.

I mimicked her movement and shook my head in agreement while silently thinking, *Wow, change from fifty pounds for a face mask? Bargain!* My favourite La Mer mask cost £185 for a tiny pot.

'Fab, thanks, Susie.'

'Enjoy,' she replied, waving me away. 'Remember, Bella, don't mess it up.'

So, there was a minor mishap in my DIY pamper session. Just the minuscule, teeny-tiny issue of my face turning yellow. *Yellow.* And not a subtle glow – not a gentle hue that could be concealed with a high-coverage foundation. No, my face was a luminous yellow. As in, *The Simpsons* yellow.

I retraced my steps while scrubbing my skin raw with a rough flannel. The ingredients were laid out on the kitchen counter. Greek yoghurt, honey and turmeric. How did it go wrong? They were all organic, for goodness' sake. Were they faulty? Expired? Was it because they weren't from Waitrose? I paced up and down, feeling like I was taking off a thin layer of skin with every step.

I'm not stupid. Obviously I googled it first, but the powers that be on the beauty website said turmeric was an antioxidant – an active ingredient that was supposed to *combat* inflamed skin, not bloody *cause* it! Even worse, it was my first day at work tomorrow. And if my reflection was anything to go by, I was going to turn up looking like a cross between an iPhone emoji and a Minion, with my face smelling like a curry. A delicious curry, but still, a curry.

Perching on the sofa, I scoured beauty forums for tips. My newly painted nails were already chipped from the panicked typing and aggressive scrubbing. The top recommendations were baking soda, rosewater, cooking oil, sugar and washing your face with milk. At least the other panicked messages offered some level of comfort that I wasn't the only person in the world to have suffered such a mortifying mishap.

I accepted the general consensus that I'd added too much turmeric and not enough yoghurt or water. But most frustratingly, it was going to take *twenty-four hours* to calm down! I was too embarrassed to tell Susie, so I picked up my phone to call Dan and break the news that I couldn't make it in tomorrow. I knew I was already on thin ice, after persuading Susie I could be trusted with the job. I dialled the number Susie had given me, and my stomach clenched tighter with every ring.

THIRTEEN

One day later than planned, and after incurring the full wrath of Dan's moody attitude when I called in sick, I was excited for the first day of my trial. If I got the job, it would be the first job I'd ever had that didn't involve the family business or my dad's contacts from the golf course. I would officially be a cook and general helper at Dan's Kitchen; I would *officially* be standing on my own two feet. The fact that those feet wore shoes that looked like they cost less than a pedicure at a sub-standard salon was something I was trying to put to the back of my mind.

I'd eventually relented and changed from my original choice of outfit (an adorable Zimmermann dress) after Susie's lecture about it being 'inappropriate' for 'real work'. FYI, it wasn't, it had *pockets* – totally practical! And my Prada heels were a measly two inches; they were basically flats.

Anyway, I forced myself to keep my mouth shut and not inform her that I did, in fact, know what 'real work' was – had she ever sat through a twelve-course networking dinner with my father's golfing buddies? I thought not.

After Susie's insistence on dressing casually, I instead opted for jeans, vest top and checked shirt (all Balmain, but she didn't need to know that), while she lent me some 'bargain' pumps from her favourite vintage shop. It was good to know Susie and I were both on the same page when it came to a shared passion for pre-loved bargains. I'd been collecting vintage Chanel hand-bags for years.

As I darted down the road from my flat to the soup kitchen, I couldn't miss the petite lavender-covered figure scurrying along the pavement. 'Elsie!' I shouted, as she rushed past in her (totally on-trend) purple ballet flats. 'Hey, Elsie!' I tried again. She was surprisingly sprightly for someone who must've been in their eighties, and I was surprisingly unfit for a twenty-four-year-old. Breaking out into a sprint, I weaved in front of her while waving enthusiastically.

'Crikey Moses, you gave me a fright!' Elsie jumped, holding her chest.

What I didn't expect was for her to take a set of headphones from her ears, neatly tucked away underneath a silky headscarf. 'I'm so sorry, queen, I can't hear a thing when I'm wearing these.' She gestured to the bright purple headphones. 'My grandson bought a record player for me last Christmas.' She shook her head. 'No, not a record player.' She paused for thought. 'An iBod,' she beamed.

'Yes, they're really great, those iBods, aren't they?' I couldn't bear correcting her.

'Oh, you just wouldn't believe.' Her face lit up. 'I have everything on here. All the golden oldies. All the classics. Elvis, The Beatles, Bowie, T. Rex. You name it, I've got it.' She tapped a lilac fingernail onto her matching iPod.

'Bowie and The Beatles, hey? You have excellent taste.'

'I don't want to be a cliché.' She patted my arm. 'But they just don't make music like they used to.'

'I totally agree.' I smiled, remembering drunken nights in

the kitchen with my mum and dad, dancing to Paul, John, Ringo and George. 'My family has Scouse roots, so I've always had an affinity for The Beatles, and anything to do with Liverpool, really. I just don't know it as well as I thought I did.'

'Best city in the world.' Elsie grinned, a glint in her eye. 'How about I take you out for a Liverpool tour one day? We'll have a pint in the Phil, go for a shop in Liverpool ONE, a boogie in the Cavern Club, and take a ferry across the Mersey! Though if you want to go to the footy, you'll have to count me out. Much too noisy for me.' She gestured to her ears and shuddered. 'I'll watch it on telly with you though!' she added, beaming. 'You a blue or a red?'

'Whichever,' I replied breezily. Soon I would need to make up my mind on this seemingly vital question.

'You have to pick one, queen, you can't support both!' Elsie said in mock outrage. 'Anyway, we'll have to do that one day. Then you'll agree that it's the best city in the world.'

'I'm in if you are.' I smiled as she squeezed my arm. Given that it was only the second time I'd met her, I couldn't help but warm to her friendliness and age-defying sense of adventure.

'Aw ey, and if you ever fancy a Zumba, you let me know.' Elsie winked. 'They do it down the community centre.' She wiggled her hips. 'I love it! And there's Knit and Natter too. You'll never be short of things to do round here.'

'Sounds great!' I said, though I didn't even know how to sew a button, so a knitting group probably wasn't my calling. I was sure I'd tried Zumba before – wasn't it that exotic fish you could order as sashimi? How fabulous – there was somewhere that did decent sushi round here!

'Where are you off to now anyway, queen? Did you have any luck at the job centre? I tell you, Ged is a lovely man, but good Lord is he useless. At least he's keeping the Chinese takeaway in business.' She rolled her brown eyes.

'I did, actually,' I beamed. 'I'm heading to my first day now.'

'Where?'

I pointed behind her towards the soup kitchen.

'Ooh, are you really?' Elsie's eyes, framed with lashings of mascara, twinkled with glee. 'That's wonderful news. I'll be your neighbour.'

'Hang on, you live there?'

'I do,' Elsie beamed. 'At the flat around the back. Pop round for a brew and a biccy whenever you fancy. Or I'll make you a pan of Scouse if you're peckish after work. It's widely accepted that mine is the best in the neighbourhood.' She straightened her posture proudly. Even at full height, she only reached my shoulder, and I was diddy myself.

'That sounds amazing.' I smiled.

'And you tell me if that grandson of mine is working you too hard – I'll sort him out.'

I couldn't stop my instinctual double-take. 'Dan's your grandson? Dan Rigby?'

'He is indeed.' Elsie chuckled.

Now that I knew she was Dan's grandmother, it was impossible to ignore the family resemblance in those deep, soulful eyes. Though how could she be so nice and friendly when he was always so miserable and grumpy?

'He's a good lad, our Dan,' Elsie said, as though she was reading my mind. 'He can take things a bit too seriously, and there's no denying he's got a cob on sometimes, but his heart is in the right place.'

'I'm sure it is,' I said politely, even though I was yet to witness anything except moodiness.

'You tell him he has me to answer to if he gives you a hard time.' Elsie winked.

'I will,' I half laughed, but I was absolutely serious. I knew it was worth having Elsie in my corner. She might've been in her eighties, but she was feisty. 'I might be in his bad books already, I had to call in sick on my first day.'

'You best get going then.' She checked her watch on her dainty wrist. 'Good luck, Bella, knock his socks off. Dan could use somebody like you.' Before I asked her what she meant by that, she popped her headphones back on and shimmied down the street, her shiny headscarf catching the sunlight.

I caught a glimpse of the time on my watch and clocked that our natter meant I was ten minutes late. More fuel to the fire of Dan's wrath. And not the best start to the already delayed first day of my job trial.

When I pushed open the soup kitchen door, Dan was dragging bursting bags of food through the hallway to the kitchen, with Herbie salivating at his tatty trainers.

'Morning,' he mumbled. 'And only ten minutes late. I owe Suze a tenner.'

'What? Why?' I said, a little offended.

'Well, I said you'd be twenty minutes late, but she said ten.'

'I guess she's the lesser of two evils then. And, as a matter of fact, you can blame your grandmother, she's the one who distracted me.'

'Ah, you've met Elsie?'

'Only the second time and she's already planning on taking me to the Cavern.'

'Mm-hmm,' Dan mumbled evasively, clearly not at all interested.

'Anyway, I am *so* excited for my first day!' I clapped my hands together. 'Again, Dan, I'm really sorry I couldn't make it in yesterday. I had a terrible case of...' I panicked. *Don't tell him you dyed your face luminous yellow. And don't say diarrhoea, anything but that. Think of something glamorous. A chic illness. What do supermodels get?*

Dan stared at me, awaiting my explanation.

'A stomach issue.' I held my stomach dramatically. 'It was awful. I mean, not awful. Not diarrhoea or anything. No, no.

Nothing like that.' I sounded guiltier and more embarrassed the more the words tumbled out of my mouth.

Bloody hell. *Why* on earth did I say that? The truth about my Simpsons face would've been better than insinuating it was loose bowel movements.

'Er, OK. You better now, like?' Dan grimaced. 'All OK there?' He gestured towards my stomach, which I was still clutching.

'All fine, yep. All sorted, thanks.' I had to change the subject. 'So, what are we doing first? I've always wanted to learn how to make a soufflé or master the art of sourdough. Ooh, or how about macarons?'

I followed Dan into the kitchen as he lugged the remaining bags along behind him.

'You might want to lower your expectations about what we cook here. Amazingly, there are no soufflés. Or sourdough loaves, or macarons.'

My huff was louder than I'd intended.

'Do you actually know anything about what we do here?' he grumbled.

'Yes,' I replied, crossing my arms over my chest.

Dan turned to me again, his piercing eyes waiting for me to elaborate.

'You feed homeless people and drug addicts.'

'OK, first you need to stop being so supercilious and judgemental.' Dan stood up stiffly and rested his hands on his hips.

'Me? Judgemental?' I guffawed. 'Don't you think *you're* being judgemental by saying *I'm* judgemental?' I stumbled over my words, which were getting jumbled and confused in my brain. I'd missed my morning coffee due to nerves, and I was feeling jittery enough. 'You don't know anything about me.'

'You can't just write people off as "homeless" or "drug addicts",' Dan interrupted, shaking his head. I knew he was already regretting giving me this job (or job trial) and I hadn't even been there fifteen minutes. Was it too early to call Elsie for backup? 'You being here is never going to work if you have an attitude like that.'

'I wasn't, I don't... I was just stating facts.'

'We're not here to judge people by their circumstances, OK? Have you ever heard the saying, "Never judge a man until you've walked in his shoes"?'

'Of course,' I said, trying to hide my annoyance at his condescending tone.

'Well, maybe you should bear that in mind. You have no idea what some people have been through in their lives.'

I could feel my cheeks flushing red with anger. 'What about you? Aren't you judging me? Have you walked in *my* shoes?' I looked down at my feet and wished I wasn't wearing the ugliest shoes I'd ever seen in my life. *Damn you, Susie.* 'You have no idea what *I've* been through.' I bit my lip.

Dan didn't say anything. He just stood, staring at me. A stand-off in the middle of the kitchen. Neither of us was going to back down – something only recognised by Herbie, who looked from me to Dan and back again.

'Fine,' Dan eventually relented, and I managed a suitably smug grin. He pulled his hair back into a short ponytail that really shouldn't have been as attractive as it was. 'First, we clean.'

Dan pulled a large box out from underneath the sink and began unloading the masses of bottles, sprays, cloths and rags. 'Something tells me you might not have much experience when it comes to cleaning?'

I crossed my arms defensively. 'I don't know what gives you that idea.' I hoped Susie hadn't told him about the washing-up liquid in the toilet incident.

'Susie said she walked in on you trying to clean your carpet with a mop.'

Or that minor mishap.

'Fine.' I blushed. 'You might have a point.'

'OK, here we go then: cleaning for beginners,' he said, neatly grouping the different products together. In a surprising act of chivalry, he pulled up a chair for me first, before grabbing another for himself. We were on opposite sides of the workbench in the middle of the kitchen, the distance between us acting as a barrier that would hopefully defuse the tension. Herbie made himself at home and curled up at our feet. Every now and again, his tail would thud against the floor as he dreamt of chasing pigeons and swiping leftover food.

'Perhaps we started off on the wrong foot,' Dan said, though his expression was unconvinced. Did the man ever smile? 'I don't want to sound patronising, but being a helper and a cook is a really important job here, and I do need to make sure you know what you're doing.' He pushed his sleeves up to his elbows, revealing arms that were almost completely covered in various inked illustrations.

'Everything we do is for the local community, people who are in difficult circumstances and are struggling one way or another. We're not here to judge, we're here to help. It probably goes without saying that we don't have much money to do what we do' – Dan crossed his arms over himself self-consciously – 'but we make the best of everything we have. Sometimes it does make things a little more – challenging, shall we say. But the reason I started this soup kitchen was to give the community a safe place where they could enjoy a hot meal, made from fresh ingredients, in a clean kitchen. Something a lot of our regular visitors don't often experience.'

'I understand.' I nodded, wondering whether this was what Susie meant when she defended Dan's standoffish attitude because he had a lot on his mind. 'Have you ever tried partnering with any businesses?' I offered, remembering our charity partnerships at Whittington Soup. 'Any in the food industry, maybe. Perhaps they could help out with donations or supplies?'

Dan shook his head. 'Not really, nowhere ever seems to be interested in doing anything long-term. They'll give us the odd donation, which we're grateful for, of course. But it's mainly just for their own image, and we won't hear anything from them again. I don't mean to sound bitter, I really don't, but sometimes it just feels like we're forgotten about, or used as a PR exercise.'

Dan's eyes filled with sadness, and I opened my mouth to tell him about the initiatives at Whittington Soup before he swiftly changed his tone. 'Anyway, I digress,' he said. 'Shall we start with something easy? Do you want to tell me which products you'd use to clean the kitchen? That's one of the most important jobs as we clean it twice a day – before the meal prep and after we serve up.'

'Yes, sounds good,' I said, surprising myself with my fake confidence. 'OK, so...' I stood up from the chair and ran a finger along each of the various bottles of cleaning solutions.

'You'd probably use this?' I picked up the nearest spray bottle. 'To clean the sink?'

'That's furniture polish.'

'Some may argue that the sink is a piece of furniture...'

Dan looked at me quizzically. Herbie rolled over onto his side with a loud snore, as if he knew we were going to be here for a while.

'Right, maybe not then,' I mumbled. 'This?' I chose another bottle from the identical selection.

Dan shook his head in disappointment as I scanned the label of the window and glass cleaner. 'We really will have to start with the basics, won't we?' he said.

Half an hour later, after I'd learnt *a lot* about cleaning, Dan clasped his hands together, the black ink on each of his thumbs hugging.

'Shall we move on to cooking now?' he asked.

I shuffled from one foot to the other. Why did I feel like a nervous schoolgirl? Any cooking skill of mine, aside from soup-making, left an awful lot to be desired. And Dan was not a man who was easily impressed. I rubbed my clammy palms together. Argh, this was going to be more difficult than I thought. I was already hanging on to this job by a thread. And why did Susie tell Dan that I'd tried to clean my carpet with a mop? (And why couldn't you clean your carpet with a mop? It made perfect sense.)

'I know when we first met, you said that you could make soup,' Dan said, his blank expression unconvinced.

'Yeah, I mean, soup is probably the only thing I'm confident at.' I silently rattled off all the different combinations we created at Whittington Soup. Soup was fine, I knew how to do soup. After all, I grew up in a soup family dynasty; my great-grandfather's original recipes might as well have been tattooed onto my brain. And anyway, how wrong could you go with soup, really? Easy peasy.

'How about we start with that then?' Dan rubbed the stubble on his chin impatiently.

'Great!' I enthused, even though my heart was beating faster and faster as I realised how long it had been since I'd cooked anything, even soup.

'We've got plenty of time...' Dan's eyes darted down to his scuffed leather watch. It couldn't have been more different from Francis's impressive assortment of Patek Philippe watches; his prized collection probably cost more than the soup kitchen building and everything in it. 'Damn,' Dan said, staring at the watch face. 'I completely forgot. I need to take Elsie to Aldi and then drop her at bingo.'

'Bingo?' I half giggled. 'Are people still playing that?'

'They certainly are. Don't ever come between Elsie and her bingo. A friendly warning,' Dan joked, his icy demeanour thawing slightly.

'Noted.' I nodded earnestly.

'You'll find her down the Mecca on Tuesdays, Thursdays and Saturdays, 11 a.m. sharp. Just don't ever go with her if she invites you, that's another friendly warning,' Dan added. 'She's crazy competitive. Emphasis on the crazy. She's been barred for challenging the result and telling the caller to speak more clearly more times than I can count.'

Dan rolled his eyes affectionately and brushed a hand over his hair. He repeated the action of checking his watch, despite having only checked it a few seconds before. 'I'm really sorry,' he said, surprisingly softly. 'After I gave you such a hard time for calling in sick as well. Are you OK to crack on with the soup while I go?'

'Of course.' I waved my hand. 'I'm totally at home in the kitchen, I'll be fine. Leave it to me. Absolutely fine,' I rambled.

'Sound,' Dan nodded. 'Cheers, Bella.' I could've sworn his cheeks coloured a tint of pink as our eyes met. 'It'll be a massive help for tonight, we'll probably need enough for eighty people. All the ingredients are in the cupboard over there.' He pointed to the right-hand side of the long kitchen. 'Use whatever you need, within reason, obviously. All the fresh vegetables are in the bags and boxes, and there are fresh herbs outside in the yard.'

Dan grabbed his faded denim jacket and car keys, before backing out of the door slowly. 'You sure you'll be all right, like?' he asked nervously. 'I won't be long. Herbie will keep you company – ask him anything, he can be very vocal when it comes to food.'

'Honestly, you're leaving it in my capable hands.' I waved at him with jazz hands. What was *wrong* with me? First, the notion of my (untrue) lack of bowel control, now my (all too true) lack of hand control. 'And of course, Herbie's capable paws.'

Dan ruffled Herbie's fur and nodded at me indifferently. The heavy door made a gentle thud as he closed it behind him.

Herbie and I looked at each other. 'We've got this, Herbs,' I said with shaky confidence, as he stared up at me with his puppy-dog eyes. He wagged his tail enthusiastically. '*Woof!*' He sounded more convinced than I did.

FOURTEEN

It might've been better if I'd let Herbie make the soup. Scratch that. It absolutely, unquestionably, would've been better if I'd let Herbie make the soup. Even though he had paws instead of hands, and was, in fact, a dog.

I wiped an unidentifiable smear of sludge from my forehead with my elbow. I was past guessing what it was. The bubbling liquid inside the pot danced aggressively as I quickly turned the heat on the hob down before it spilled over. I was past guessing what was in there, too. Stock? Sauce? Gin? Who knew.

The burning sensation in my right eye made an abrupt, painful return. And I almost pulled a nerve in my neck as I tried to scratch my fiery eyeball with my shoulder. I was ninety-nine per cent convinced the burning was from the herbs I'd picked in the garden. They weren't labelled, so there was a chance I'd used nettles or something equally unpleasant. I was just hoping it wasn't something actually toxic.

My attempt to focus on the task at hand – finishing the soup (or whatever it was at this point) – was distracted by the chaos of the kitchen and the very loud, very inconsiderate ticking of the clock beside me. It was like the countdown to a mission I should've aborted long before now. Dan was due back at any minute and things were... well, things were not looking great.

I wasn't to blame, however. It was entirely the blender's fault. Who buys a blender that doesn't have an automatic lock on the lid? More importantly, *why* would anyone invent such a device? What kind of sadist wants to play roulette with *blending*? I shook my head, sprigs of herbs falling from my hair. *Must not dwell, Bella. Must get on with the task at hand. Must not throw the blender out the window. Must buy Dan a Vitamix.*

'No, Herbie, no!' I admonished my not-very-helpful sous chef as he, yet again, nuzzled into my leg and licked the countless pungent stains covering my designer jeans. I eyed up the enormous pot of soup that was my work in progress. It was steaming, as the recipe had said it should, so at least that was one thing going to plan. The problem was, my phone was covered in approximately twelve layers of various blender explosions, not to mention the residue from my oily fingers and the unfortunate salt spillage, so I couldn't see where I was up to with the recipe on the open tab of Google Chrome.

My original plan, all of one hour (it felt like one day) ago, had been to cook one of my favourite soups from memory. I was going to wow Dan – if that man was capable of being shaken from his constant underwhelmed state – with a silky-smooth roasted butternut squash and red chilli soup. He'd marvel at the velvety texture, he'd compliment me on achieving the perfect amount of chilli so that it was warming, but not knock-your-socks-off spicy. He'd lick his lips and ask for a second helping. Most importantly, I'd pass the trial and the job would be mine.

Alas, I was rusty. I was cursing all that time living in London and taking advantage of the amazing 24/7 takeaway options. Then, after moving back North, it was too easy to nab any leftovers from the staff canteen at the Whittington Soup headquarters, or Francis and I would eat out at the amazing restaurants that were literally on our doorstep. After all that time of not so much as making a bowl of pasta, I'd completely lost my knack for soup, and I wasn't willing to give soup, smoothies – or anything that involved a blender – a go. Ever again.

I ground my teeth and stomped my foot with frustration, giving poor Herbie a fright as he gobbled up the raw vegetable shavings forming a moat around my spot in the kitchen. At least he was helping in that sense; he was more efficient than a hoover. Wiping the sweat from my forehead with my rolled-up shirt sleeve, I closed my eyes and tried to remember the next steps of the recipe on the Whittington Soup blog, and how I could salvage the murky liquid bubbling on the stove. I had to prove Dan (and Susie) wrong, I had to show them both I was worthy of this job. I had to hope they wouldn't realise I'd put sugar in the recipe, instead of salt (in my defence, they look exactly the same when they're side-by-side and you're totally flustered).

I took a deep breath, right from the bottom of my belly, as I was taught on the ridiculously expensive meditation retreat in Bali that Tabs dragged me to a few years ago. Oh, Bali. I mentally digressed. How I wished I was on a beach, basking in sunshine, a cocktail in hand. But I wasn't, I was in a kitchen war zone, and I'd lost my spatula. I swivelled around, taking in the chaos. Yellow slush decorated the cupboard doors in fluorescent smudges. Everything (even myself) smelt like vegetable stock, and there was a chunk of butternut squash stuck to the ceiling, hanging by its skin. If it could talk it'd be bellowing, 'Help! Someone remove this lunatic from the kitchen!'

'Where's my spatula, Herbie?' I asked to his amused little furry face.

'I don't know, but this is very entertaining,' he told me with his eyes. 'Also, pass me another carrot, will you?'

'Gaaahhh!' I cried, scanning the anarchy around me. 'It was right here.' I held my hands out and leant over the messy surface, dirtied with all manner of ingredients, as well as my blood, sweat and tears. Literally, because I'd cut my finger within the first five minutes. 'It was right here...'

The pot bubbled teasingly, as if it knew that it held the answer. I lifted the lid tentatively. Phew, the spatula was in there. I grabbed a stained dishcloth and lifted it from the heat. But only half of it came away. Where was the other half? Had it always looked like that? But how had I been stirring the soup? I turned the heat off so that the liquid calmed to stillness. I dipped the half-spatula in, and it hit something hard. 'No!' I cried as I tapped it, splashing myself (again) in the process. The plastic spatula had melted into the boiling pot. It had *actually melted* into the soup. I was pretty sure a special of 'Spatula Soup, complete with mouth-watering melted plastic' wasn't what Dan had in mind for his soup kitchen customers that evening.

I slid down next to the cooker and didn't even bother trying to stop Herbie as he leapt into my lap and sniffed at my stained clothes with his twitching nose. I clocked my reflection in the glass cupboard in front of me. I looked like a woman possessed, with ragged hair and frantic eyes. My clothes were ruined. Although every now and again, Gucci's latest collection featured clothes with holes and stains, so perhaps my outfit was a look I could pull off.

But to my surprise, my mind wasn't on my expensive shirt which was blotted with luminous vegetable juice, or my jeans that would forever smell of vegetable bouillon (I still hadn't mastered the art of the washing machine – so many buttons!).

No, my mind was on my gargantuan failure. I'd failed at the one thing I was good at, my one saving grace for the job that I'd convinced Susie and Dan I could do. I'd failed both of them. Worse still, I'd failed the people who were depending on the soup kitchen for their next meal – a task I'd been entrusted with. There was no way Dan was going to let me stay at the soup kitchen now. And I didn't deserve to. I buried my head in Herbie's fur and watched through blurry eyes as my tears nestled between his wiry curls.

The security lock clicked, and I held my breath as the kitchen door opened. Herbie barked and padded over, his tail wagging with glee as he recognised the face that emerged from behind it. But the face – Dan's face – wore an expression that transformed from neutral to horrified in milliseconds.

'What the hell...'

'I can explain,' I whimpered.

When I was slumped on the floor with Herbie curled into my legs, I decided I had two options – well, three, if you counted doing a runner (the most tempting choice, if I was being completely honest). The first option was to forget about the soup and focus on cleaning up the disaster zone that was the kitchen. The second was to ignore the mess, work around it, and get a new batch of soup finished in time for Dan's return. That way, he'd at least have something to serve for the evening meal. A meal that, ideally, didn't include a melted kitchen utensil in its list of ingredients.

'What the...' Dan repeated, aghast.

I'd gone with option number two. I'd thrown away the soup that looked like pond water (*not* the look I was going for) and started again, pulling the recipe from the depths of my memory. The kitchen was still splattered in a kaleidoscope of colours from the inside of the blender (again, I must emphasise, *not* my fault). The sink was overflowing with dirty pots and pans. It was impossible to tell what colour the kitchen countertops were thanks to the various peelings and spillages, and there was still a sizeable chunk of butternut squash stuck to the ceiling. The floor was clear though; my furry sous chef had pulled his weight in that department, at least.

'I can explain.' I held my hands up to Dan in surrender, as if he was the Mess Police. 'Please.'

Dan rested one arm across his stomach and chewed on his already bitten-down thumbnail, drawing attention to the point where his top tightened over his biceps. They were distractingly muscular, like a rugby player's. I blinked myself back to reality, although suddenly I was all too aware what a total mess I looked.

While Dan surveyed the state of the room in shocked silence, I surreptitiously smoothed down my hair and checked my flushed face in the reflection of a stray spoon.

'I knew this was a mistake,' he said eventually, shaking his head, his shoulders stiff and tense.

'It looks worse than it is,' I pleaded. 'I've finished the soup for this evening's service. I just had a bit of an issue with the... never mind.' I rubbed my head and was all too aware of my tatty hair, piled high on the top of my scalp in the sort of knot that a hipster barista in a trendy coffee shop would've been proud of. 'But the soup is done, at least, and I'll clear all this up now, I promise.'

'I think you should leave,' Dan said, assessing the damage again. 'I don't think this is a good idea.' His dark eyes cut through the space between us.

'But I—'

'Please,' Dan said, looking away from me and up at the ceiling. 'I'm sorry, Bella. I know Susie said this might work, but I don't think it will.'

Herbie padded over to me and lowered his body onto the floor. He looked up at me with sad eyes as if he was trying to say, 'Sorry, I know you tried.'

'OK,' I said. There was no point in arguing with Dan. I

knew he meant it. I could see it in his eyes, hear it in his voice. I'd messed up, I'd ruined it.

I resignedly picked up my jacket and handbag. I could feel Dan's stare follow me all the way through the kitchen, until the door shut behind me. I walked back to my flat, each step fighting back a new tear.

FIFTEEN

The walls around me felt claustrophobic as I paced my studio flat. I was still reeling from my disastrous trial at the soup kitchen. I knew if Mum was here, she'd give me a good shake and tell me to stop catastrophising (ironic, given Mum was by far the most dramatic person I knew). But I'd cringe and shudder with every memory of what the kitchen looked like when I left, and I couldn't shake off the disappointed expression on Dan's face as he watched me walk out of the door.

Deciding some fresh air would probably do me good and distract my anxious mind, I slipped into my trainers, grabbed my keys and headed out of the door. The temptation to run away and join Mum and Dad in France was an urge I was struggling to fight. Instead, I hoped my new neighbourhood would give me some sort of sign that this was where I should be.

As I walked around the area in the daylight and properly took in the sights, I passed scenes and buildings I hadn't noticed before. A square of lush greenery, surrounded by grand town-houses, reminded me of Eaton Square in Belgravia, where a house wouldn't offer change from £5 million. Further down the road, there was a magnificent synagogue that stopped me in my tracks, and I stood to admire the bright terracotta bricks and the incredible wheel window dominating the striking facade. Even the local library was impressive, with its majestic sash windows and carved etchings above the imposing entrance.

I was surprised to find the dilapidated church was another stunning sight in the light of day, rather than the spooky silhouette that I'd previously marched past. The sun illuminated its original Gothic features; the windows were empty of glass, but still offered a glimpse to the trees growing inside, and the green moss winding up the walls. Its tall steeple pierced like a needle into the clouds above, while the vibrant colours of the graffiti on the walls transformed it from times gone by to the present day, and birds nested cosily along the slate roof, grateful of the shelter that could be found in its crevices.

It was as I walked along the tree-lined Princes Boulevard, a leafy avenue in the heart of Toxteth, while the warm sunshine dappled the emerald leaves, that I admitted defeat – I was seeing the area with new, sober eyes and I was ashamed of how fast I was to judge it at first.

Magnificent Georgian mansions stood majestically on the roads either side of the newly refurbished walking avenue. Victorian street lights lined the pedestrian pathways, with wooden benches where locals sat, enjoying the blue skies above and listening to the birds singing. An elderly couple, holding hands, smiled and nodded at me as I walked past. An artistic 'L8' sculpture along a leafy patch of grass reminded me where I was.

The boulevard was a hive of activity on such a beautiful day. Cyclists pulled over from the designated cycle lanes and gulped from fluorescent sports bottles. Visitors stopped to marvel at the art installations and read the plaques that revealed the history of the area. I stood alongside the groups and pored over the amazing heritage. Each plaque explored a different topic – the religious buildings reflecting its multi-faith community, its once thriving nightlife, the history of activism and the legacy of Liverpool's role as a major port city.

Through my ignorance, all I'd associated Toxteth with was the riots, but here it was, resplendent in its regeneration and the proud community basking in its glory.

An installation at one end of the boulevard – just before the inviting, gold-adorned gates of leafy Princes Park – was especially eye-catching, with striking golden text and gilded patterns inscribed in the stone stating: 'Our Home, Our Life, Our Future'. Would it be my home, my life and my future too?

The freshly laid, pastel grey pavement was decorated with the occasional mosaic showcasing inspirational quotes. I stood above the one featuring words once spoken by Nelson Mandela: 'The greatest glory in living is not in never falling, but in rising every time we fall.'

I had my answer; Toxteth had given it to me. I turned and headed back to my flat – back home.

Knock, knock. I assumed the gentle thump at the door was Susie asking to borrow something random again. 'Hang on a minute,' I said through a mouthful of double-sized crumpet, soaked in butter. After my unceremonious firing from the soup kitchen (although I reassured myself that you couldn't technically be fired from a job trial), I was back to combing through job adverts. As well as getting a job, I was also determined to revive my soup-making skills. So, I had a batch bubbling away on the hob, which I was considering taking to Dan as an apology.

My eyes were half on the TV showing a rerun of my favourite *Friends* episode ('The One With Ross's Tan' – it always reminded me of the time when the same thing happened to Mum the day before she was due to attend a big celebrity wedding in St Barts).

'Hang on!' I shouted again, as another knock thumped on the door. Wiping a greasy hand on my pyjamas, I whipped the door open. 'Oh,' I said, pulling the crumpet away from my mouth as I looked from the TV to the person in the doorway. 'Hello.' I wiped a drop of melted butter away from my lip.

'Hi.' Dan shuffled awkwardly from side to side with his hands in his pockets. 'Look,' he said eventually, still not meeting my eye. 'I came to say...' He stopped distractedly and sniffed the aromas lingering from the kitchen. 'Are you cooking soup again?' he asked.

'Yep.'

'It smells amazing,' he said, looking towards the kitchen behind me.

'It's creamy mushroom and thyme.' I wiped the remnants of the crumpet crumbs over my unicorn-covered pyjamas pants again, and in doing so, noticed a rather sizeable chocolate stain on them. The silence of the moment between us was filled with the roar of the studio audience on the TV behind me. As Chandler would say, could this *be* any better timing?

'I came to say I'm sorry. I was out of line,' Dan continued, seemingly – and thankfully – oblivious to my haphazard appearance. 'The kitchen looked like a bombsite, and I was stressed. We've been looking for the right person to join the team for so long and I took my frustrations out on you. It was wrong of me, and I'm sorry.'

Dan's steely eyes locked onto mine as he rested one arm on the door frame. Maybe my initial impression was right. Maybe he *did* have a look of Regé-Jean Page.

With that realisation, I was suddenly all too aware of my lack of make-up, something I wouldn't entertain in my past life when careful make-up application was as much a part of my morning routine as brushing my teeth. I wished I'd at least applied a smudge of eyeliner or a dash of mascara that morning.

I looked away, over Dan's shoulder, trying to break the

intense eye contact that made me feel funny inside – though that could've also been the impressive (and alarming) amount of Nutella I'd already consumed with my crumpets while making the soup.

'You *were* a bit harsh.' I folded my arms over myself. Partly to make him work for his apology, partly because I was sure the chocolate stain I'd already identified was unlikely to be a lone ranger.

'I tried your soup.' Dan smiled at me properly for the first time, his lovely, pillowy lips framing his perfect teeth. 'It was... well, it was incredible, Bella.' He smiled again, the faint scar from what looked like a teenage lip piercing stretching as he beamed.

'Ah, it was nothing.' I flapped my hand and shrugged, ignoring the flutter in my stomach and the internal voice screaming, 'He thought my soup was incredible!'

'You think that was nothing? Really?' he asked, leaning his well-built frame against the door. 'Was it your own recipe? How did you get the texture so smooth? How much chilli did you put in to get the warmth just right?' He laughed, a deep, throaty laugh. It was nice hearing that properly for the first time too. 'Sorry, so many questions. I'm a food geek.'

'It's OK,' I said, my heart doing a little happy dance. Soup Mission: Accomplished.

'I can't be without that soup, to be honest. And my mouth is watering at the smell of the soup you're cooking now. So, I'm here to beg for your forgiveness, and to beg for you to come back.' He sighed, silently asking me not to make him beg. Something told me Dan Rigby was not a man used to begging.

'Well, I *am* rather busy at the moment,' I said with a flourish, gesturing to my pyjamas and cosy sofa set-up.

'Of course,' Dan replied with a bright smile. 'I wouldn't want to intrude. But if you can take the time out of your terribly busy schedule...' he joked.

I nodded. His shoulders relaxed. I liked this side of Dan.

'We could really do with your help later on, say 3 p.m.? A few of our regulars have requested the same chef who made that *boss* butternut squash soup, would you believe?'

'Would you believe...' I shook my head at him mockingly.

'She could do with honing her cleaning skills though.' He straightened his posture. 'And she's banned from using any blending equipment. Indefinitely.'

'She will bear that in mind.'

Dan smiled at me again, before turning and walking down towards the stairs. 'See you later, Bella,' he said over his shoulder with the faint hint of a smile in his voice.

'See you later, Dan.'

I shut the door behind me, leant against it and closed my eyes. I had my job back! That was why my heart was beating so fast. That was definitely why my heart was beating so fast.

SIXTEEN

After learning how to make everything sparkle in a kitchen, bathroom, and any room at all, I was half tempted to go back to Ged at the job centre and plead for a second look at any of the other jobs he'd told me about.

Only *half* tempted, though. Despite the hard work. No, let me rephrase. Despite the back-breaking work, I had a genuine smile on my face for the first time in a while. Although I didn't enjoy the cleaning side of things as much, I was revelling in the cooking. Granted, it wasn't exactly Michelin star level. And as Dan was a passionate advocate for animal rights, it was also entirely vegan, which was a new experience for me. Still, it was decent, comforting, homely food. And the majority of it was soup, so at least I knew I was doing one thing right, once I got into the swing of it again, and stayed away from the blender.

My soup-making skills were probably the only thing that explicitly impressed the hard-to-read Dan Rigby. One minute he was joking with me about my inability to turn on the dish-washer (so many settings!), the next he was distant and completely lost in his own thoughts. He'd sometimes put earphones in and finish his never-ending list of tasks in silence. I didn't mind, but I couldn't fight the feeling that sometimes he wanted to be left alone. I was still learning the ropes and hated how I kept disturbing him with my endless questions – and he did answer *most* of them with the glimmer of a faint, yet patient, smile – but he was haunted by something, something that followed him around like a permanent grey rain cloud.

Today, while Dan was dropping Elsie off at her Zumba class (not a type of sushi, I'd since learnt), I had some down time. So, I decided to bake a cake to try and defrost the sometimes-icy atmosphere between us. But wow, baking a cake was *hard*. Baking felt like so much more of an exact science than cooking, and Dan was due back any minute but the cake was nowhere near finished.

I did what the contestants do on *The Great British Bake Off* and sat on the kitchen floor, staring through the glass window of the oven, willing my creation to rise. But despite my pleading stares, it stubbornly refused to grow more than a centimetre. Thank goodness I hadn't attempted the soufflé like I'd originally planned.

I wasn't passing the blame for the unrisen cake, but it *really* wasn't my fault. It was all the vegan ingredients I had to use. I thought 'aquafaba' was a Farrow & Ball paint colour until today. But I learnt that it was, in fact, the liquid left over from tinned chickpeas – a revelation! I wasn't completely convinced, but apparently if you whipped the 'aquafaba', you could use it as an egg replacement. However, the cake was looking a little *sludgy* – the type that Paul Hollywood might scowl at, before Prue Leith offered words of encouragement. It had been in the oven for longer than the recipe instructed, so I couldn't understand why it looked so gooey. Maybe it was supposed to? Maybe that was how vegans liked their cakes?

'Smells amazing in here!' Dan exclaimed, as he walked through the kitchen door.

Dan's uncharacteristic enthusiasm startled me, and I moved a few inches so he couldn't see the melting mess inside the oven.

'Thanks!' I said, tucking a curl behind my ear. 'I'm making a vegan chocolate cake, I'm using *aquafaba*!' I enthused, clapping both hands together.

'Great,' Dan replied, brushing crumbs off the worktop. My cleaning had improved since my soup-making disaster, but it still wasn't up to his impossibly high standards.

'I *hope* it's going to be great. I don't know if it's a bit... melty.' I grimaced. I hadn't even had a chance to decorate it with the special vegan buttercream icing I'd made with vegan butter (after originally using standard butter and forgetting its rather obvious animal origins).

'Don't worry, everyone has to start somewhere.' Dan was being nice, for once. Well, nice but still a little stern. Would it kill the man to smile? 'Suze isn't in until later, so we have the whole afternoon to ourselves.' I swore I saw Dan's cheeks flush. 'To enjoy the cake, I mean,' he added hastily.

I stole a sly glance at the oven. Why wasn't it *rising*? Why wasn't it doing *anything*? Damn aquafaba. That vegan website was probably having me on. It sounded too good to be true – how would chickpea liquid create a cake?

'Erm, Bella,' Dan said as he stood in front of the sink.

'Mmm?' I replied, glaring at the oven that must've broken overnight.

'What's this?' Dan picked up the new handwash I'd ordered from petty cash.

'Handwash,' I smiled, with a little 'duh' expression.

'What about the handwash we usually have in?'

'Pfft,' I grunted. 'The ingredients in those brands are too harsh for your hands, Dan. There were all sorts of unnatural chemicals in them.'

There weren't. I mean, there might've been, I didn't check. I just missed the smell of my beloved orange and bergamot

Molton Brown soap and thought Dan's hands would benefit from some serious paraben and phthalate-free moisture. Plus, it smelt like Sevillian orange – sublime!

'How much did this cost, Bella?' Dan asked, shaking the bright citrus-coloured bottle at me.

'Not much,' I insisted, as I realised my buttercream icing was starting to solidify. *How?* I wondered desperately. I couldn't even get the spoon through the icing now.

'How much is not much?'

Bloody hell, he was like a dog with a bone.

'I think it was like, twenty pounds?'

'Twenty pounds *a bottle?*' Dan said, his eyes wide, his nostrils flaring.

I decided at that point not to mention the matching hand lotion I'd put in the other bathrooms.

Dan read the back of the bottle in disbelief: 'A courtyard of orange trees in dappled shade. Lively citrus airs dancing the flamenco at dawn. Azure blue skies above. Awaken your spirits with our modern classic, plucked from the naranja grove...' He shook his head. 'Bella, we don't need things like this. We can't *afford* things like this.'

'But it has nourishing qualities, Dan,' I reasoned. 'I just thought it might soften your dry hands—'

'I don't care about my hands,' Dan said impatiently, the volume of his voice rising with every word. 'I don't care about the nourishing qualities of hand soap.'

'But—'

'Please, Bella,' Dan interjected. 'Our usual soap costs a tenth of the price of this stuff, and it does the job just fine.'

I turned my attention back to my sad-looking cake to hide my frustration. I mumbled to myself about his calloused hands and neglected cuticles while he muttered inaudibly on the other side of the kitchen, while thudding and banging pots and pans around to prepare for dinner service.

'Bella,' Dan said, as he set the well-worn saucepans down on the countertop next to me. I turned towards him and he sighed, rubbing his face which was etched with stress. 'You do know the oven isn't on, don't you?'

SEVENTEEN

Miraculously, I'd made it one month at the soup kitchen. Though not through my baking skills, as Dan made me promise that I'd never make another 'chickpea catastrophe' – his semi-polite way of referring to my first attempt at a vegan chocolate cake that managed to both melt *and* solidify into a total inedible mess.

It broke the ice between us, at least. I managed to get a refund on the unopened bottles of Molton Brown handwash and hand cream – and we agreed on a compromise that Dan would start to use hand lotion. Apparently cuticle oil was one step too far, but I was still working on it.

Friday had rolled round, and I'd invited Susie over to my flat so we could toast my one-month anniversary at work. In my old life, that sort of celebration (or simply the fact that it was Friday) would call for champagne. But that was out of the question on my lemonade budget. However, lemonade was also out of the question after the month I'd had – there was no doubt that the occasion called for alcohol. So we settled for a cheap bottle of cava and a Ben & Jerry's rip-off called Bev & Kerry's.

Mine and Susie's Friday night wine and trashy TV evenings

had become a tradition over the last month. I needed them at the end of a long week at the soup kitchen. I'd been working twelve-hour days, six days a week. But not only had the long hours of scrubbing, buffing and dusting paid off superficially (my toned biceps were beginning to rival Jennifer Aniston's), I was actually starting to feel at home in the soup kitchen, and perhaps most surprisingly, in Toxteth.

Despite there being absolutely nowhere that sold sushi, there was a community feeling that you didn't get in many places – certainly not when I lived in Chelsea, back in my London days. Not unless you were lobbying together with your neighbours to stop the non-residential parking outside your apartment building, of course. Important issues like that always bonded neighbours.

Luckily, Dan and Susie hadn't asked many questions about my background or why I'd moved to Toxteth. Susie assumed it was a bad break-up, while Dan didn't have much to say most of the time anyway. They just laughed about my 'alien ways', as Susie always said. For example, when she discovered that despite knowing how to cook at least eighty-six different varieties of soup, I didn't know how to boil an egg. Or why you shouldn't mix reds with whites when doing your laundry (RIP beautiful Lanvin silk shirt, I miss you every day).

Even though only a couple of months had passed since they'd welcomed me open-armed into their lives, no questions asked, I couldn't help the nagging feeling in the back of my mind that I still couldn't tell them who I really was – Arabella Allegra Whittington, (former) heiress to the multimillion-pound Whittington Soup company. They still knew me as Bella Whitson, and luckily, their part-time accountant hadn't noticed my real name, now that I was officially a member of the team. How could I tell them that my mother's jewellery collection (before she sold it) was probably worth more than mine and Susie's apartments put together? Or that my old monthly shopping bills totalled more than what they'd both spend on food in a year?

These were people who spent their lives helping those who didn't even have a roof over their head, or assisting parents who were forced to rely on surplus handouts from Dan's soup kitchen to feed their hungry children. A soup kitchen that Dan established because he could see that nothing was being done to help the homeless and the vulnerable, or the people lining the pavements at night, comatose from a toxic cocktail of drink or drugs, or both.

As an heiress – which already felt like a distant dream – I'd never met people like Susie, Dan and Elsie. I'd experienced the ruthless side of the business world, where there was no room even for successful and kind-hearted people like my dad when push came to shove. But not just that, I'd also learnt the hard way that my foundation of friendships was built on a shallow, shared love of partying, gossip and Instagrammable brunch spots. I was struggling to enjoy the memories of a #BrunchGoals £25 eggs royale, knowing that a treat for some kids at the soup kitchen was bread and butter with sugar sprinkled on top.

Even though I'd only known him a relatively short time, I recognised that Dan took every challenge in his stride. Despite limited (pretty much non-existent) funding for the soup kitchen, he somehow managed to keep it ticking over. The paint was still peeling from the doors and most of the children's toys were missing at least one limb, but a small government grant, minuscule donations from well-wishers, and occasional charity drives meant he could continue to open the doors to the decrepit building 365 days a year.

'Margherita pizza or roasted vegetable pizza?' Susie shouted from the tiny kitchen area in my studio flat.

'I take it you didn't get a meat feast?' I sighed.

'Of course not.' Susie squirmed in disgust.

'Roasted veggies then, I suppose,' I said, making a mental

note to keep a packet of ham in the fridge to add to my pizza whenever it was Susie's choice. She handed me a plate that was piled high with meat-free, cheese-free pizza.

My apartment was still very much a work-in-progress. We were perched on oversized beanbags at my second-hand coffee table, drinking wine out of mugs. I knew I had to get round to buying furniture eventually, but my demanding work schedule and limited income meant it wasn't a top priority.

I'd hidden the majority of my mountainous piles of designer clothes, shoes, handbags and accessories. They were either in storage or tucked away in cardboard boxes and bin bags (please forgive me, Louboutin collection) inside a spare cupboard. Realistically, I didn't know when I was going to wear them again. It was a case of 'out of sight, out of mind', and the optimistic hope that cashmere would survive the winter in a slightly damp cupboard. It was a hardy fabric, wasn't it?

'How's work been this week?' Susie asked, mid-pizza bite.

'Fine,' I shrugged, 'though Dan has been a little quiet... quieter than normal.'

'Oh bollocks,' Susie interrupted, dropping the pizza onto her plate and wiping the crumbs on her paint-covered overalls. 'What's the date today?'

'Erm.' My phone lit up as I nudged it with my elbow. 'The sixth of September?'

'Dammit, I completely forgot,' Susie mumbled, before frantically typing on her phone.

'Forgot what?'

'Tomorrow is mine and Dan's monthly bingo outing with Elsie.' She pushed her wild, ruby-coloured hair back from her face and tucked it into her bandana. 'I've been so busy working on my new paintings, it completely slipped my mind.'

'Oh, that is too cute,' I said. 'How long have you guys been doing that?'

'As long as I can remember.' Susie sighed. 'I don't even like bingo! I only do it for Dan, and he only does it for Elsie.' She set her phone down and took a swig of wine.

I desperately wanted to ask Susie if she and Dan had any history (or for any inside information about his relationship status), but every moment felt inappropriate. I took a gulp of wine, partly for Dutch courage, but then was interrupted when Susie glanced at her phone as it buzzed to life. 'Dan said would you like to come with us?'

'Oh, gosh no.' I shook my head. 'I have lots of stuff to sort out,' I lied. 'And I wouldn't want to intrude.'

'I don't think he'd suggest it if he thought you were intruding,' Susie answered with a cheeky smile.

'Oh.' I looked down at my pizza again to try and hide my blushing cheeks. I was torn. Part of me wanted to join them, but another really didn't want to intrude on their tradition. I'd already imposed myself on them and their lives enough. 'No, I'd better not,' I said firmly.

Susie typed a message, and her phone pinged again just a few seconds later. She picked it up in frustration at having to swap it for the pizza slice she was nibbling. 'Dan said how about meeting us in the pub later on then?'

'Yeah, I guess I could come along to that,' I said. 'It'd be rude not to. You know, if he's invited me,' I added hastily.

'Yeah, you don't want to be rude. Nothing about wanting to see Dan. Nothing at all.' Susie grinned mischievously at me as I threw my pizza crust at her.

EIGHTEEN

I followed Susie's instructions and headed in the direction of the Georgian Quarter to my new 'local' – The Blackburne Arms. Apparently, it had been a local pub for almost a hundred years, so I expected it to look like that too; I imagined its dated decor, sticky floors and the smell of stale cigarettes embedded in the wallpaper, despite the smoking ban being in place for more than a decade. Oh well, if my soles did stick to the floor, at least I still had custody of Susie's shoes.

I was getting used to my now everyday (and secretly designer) uniform of jeans, a plain T-shirt and either a hoodie or jumper with borrowed flat pumps. This was paired with a minimal make-up routine (I'd only sweat it off in the hot kitchen) and my hair tied back in a ponytail (nobody wanted a hair in their soup, even if it had been expertly highlighted by the best hairdresser in Liverpool).

Thankfully, the morning's DIY pamper session had been more successful than the last one. Susie's tip to use coconut oil as a hair mask meant my locks were smooth and shiny, while my exhausted eyes were invigorated, thanks to the cold teabags I placed on them before I napped on the sofa. I didn't trust

Susie's insistence that you could also do a bikini wax at home, however. And I still didn't fully trust my DIY skills after dyeing my face luminous yellow.

When I turned the corner, I did a double-take as I saw the striking building on the corner, the copper lettering outside identifying it as the pub where I was meeting them. The building's exterior was the perfect representation of the Georgian architectural style of the area, with its impeccable symmetry and embellished headers above the enormous sash windows which framed the warm glow from the inside of the pub.

Pushing open the door, I recognised the Farrow & Ball paint on the walls – it was the same colour my parents had on the walls of the dining room in their Southport mansion. Instead of sticky floors, there was an immaculate carpet that complemented the interior's chic colour scheme. And there wasn't a single whiff of cigarette smoke; instead, there were mouthwatering smells from the kitchen – and if the plates that the waiting staff carried past were anything to go by, the food was as good as it smelt.

The eyes of the pub's guests landed on me as I surveyed the room, before recognising the sounds of laughter coming from the corner where Dan, Elsie and Susie were huddled cosily. Susie was slapping the wooden table as she giggled, while Dan held his head in his hands and Elsie wiped her eyes with a lilac handkerchief.

'Bella!' Susie beamed as she clocked me making my way towards them.

'Hi, guys,' I said, greeting them with an awkward wave and ignoring the butterflies in my stomach. 'Sounds like I missed something funny?'

'Elsie was just telling us a story about Dan and a very determined, but very tiny, goat that chased him around a petting zoo when he was five.'

Elsie dabbed her eyes again. 'He had to climb a tree to get

away from it. I've never seen anyone so scared of something the size of a puppy.'

Dan caught my eye, rolled his eyes jokingly and smiled as he sipped the last dregs of his beer. 'No puppy I've ever seen,' he said defensively, to Susie and Elsie's giggles. Then he stood, yawned, and stretched his arms up, revealing a cluster of tattoos around his dark snail trail. 'Fancy a bevvy?' he asked me.

'I'll have what you're having,' I replied, making a conscious effort not to stare at his distractingly toned stomach.

'An alcohol-free beer?' Dan said, feigning shock.

'Erm, no. In that case, I'll have a rosé, please.'

'One rosé coming up,' he said, pulling a tatty wallet from the pocket of his ripped jeans. 'Els? Suze?'

'Would you *look* at the time!' Elsie said, dramatically checking her watch and grabbing the deep purple furry jacket beside her.

'Seven?' Dan answered quizzically.

'It's nearly time for the *Corrie* rerun. I'm sorry, I have to go. I can't miss it. You know what I'm like.'

'No, actually I don't. Since when do you watch *Coronation Street*?' Dan replied, puzzled.

'Since... since before you were born, soft lad.'

'I've never seen you watch—'

'Anyway, ta-ra!' Elsie interrupted, before she rushed over and kissed Susie and Dan on their foreheads in quick succession. 'Ta-ra, Bella love, nice to see you. I'm so sorry we couldn't catch up properly, but you know...'

'*Corrie* calls?' I smiled as she stroked my hair in a hasty farewell. She hurried to the door after bidding farewell to all the other people she knew in the pub (most of them), who each waved and smiled affectionately at her.

'Suze? What can I get you?' Dan gestured to the bar.

'I'm actually going to head off too,' Susie replied, collecting her backpack and wrapping a blanket scarf around her neck and shoulders.

'What?' I said, slightly panicked, knowing that this would leave just me and Dan together. Despite spending almost every day working together side by side (literally, the workspace in the soup kitchen was quite narrow), we'd never 'hung out' just the two of us. Not in a non-work capacity, anyway.

'Yeah, erm, I've got that thing, you know?' She clicked her fingers. 'You know... that thing. I've definitely told you both about it.'

Dan raised his eyebrows. 'Funny that, I don't remember you saying anything about having any plans today.'

'Me neither.' I glared at her.

'Clearly you both have terrible memories.' She stood up and straightened out her bright orange dungarees before legging it towards the door. 'See ya, kids, don't do anything I wouldn't do!'

Dan smiled at me. 'I think the question is, what wouldn't Susie do?'

'I dread to think.' I laughed.

'I'll get us a couple more bevvies then,' Dan said, before heading to the bar.

This will be fine, I tried to convince myself. *Absolutely fine. Tickety-boo.* We were colleagues, after all.

We'd perfected our daily rhythm at the soup kitchen. In the morning, after two cups of coffee, I'd clean the kitchen while he sorted through the bags of daily ingredients and donations. We'd prepare and cook the food together while arguing over what music to listen to, only ever agreeing on The Beatles.

After the volunteers helped us serve lunch, and Herbie devoured any leftovers that fell from the table, I'd clean again, before hanging out with some of the mums who brought their children in to play with the toys. Dan's afternoons were usually back-to-back meetings with the people he sponsored through Alcoholics Anonymous and Drug Addicts Together. When he wasn't doing that, he was furiously typing letters on his ancient laptop. He said they were to the council and the local MP, and that he was lobbying them for more funds, but inevitably to no avail.

'A rosé for the lady.' Dan placed the glass down in front of me. It was filled with a delicate, blush-coloured Côtes de Provence. He leant back next to me and took a swig from his Beck's Blue.

'I'm sorry if I interrupted your evening,' I said, as we watched plate after plate of beautifully presented food leave the kitchen and arrive at the tables of diners, who licked their lips in anticipation before tucking in. 'I told Susie I shouldn't have come, I didn't want to intrude.'

Dan shook his head and turned back towards me. 'Not at all, I wanted you to come.' He rested his arm over the back of my seat, so his whole body was facing me. 'I think I owe you an apology,' he said.

'Please don't say you're going to make me clean the gents' toilets again.' I shuddered at the memory of the urinals.

'No, I promise, from now on, the gents' toilets are my cleaning responsibility,' he laughed. 'I want to say I'm sorry for misjudging you. I know I was a bit standoffish when we first met.'

I raised my eyebrows. Standoffish was one way to put it.

'But I just thought you were a bit, I don't know...' His eyes took in our surroundings as he thought about his words. 'Snobby,' he winced jokingly as he gauged my reaction.

'Snobby?' I guffawed. 'Me?'

Dan shrugged his shoulders and took a gulp of his drink.

What a hilarious thought – me, *snobby*. I was about to tell him he was embarrassingly incorrect. I was anything *but* snobby. I've flown with a budget airline, for goodness' sake. Granted it was for my cousin's wedding in Tuscany and we all booked a row each so we'd have some space for ourselves, but still, it was a *budget airline*. I wasn't snobby. In fact, I was an anti-snob. That was me. The Anti-Snob.

'Oh, bugger!' I said, grateful for an excuse to dispel Dan's amused gaze as I considered my argument against his rather offensive (and incorrect) first impression of me. 'I've just remembered I forgot to leave the empty bin bags outside for the food donations tomorrow.'

'Don't worry about it,' Dan said, raising the bottle to his lips.

'Can I ask you something?' I said, noticing how his legs were so close to mine under the small wooden table that our jeans were almost touching.

'Only if it isn't about work.' Dan smiled, circling the top of his beer bottle with a tattooed thumb. 'You know, this is the first occasion we've spent time together outside work.'

I stopped myself from taking another sip of rosé, realising he'd notice that my skin tone nearly matched the shade of pink if I put it next to my face.

'Perhaps if Ringo wasn't your favourite Beatle and "Yellow Submarine" wasn't your favourite song then we could spend a bit more time together,' I said.

'When did I say "Yellow Submarine" was my favourite?'

'You said it's a classic.'

'It *is* a classic!' he enthused, as the other punters glanced over at our animated chatter. 'And Ringo is an exceptionally talented man. His childhood home is just around the corner from here, you know?'

I raised my eyebrows impassively.

Dan ignored my lack of enthusiasm. 'He played the drums in the best band in musical history with his right hand when he's left-handed. Fun fact.' Dan tilted his beer towards my glass as a victorious 'cheers'.

'Even John said he wasn't the best drummer in the band.'

'He was joking!' Dan said, wide-eyed. 'The journalist didn't understand Scouse humour.'

'Sure.' I nodded. 'Although I bet Elsie doesn't even agree with you on this.'

'She doesn't, and you have to promise me you won't ever get her started on the topic.' He grabbed my little finger with his so fast that I almost knocked over my wine glass. 'Promise?' The soft wrinkles around his eyes creased as he smiled.

'Fine, I promise.' I squeezed his pinky together with mine as I said it. He held mine wrapped up in his for a little longer than necessary, before we were interrupted with the familiar intro of 'Yellow Submarine' filling the pub.

'Cheers, Barry mate!' Dan gestured to the barman blatantly eavesdropping on our conversation, who replied with a thumbs up.

'So now we have the evening's soundtrack sorted' – he smirked at my expression of contempt – 'what was it that you wanted to ask me?'

'Oh yes,' I remembered, after a sip of the delicious wine. 'I was wondering. Well, I've been wondering for a while now...' Dan's eyes held mine. 'Those massive bin bags of food that we use in the kitchen every day. Where do they come from?'

Dan settled back in his seat, seemingly disappointed at the dullness of my work-related question.

'I know we get some of the food from donations,' I said. 'But there's just *so* much in those bags – enough to feed everyone who comes through the door, the volunteers and us too, not to mention Herbie's insatiable appetite. There are decent ingredients in there as well.' I shrugged my shoulders. 'I don't know, I've just wondered.'

'What time is it?' Dan checked his old watch. 'Seven thirty,' he said, answering his own question. I didn't wear a watch any more – I hadn't worn my precious Cartier since I'd moved, instead hiding it above one of the many loose ceiling panels in my bathroom.

'I can show you in precisely two hours. If you're up for it, that is.'

'Up for what?' I asked nervously.

Dan stood up and gestured to my glass. 'You'll be fine. But you might want to down the rest of your wine.'

I sipped, contemplating exactly what he meant and whether I should be worried.

'Have you eaten?' he asked.

'Nope.' I shook my head. 'Not since lunch.'

I'd been experimenting with a new soup flavour that I hoped Dan was going to love, but I needed to perfect my recipe first. It was a carrot, tarragon and white bean soup, with crispy sage and apple croutons. Absolutely delicious, but the apple croutons still needed refining. It would be an ideal recipe to use up the surplus of carrots and apples that were constantly over-flowing from the bags in the soup kitchen – the bin bags I'd soon discover the origins of.

'Would you fancy getting something to eat first?' Dan asked shyly, which was a little out of character for him.

'Sure.' I smiled, before downing the last of my wine. 'Here?'

'We could do, or there's an amazing Middle Eastern restaurant over on Lodge Lane. Do you like Arabic food?'

'Of course!' I grabbed my jacket and handbag. 'I grew up holidaying in Dubai.' I regretted the words as they came out. My extravagant holidays were not part of my new identity and the Bella that Dan and Susie knew.

'Ooh, Dubai, 'ey?' Dan teased, nudging me. 'But this place is the real deal. Totally authentic.'

'And what makes you think that what or where I ate in Dubai wasn't authentic?'

Dan eyed me cynically.

'Fine, you might have a point.' I surrendered as I was transported back to holidays with the girls, and how cultured I thought I was as I posed for Instagram shots on a quad bike next to a camel in the desert, or on the bow of a yacht in front of the Burj Al Arab. And how despite it being technically a dry country, we'd spend most of our time at the notoriously alcohol-soaked brunches.

Dan held the door open for me and I checked my reflection in the window again as I walked through it. What was supposed to be a quiet drink, the four of us, had now turned into a dinner date with Dan. Was it a date? That I didn't know, but I did know I liked how he walked so close beside me that I could smell his aftershave.

NINETEEN

The evening had changed dramatically from just an hour earlier when we'd shared an amazing, authentic Arabic feast. We'd both apologised profusely as we each reached for the final scoop of fattoush, argued over who deserved the final kibbeh, and debated whether we were too full for luqaimat (we were, but it was worth it). As much as it pained me to admit, Dan was right. Before our dinner together, I thought that eating hummus and pitta bread while sipping cocktails beside the pool at a five-star hotel was me embracing genuine Arabic cuisine.

However, I was already regretting asking Dan where the big bin bags originated from. We'd gone from the candlelight of an intimate restaurant to standing in the middle of an industrial-sized bin. A *bin*! The beams from our flashlights and head torches illuminated the remnants of a supermarket's unwanted produce. The dancing spotlights broke up the darkness, reminding me of how I used to spend my weekends – drinking champagne in pretentious bars, wearing my highest heels and my prettiest dress.

'Is this legal?' I whispered to Dan, who was expertly tiptoeing over the precariously stacked bin bags.

'Technically, yes.' He stopped to tie his hair back into a short ponytail, holding the bin liners in his teeth as he did it. 'In the UK, "dumpster diving" as an act is legal. You can't be prosecuted for stealing abandoned goods because abandoned goods can't be stolen.' He tapped his nose, with a matter-of-fact nod. 'But...'

'How did I know there would be a but?' I groaned, feeling the squelch of another pile of fruit exploding over my Hunter wellies, which Dan had ordered me to grab from my flat.

'We could get arrested for trespassing,' he added.

'Aargh!' I squealed, feeling myself slipping into a ripped bag that was leaking with a stench that could only be described as a combination of rotting eggs and sour yoghurt. As I braced for impact, I felt Dan grab my right arm and smoothly hoist me up next to him.

'That's why we have to be quiet,' he mock-whispered, gently pulling a few herb sprigs from my hair.

'I don't think I'm cut out for this.' I winced. I looked down at my Armani jeans, which were previously jet black but were now a dirty grey from all the moist, foul-smelling sludge that I was almost thigh-deep in.

'I told you to grab your cheapest wellies,' Dan said, gently holding on to my arm and expertly navigating me through the enormous bin. 'Hunters weren't exactly what I had in mind.'

'They're the only ones I have.' I shrugged.

'They're dear though, aren't they? Must've set you back at least a hundred pounds?'

'Nah, I can't remember.' I tried to brush him off and change the subject from my custom-made £800 Hunters. 'I bought them a while ago for Glastonbury,' I said nonchalantly. Tabs and I had matching ones made; it was one of my most liked photos on Instagram.

'Oh wow,' Dan said. 'I've always wanted to go to Glasto. For the actual music though, not "for the gram".'

'Hey, I went for the "actual music",' I mocked, while concentrating on my footing and not the relentless reek of rotten vegetables.

Dan turned away, but I was sure I clocked a smile from underneath the blinding glow of his head torch. 'Just a little further this way,' he said.

Dan carefully guided us to the opposite end of the bin, where the smell was much less vomit-inducing.

'Right,' he declared, as if he was a world adventurer conquering new land for the first time. He pulled the thick rubber gloves up to his elbows and separated the pile of bin bags. 'Here you go,' he said, throwing a small stack to me. 'Four bags each, you should be able to manage that.'

'Four bags of what?'

'Of this,' Dan said, his arms outstretched and his smile like a Cheshire cat. Though I was certain a cat in Cheshire would have much higher standards. 'Only fruit, vegetables and store cupboard ingredients though. And no meat or dairy, obviously.'

'Is *this* why you only cook vegan food at the soup kitchen?'

'Partly,' Dan answered. 'It would be riskier to scavenge meat in case it's gone off, of course. But I also love animals. Each to their own, like, and I don't want to be preachy, but I don't think there's any need for us to eat them if we don't have to.'

I nodded, but was quickly distracted by the overwhelming stench where I was standing. 'I'm sure it's all expired. It stinks.' I pinched my nose together.

'Not all of it. Trust me. It's a treasure trove.'

That was the moment I realised Dan Rigby and I most definitely had different ideas of 'treasure'.

Dan got to work quickly. He expertly identified the waste that looked fresh and filled the bin bags with perfectly sealed, but slightly bashed, packets of biscuits, rice and pasta.

'See what I mean?' He used his torch to show me the inside of the bag, which was soon bursting with cupboard goods, together with fresh, but wonky, vegetables and fruit that mustn't have sold because of the imperfect shapes.

I reasoned that it must've been a fluke. Surely the bags that Dan had unearthed were lucky finds.

'How did you find all that? How do you know what to pick and what to leave?'

'Pretty easy really,' Dan replied casually. 'Use your nose and your eyes. Like people did for thousands of years before the food industry invented sell-by stickers and best before dates.

'Here, check this one.' He passed over a supermarket-branded plastic bag that was fit to burst, while balancing on his knees.

Rifling through it, I couldn't believe how ridiculous it was. Freshly baked loaves of bread, perfectly intact. Artisan salted caramel biscuits with reduced price stickers. Just a couple of hours earlier, everything would've been sitting on a shelf in the shop.

There were plenty of expensive brands too. I recognised a familiar pot of truffle mustard – all sleek packaging with calligraphy letters. Its best before date was only today's date. There were abandoned bouquets of flowers dotted around the food graveyard as well. I grabbed a handful of roses that didn't get the chance to bloom, but a little water and TLC might save them.

I beamed as I proudly showed Dan my wares. Before I knew it, we'd both filled our four bags. Each one was carefully placed to the side of the ten-foot-tall bin so that we could carry them back to the van once we'd finished.

'That's enough for today.' Dan nodded.

He scaled the bin like a pro, then guided me (certainly not a pro) down afterwards. The minute he decided the coast was clear, we both grabbed the bags and ran through the car park of Super Saver supermarket around the corner to where his bright yellow VW camper van was parked.

'What a haul!' Dan gushed, climbing into the driver's seat after we'd piled the bags into the boot.

I smiled as the word 'haul' reminded me of endless hours spent watching my favourite fashion vloggers unpacking and unwrapping their shopping sprees of the new season's designer goods.

'What a haul indeed,' I agreed, silently laughing at the parallel of my new life – swapping Balenciaga for bananas, Hermès for herbs and diamonds for dumpster diving.

'I bet this isn't the answer you expected when you asked where the food bags came from,' Dan said, wiping an unidentifiable liquid from his neck with a stack of baby wipes.

'Not exactly,' I agreed, as I clocked that I too probably needed to wipe the bin juice off myself. 'But at least the mystery has now been solved.'

'To be honest, I'm a little surprised by how much you embraced it.' Dan cast his used wipes to one side and turned to face me. 'Suze won't believe it either.'

'And why not?' I said incredulously, trying to mask my outrage.

'Are you kidding?' Dan laughed. 'Don't take this the wrong way, Bella, but you do come across as a little bit of a princess.'

'What?' I said, aghast. 'Give me one example where I've been "princessy",' I air-quoted.

'I think there might be too many to count.' Dan laughed. 'Ordering the most expensive blender you could find might be one...'

'I'll have you know that Vitamix is *the* best blender brand. It would've totally changed your life if you hadn't sent it back, it was an entirely selfless act.'

'It cost nearly seven hundred pounds!' Dan exclaimed.

I shrugged; there was no need to keep going over the argument now, was there? I'd already told him I'd actually reined myself in and bought the cheaper model out of the two I had my eye on.

'Or your hatred for dusting?' Dan offered.

'The dust gets *everywhere!*'

'And hoovering?'

'It makes my arms ache. Hoovers are *heavy.*'

Dan bit his lip to stop his stifled laugh. 'It's a good job you make amazing soup then, isn't it?'

'Mm-hmm.' I smiled.

'I've got to admit, it's getting better. The cleaning, I mean.'

'A little better all the time, I'd say.'

The smell of bin juice, baby wipes and his aftershave filled the van as we looked at each other. A moment between us. That was, before a loud knock at Dan's window made us both jump out of our seats.

Dan clocked the security guard and rolled the window down. 'Good evening,' he said innocently.

'Just checking why you're parked here at 10.30 p.m. on a Saturday night,' the security guard said suspiciously, eyeing our baby wipes in the middle of the seats.

'We're just out for a drive,' Dan replied. 'Seeing the sights.'

'Round 'ere? Good luck finding them,' he scoffed, taking a cigarette from the pocket of his shirt. 'Not to worry, mate. Drive on. Just checking you're not up to no good.' He winked, slapping the side of the van as he walked back to his post.

Dan started the knackered engine of the scruffy Volkswagen. 'Let's get all this food back to the fridge at the kitchen. We can sort through it in the morning,' he said.

His hand brushed mine as I reached over to turn the radio on, and he changed gear. 'Sorry,' we mumbled at the same time, but I couldn't ignore the rush of excitement I felt when our skin touched.

I averted my eyes from Dan to the window and watched his

reflection in the driver's seat as we trundled through the dark streets.

'You survived your first dumpster diving trip then,' Dan said, breaking the tension between us.

'It appears so,' I agreed.

'I don't suppose you're free tomorrow afternoon, after work, are you?'

My stomach did a teeny flip.

'Don't worry if you're busy,' Dan added quickly, casually putting one hand on the wheel, with the other tapping on the door to the beat of the music.

'I'm free,' I said. 'Though I'll have to check with my boss,' I grinned.

'Eugh, Dan Rigby? I hear he's a right misery guts.' Dan glanced at me.

'He's all right,' I said, shrugging my shoulders.

'Well, if you manage to get away from him, I'd love to take you somewhere.'

I turned away again to hide my smile. 'Sounds good,' I said. 'As long as it doesn't involve any more bin juice.'

'No bin juice,' he nodded. 'That's a promise.'

TWENTY

Thanks to a busy lunch period at the soup kitchen, I was already running late and feeling frazzled. The kitchen closed early on Sundays, so after locking up, Dan and I went our separate ways before agreeing to meet at my flat in half an hour.

I felt sufficiently out of practice in all things hair and make-up; I didn't even have time to get changed by the time I'd made myself look mildly presentable. Although I was still undecided as to whether it was definitely a date, Susie had excitedly assured me it was, and that she was to be my Chief Bridesmaid if Dan didn't choose her as his Best Woman.

If Susie was right, then never in my life had I worn jeans, trainers and a jumper as an outfit of choice for a first date. So, I tried to dress it up a little and add a bit of pizazz by throwing on a gorgeous (Stella McCartney) trench coat.

The buzzer rang and I shoved all the essentials into my oversized handbag, rushed out the door and down the stairs. Pushing the front door in the communal entrance open, I was immediately greeted with the sight of Dan, and Herbie at his feet.

'Hello, you!' I made a beeline for Herbie. 'I didn't know you were joining us,' I said to him as he tried to lick my face.

'Hello to you too.' Dan smiled, holding Herbie's lead loosely around his wrist.

'Sorry,' I said, standing up. 'I can't resist Herbie cuddles.' Herbie sat next to me and pawed my knee, willing me to carry on with my scratches behind his floppy ears.

'I don't think he can resist them either.' Dan laughed at the scruffy pooch looking up at us with his big eyes. 'Come on, Herb,' he said, gently pulling the lead so he got to his feet again, but not before a big downward dog stretch and an enormous yawn.

'Honestly, you'd think he hadn't just spent the entire day sleeping,' Dan teased. 'Although he *has* been with Elsie, so there's a good chance he's worn out from being spoilt by her home-baked dog treats.'

'I feel your pain, Herbie. Carb coma?' He looked up, as if in agreement, while he plodded along the pavement between Dan and me.

We headed down the high street, past the pizza restaurant that was my first experience of the area. I wasn't sure whether my Italian food standards had dropped, or if I had developed some sort of immunity to second-rate pizza, but I was surprised how much I'd grown to like it after the disastrous first visit with my parents.

'Are you going to tell me where we're going?' I asked Dan. Judging from his damp hair and strong scent of woody after-shave, he'd managed to find the time to fit in a quick shower and change of clothes during our thirty-minute window.

Dan pointed in front of us.

'We're going to Brunswick train station?' I asked, puzzled.

'Not as our final destination, no,' he laughed, 'but we need to go on the train to get there. Just one stop, like.'

I stopped suddenly.

'We're getting the train?' I said, trying but failing to hide my tone, so high-pitched that it was probably only Herbie who heard me.

'Erm, yeah?' Dan nodded before stepping closer to me, as if approaching a wild animal that might bolt at any moment. 'Is that OK? Are you OK?' He eyed my hands fidgeting with the slightly torn leather on my handbag.

'Yeah,' I lied. 'I'm fine.'

'You don't seem fine,' he replied. 'What's the matter?'

'Nothing.' I shook my head. 'It's just... well...'

Herbie brushed past my legs and yawned, bored with our conversation. He obviously had places to be – sticks to find, wees to do, dogs' bottoms to sniff.

'I've never been on the train before. I mean, not like a normal train. I've only ever been on the Eurostar,' I clarified.

Dan raised his eyebrows in surprise. 'Really?'

'Mm-hmm,' I said, still fidgeting with my poor handbag. It wouldn't have any leather left if I carried on and I didn't have enough money for a new Mulberry Bayswater, even in the seasonal sale. I always used the least conspicuous bags in my collection – any that didn't have an instantly recognisable label and logo, and any that I didn't mind accidentally filling with the constant stream of vegetable peelings that somehow always managed to end up inside.

'And you've lived in Liverpool for how long?' Dan asked, rubbing his chin.

'Not long, I guess. I grew up in Southport though, so I feel like I've lived nearby my whole life – apart from a few years in London.' My stomach clenched whenever I accidentally gave away any details of my background. I was living my life on tenterhooks, scared that at any moment Dan and Susie were going to realise who I really was. I was grateful that neither of them used social media and hadn't accidentally stumbled upon my old profile, despite my fake name and different appearance.

'OK, we have two options,' Dan said, swiftly changing the subject as he sensed my discomfort. 'First option, we can go ahead and give you your first lesson in train travel. Herbie's a pro, so he can lead the way.' Herbie wagged his tail at the mention of his name. 'Or I can go back, get the van and we can drive there. Though we might hit the gridlock weekend traffic.' Dan grimaced as he checked his watch.

'Let's do it, let's get the train.' I almost checked over my shoulder to see who was talking as I injected a false sense of confidence in my answer.

'Are you sure? We don't have to.'

'Let's go for it. I can learn from the experts.' I smiled.

Dan grinned and held his arm out for me to hook mine into. 'We'd be honoured to be your tour guides, if you'll have us.'

As our arms touched, I felt the same butterflies in my stomach that fluttered every time he brushed past me in the kitchen, or whenever his hand accidentally touched mine while we were washing the dishes or chopping mountains of vegetables.

Dan demonstrated how to use the ticket machine and bought a return ticket for me, while selling me the benefits of a travel pass if I was going to use the train regularly.

'Keep it handy,' he instructed, stopping me as I whipped out my purse to put the ticket away. 'Especially when you're going through the barriers.' He demonstrated swiping the card over the screen and dashing through the barrier with Herbie in tow, waiting for me on the other side.

'Noted.' I nodded, quickly following them.

'Fun fact for you,' Dan said. 'Dogs travel for free on the train, but you have to carry them on the escalators. And no sitting on the seats.' I could've sworn I saw a subtle roll of the eye from Herbie, as he trotted confidently down the stairs.

'That's so cool,' I said, in support of my favourite four-legged friend.

'Yeah, there's been a whole campaign about it, it's called "Mutts on Merseyside".' Dan smiled. 'Herbie definitely approves. Especially if I take him to Crosby Beach or Formby sand dunes.'

'I've always wanted to visit the Antony Gormley statues on Crosby Beach!' I said. 'Francis... my ex,' I clarified. 'He wasn't really a beach kind of guy, unless it was the Maldives.' I shook my head as thoughts of Francis popped in. They were always entirely uninvited, but still made an occasional appearance. It was easier to forget him and my old life when I was with Dan.

Dan raised his eyebrows. 'Well, I much prefer Merseyside over the Maldives. Not that I've ever been.' He laughed, but crossed his arms over his chest defensively. 'We can go there one day, to Crosby Beach, if you like? Herbie will gladly oblige, I'm sure. Although he does like to pee on the statues.'

I ruffled the fur on Herbie's head as he looked up at me.

'Herbie says you're lying.' I glanced from Herbie's big eyes to Dan's. 'He's saying, "This is completely untrue, don't believe a word my human says. I would never pee on the statues. I am an upstanding member of dog society, with excellent manners and honourable toilet etiquette."'

'You need to stop anthropomorphising him,' Dan said, but he couldn't stop a smile stretching across his face as he shook his head.

I gave Herbie a look to say, 'Don't worry, I understand you,' and his expression told me he was grateful that someone finally did, before he started trying to sniff his own bottom, signalling the end of our telepathic conversation.

'All OK so far?' Dan said.

'Fine.' I grinned. 'I'm actually quite enjoying it!'

'Sound,' Dan said, seemingly pleased with his work as a train guide of Liverpool so far.

A burst of noise blasted through the platform as the train trundled across the railway line and stopped in front of us. The train doors opened, and I took a step towards the carriage as the flurry of passengers rushed past us.

'Hang on a sec,' Dan said quietly, holding his hand out in front of us both. 'Next lesson: never get on the train before everyone else has got off.'

Dan's hand rested gently on my back as we jumped on after the crowds hurried away, before hesitating and swiftly placing his hand back into his pocket. He found a seat, sat down with Herbie at his feet, and gestured to the space next to him. Herbie panted happily as the train picked up speed and he watched the fellow passengers, a few of them making a fuss of him.

'Yer gorgeous, you are, lad.' An old man crouched down and tickled Herbie's chin as he passed through the carriageway.

'He's boss him, like.' A teenager in a grey tracksuit nodded to Dan, after asking Herbie for a high five, to which he happily performed the rest of his repertoire of tricks. Such a show-off.

I looked around as we sped along, the Liverpool suburbs zooming by in a rush of colours and blurred scenery. *I could get used to this*, I thought. What was I so worried about?

'So, when does the refreshments trolley come along?' I asked Dan.

'Y'what?' he beamed, a glint in his eyes.

'You know, the food and drinks trolley?' I looked around. 'I'd love a coffee, or maybe a G&T?' I smiled at him.

Dan looked down and pressed his lips together. 'It must be their day off today,' he said eventually. 'It is Sunday, after all.'

'Ah, of course.' I nodded. Oh well, a drink could wait. 'So, my official tour guide and train travel aficionado.' I turned to Dan. 'Are you going to tell me some fun facts?'

'I suppose I'd be a pretty rubbish guide if I didn't,' Dan replied. 'Seeing as we're on a train, did you know that the world's first passenger railway line was built from Liverpool to Manchester in 1830?'

'I didn't.'

'Hmm.' Dan rubbed the stubble over his jawline. Herbie wagged his tail at Dan and offered a quiet bark.

'Of course, Herb. How could I forget?' Dan rubbed Herbie behind the ear. 'Would you like to know Herbie's fact?'

'Absolutely.'

'Herbie's home before mine was the RSPCA, and the RSPCA was actually founded in a coffee shop on Bold Street in 1809, making the Liverpool branch the oldest animal charity in the world.'

Herbie trundled forward from Dan and nuzzled against my knee in confirmation.

'I have one,' I said. 'Did you know that the existing Cavern Club isn't the original one?'

'Of course.' Dan wiggled his eyebrows. 'Everyone knows that. The original entrance was where the fire exit is now.'

'Yeah, I know,' I said insecurely, having only found out that morning when I hastily googled things about Liverpool to try and impress Dan. Or at least so he wouldn't think I was totally ignorant about the city he loved so much. 'I was just checking *you* knew.'

I caught a glimpse of Dan's amused smile as he turned to face the window. The train slowed before pulling into the station and Dan slapped his hands onto his jean-clad knees. 'Our stop,' he announced, nudging Herbie up.

We stepped from the train onto the platform and headed up the stairs. 'We're fine today and there are no escalators here, but if you ever go to Moorfields, or any station, during rush hour, remember to always stand to the right on the escalators, never on the left side.'

I walked beside Dan and Herbie up the stairs, not touching

the handrail, even with my elbow. I shuddered as I imagined the germs. Mum would've been having a meltdown if she was here.

'Promise me and Herb you'll stick to the right at all times?'

'The right at all times,' I repeated.

'Good.' Dan smiled. 'And do you have your ticket ready?'

'I do,' I said gleefully, pulling it from the pocket of my jeans.

'See, you'll be a natural train user in no time,' Dan beamed.

TWENTY-ONE

The fresh air hit us the moment we stepped out of the station. I'd successfully taken my first train journey. *Wait until my parents hear this*, I thought, doing a mental victory dance – I'd ticked off the bus *and* the train! I was officially a public transport aficionado. Though probably best not to tell my germophobic mother if I didn't want to give her sleepless nights, and inevitably receive an industrial crate of hand sanitiser she'd order for me in a panic.

'Where are we going?' I asked.

'This way,' Dan replied, taking strides I was struggling to keep up with.

'Herbie clearly knows where he's going.' I laughed, as he trotted confidently in front.

'He certainly does,' Dan answered.

We walked around an area of Liverpool I'd never seen before, through some woods and across a main road before arriving at the entrance to a park (I was relieved I was wearing trainers and not my usual date staple of six-inch platform heels). Herbie looked back at us and wagged his tail, before urgently dragging the lead inside. Dan unhooked the lead from his collar, and he bolted like a bullet from a gun.

'Herbie!' I yelled at the blurred shape getting further and further away from us.

'Don't worry,' Dan said. 'He knows where he's going. This is like his second home – aside from the soup kitchen and Elsie's, obviously.'

'What is this place?' I looked around at the lush greenery and blooming flowers while inhaling the heady scent of freshly cut grass. I wondered if the train had actually taken us out of Liverpool altogether; it didn't feel like we were anywhere near a city any more. There were bright red pagodas over the waterways, where the reflection of the blue sky shimmered.

'Festival Gardens,' Dan answered. 'My parents used to bring me when I was younger.' He looked around the vast space, mostly empty except for a handful of fellow dog walkers. 'They loved it here.'

'I can see why.' I smiled at the flower-lined paths and the ponds with water features quietly trickling.

'This way,' he gestured to me. 'I promise we're only a minute away now.'

'Good.' I laughed as my stomach rumbled. 'Otherwise you might have to carry me.'

We followed the path around the park and passed through a hidden cluster of trees. As we turned the corner through the shrubbery, we were greeted with a bench that offered a breath-taking view of Liverpool. Herbie wagged his tail as he clocked our arrival from his place next to the bench.

'Wow,' I breathed.

'I know,' Dan whispered next to me. 'The view never gets old, no matter how many times I see it.'

Herbie sniffed Dan's backpack excitedly as Dan knelt down on the grass and began to unload. 'I know what you want,' he said, passing Herbie a bone that was almost the size of his head.

He happily sauntered off to enjoy it under the shade of a nearby willow tree.

'And I know what you want too,' Dan smiled. 'A G&T, as promised,' he said, handing over a pre-mixed can.

'Thanks,' I said. *A G&T in a can? First time for everything*, I thought, as I examined it suspiciously before clicking it open.

I sat down on the bench and wrapped myself up in one of the many blankets that Dan had squeezed into his backpack. As I put my handbag down, I noticed the names engraved into a small silver plaque on the bench.

Eleanor and David Rigby
In our hearts forever

'Is this...' I felt the hairs on my arms stand up.

'Yeah, it's my parents,' Dan said. He stopped unpacking the bag for a moment. 'Elsie paid for the bench and the inscription. It's our way of remembering them. She didn't want me to spend my life mourning them in a graveyard, so she arranged this instead and we scattered their ashes here.'

'It's beautiful,' I said softly. 'It's a beautiful way to remember them.'

'Mm-hmm.' Dan nodded, turning back to the bag.

'What happened?' I swallowed the lump in my throat. 'We don't have to talk about it, of course...'

'It's OK,' he said, sitting down next to the bag. His eyes looked unguarded for the first time since I met him, as if the dark clouds had temporarily stopped following him. 'They died when I was sixteen, within a year of each other. We were a close-knit unit, so it was tough. I'm an only child so I had no other family apart from them and Elsie, and we'd always done everything together.'

Dan fiddled with the blades of grass in front of him. 'Mum had a brain tumour. It happened so fast. She was fit and healthy, but then she woke up one day, felt really dizzy and couldn't see properly. She went to the doctors, and they discovered an enormous tumour that was eating away at her brain.'

'That's horrific,' I whispered.

'Mm-hmm,' he agreed. 'She was dead within three months, didn't leave the hospital after she went in. Dad just couldn't cope, he drank and drugged himself into oblivion. He died from an overdose six months later. I think he died of a broken heart. He couldn't live without her, they'd been together since they were teenagers.'

Dan bent his knees up and leant his arms over them. 'We didn't have much money growing up, but they made sure I did well at school and encouraged me to follow my dream of being a chef.'

'So that explains the soup kitchen?' I asked.

'Kind of,' he said hesitantly. 'I'd won a scholarship to a prestigious cookery school. But after my parents died, I...' He paused, searching for the right words. 'I went a bit... off the rails.'

'Off the rails?'

'I got in with the wrong crowd.' He shrugged slowly, as if that story was too heavy to unload onto me. 'One thing led to another... I don't remember the exact details. But I was drinking far too much, dabbling in other things too, and I eventually ended up homeless.'

'Homeless? You?' I said with disbelief. Although I didn't know him well, Dan just didn't seem the type to be homeless. But who was 'the type' to be homeless? I was learning that you could never predict what life had in store for you, no matter how much you planned.

'I don't talk about it much. It was a dark period.' His protective wall went up again and he looked away, out over the views of luscious green grass and lapping water.

I knew it was the end of that part of the conversation. 'How did you get through it? How did Dan's Kitchen come about?' I asked, changing the subject.

There was a change in atmosphere as Dan's body language shifted and he smiled at me, while squinting from the light of the sun. 'I'll give you one guess: she dresses like a real-life purple Quality Street.'

'Elsie?'

Dan nodded. 'She never got over the grief of losing her daughter, but she looked after me. Eventually, she managed to pull me out of the dark hole. She'd been trying to persuade me to live with her, obviously hating the idea of me on the streets. But I was in self-destruct mode for a while. I wanted to hide exactly what I was doing from her and I refused any help.'

Dan breathed deeply. 'But I'd reached rock bottom, and deep down, I knew that if I carried on the way I was going I'd almost certainly...' He shook his head and quickly moved on. 'Anyway, I didn't know it at the time, but my mum and dad saved every penny they could. They both worked two jobs, and they put everything in an account that I couldn't touch until I was twenty-one, unless Elsie applied for it to be released in "emergency" circumstances. Elsie was taking the risk that I might use the money to run away and spend it on what I was numbing the pain with. But she trusted me and told me to use the money as a second chance to rebuild my life.'

I nodded, captivated by Dan's story, and the courage he had to rebuild his life from scratch – it was exactly what I needed to hear, even though I obviously couldn't compare my circumstances to what Dan had lived through.

'I bought the building that's now the soup kitchen, and Elsie sold her house and bought the flat at the back. It was the perfect situation – Elsie always joked that she could keep an eye on me from there.' I noticed how Dan's eyes always lit up at any mention of his grandmother. 'And I guess you could say that it gave me a new lease of life. I could pursue my dream of being a chef, while giving something back to the homeless community that I'd come to know so well. But I guess, most importantly, it gave me a purpose – a reason to wake up in the morning.'

I wished Dan was sitting next to me, so I could hug him, or at least touch him. The distance between us felt so far, but in some ways, we were closer than ever. Finally, I was starting to understand why he seemed to carry the weight of the world on his shoulders. He'd been through more hardship and heartache than most people could ever imagine.

'I think it's always stuck with me that my dad was just crying out for help,' Dan said. 'He wasn't a bad man by any means, he just couldn't deal with his new reality. That's why I want to help the locals with drink and drug problems. I let the council hold counselling sessions there every week and I'm a sponsor for a few guys too. Still, it has its challenges. A lack of funding and support being the main ones, but that's another story...' He looked at his backpack and shook himself back to the present moment. 'Bloody hell, sorry Bella, there's me talking your ear off when we could be tucking into this feast.'

'It's fine,' I said. 'I'm glad you told me... I'm really, really glad you told me.'

He stopped unpacking the neat stacks of food from the piles of Tupperware and smiled at me. 'I've never actually brought anyone here before. Except Suze, of course. I come here whenever I finish early on a Sunday. Herbie loves it because he can run around off the lead, it's always pretty quiet.'

'I can't believe it isn't busier.' I looked at the leafy oasis around us. The trees were caught in the mid-point as autumn turned to winter; some with bushy branches and jade-green leaves, while others were bare, with only a sprinkling of amber sprigs. Our surroundings were completely silent, except the trickle of the water features, and Herbie munching on his giant bone.

'It's a well-kept secret.' Dan grinned. He stood up, holding a reusable plastic plate in either hand. 'I thought you might like getting out of Toxteth for some fresh air. Not that there's anything wrong with Toxteth, or the air there.' He handed a plate to me.

'This looks delicious,' I said, as I surveyed the mouthwatering finger food he'd unpacked from the stack of containers – bruschetta topped with juicy tomatoes and fresh basil, rice paper rolls packed with fresh veggies, paprika-roasted sweet potato and hummus with crudités and falafels.

'All home-made and all vegan.' Dan nodded. 'I know you still need convincing on the vegan element.' He cocked his head.

I couldn't deny it. A Sunday morning without a bacon butty was a Sunday morning I wanted no part of.

'If anything's coming close to my vegan conversion then it's this, and maybe your chocolate and cherry brownies.'

Dan laughed. 'I'll do you a deal then. I'll show you how to make those brownies, and you show me how you manage to make every flavour of soup taste so amazing.' He chuckled again. 'I don't think I'll ever be as good as you when it comes to soup-making.'

I blushed and took another sip from my G&T. The unseasonably warm autumn afternoon passed by in a haze of delicious picnic food and cans of drinks, our conversations only disrupted by the occasional giggle at Herbie's deafening snoring or sleep-barking.

We watched the changing colours of the backdrop to the Liverpool skyline, before the sun eventually hid behind the clouds and the dazzling blue blanket of sky turned to a dull grey, threatening a torrential downpour.

'Question,' I said, cracking open another tinned gin (quite the discovery!) while Dan sipped his Pepsi Max. 'Why have you named your dog after a car?'

'Ey? I haven't,' Dan answered, puzzled.

'Oh, is it a nod to his fondness for eating the fresh herbs in the herb garden?'

Herbie lazily opened one eye from his post-bone slumber.

'Neither,' Dan said. 'He's named after Herbie Hancock, the jazz musician. I'm not big into cars – you've seen my van. I'm always astounded when that thing passes its MOT. No, my mum and dad were both music obsessed, and they loved jazz. I grew up listening to all the classics – Herbie Hancock, Miles Davis, John Coltrane...'

'You're in good company,' I said, taking a sip. 'My dad is jazz mad, especially Miles Davis. He knows every millisecond of *Kind of Blue*. I feel like I do too, I grew up listening to it.'

'One of my favourite albums,' Dan said, looking out over the view. 'Bittersweet memories though. I love listening to it because I can close my eyes and feel my parents next to me – it's such a strong feeling. But then, I open my eyes and they're not there.'

In a bold move of confidence, sponsored by the revelation that was gin in a tin, I put my hand in his. He stroked my thumb gently as we sat side by side, and took a deep breath. 'It isn't easy losing your parents at sixteen, but I'm not proud of how I dealt with it.'

'You were just a kid,' I said, 'it's understandable.'

'Maybe, but still.' He shook his head. 'I often wonder what life would be like if they were still here. My mum would've given me what for if she knew what I'd got up to in those early days when my head was a mess. But what about now? How would life be different? I probably wouldn't have the soup kitchen, for a start.'

'They'd be proud of you,' I said quietly.

'I hope so,' he replied. 'I know I'd be dead if it wasn't for Elsie. She saved my life. I was a few drinks or drugs away from never waking up again, so the doctors told me. But Els gave me the option to carry on, and she trusted me when I said that I would. I could've easily taken a different path and numbed the pain forever.' Dan shuffled uncomfortably in his seat. 'I honestly don't know what I'd do without her.'

Herbie trotted over from his sleeping position under the tree and rested his head on Dan's knee. 'I don't know what I'd do without you either, mate.' He ruffled the top of Herbie's head. 'Herbie was homeless too. In an animal shelter, I mean. He'd been there for almost a year, nobody wanted him apparently.'

'How could nobody want him? Look at that little face.' I rubbed his favourite spot behind his ear.

'He's mixed breed, a bit older, not exactly an "Instagram" dog,' Dan air-quoted. 'No offence, Herbs.' Luckily, he was too distracted by the ear scratching to hear. 'But I knew he was the dog for me from the minute he greeted me from inside his cage.' Dan smiled at him in the warm and fuzzy way that dog owners look at their four-legged friends. Pure adoration. 'You couldn't ask for a better buddy.'

'You really couldn't. I'm a bit in love with him,' I said.

Dan and I met each other's eyes before quickly looking back towards the view.

'We should be making a move soon,' Dan said, jumping to his feet. He began tidying the rubbish and packing away the few leftovers there were, offering some to Herbie who licked his lips with glee.

'I'll help,' I offered.

'Not at all,' Dan said. 'You enjoy the last of the view before the sun goes down.'

'If you insist,' I said, as I sat back on the bench and pulled the picnic blanket around me for warmth against the early evening chill. I looked ahead as the sun started to sink into the mesmerising view of the horizon, but found I was more distracted by watching Dan pack away the last of our picnic in front of me.

'Ready?' he asked, after a few minutes.

I pushed myself from the bench, still wrapped in the blanket, and took his hand. We stood in front of each other as tiny droplets of rain landed on our noses and eyelashes. He touched a raindrop that fell on one of my messy curls, before his rough hands were entwined in my hair and his lips were on mine. His heavily tattooed fingers gently outlined the shape of my chin as he planted the softest kisses on my lips.

'I've been wanting to do that for a while,' he whispered.

'I think I've been wanting you to do that for a while too,' I replied as I touched my mouth, feeling where his lips had been just seconds before.

'You *think* you've been wanting me to?' he smiled.

'You can be a little hard to read sometimes.'

Before I could say anything else, he wrapped his arms underneath the blanket and pulled me by my waist into his warm body. His stubble brushed against my skin as he kissed my neck delicately before whispering, 'I hope this is a little easier to read.'

TWENTY-TWO

From: Queenofthehousehold@whittingtonfamily.co.uk

To: Arabella@whittingtonfamily.co.uk

Mon amour,

How on earth are you, mon petit chou?

How are you coping in that godforsaken apartment? I still can't believe we left you there, my love. Please forgive us. And please do reply so we know that you haven't been murdered.

Daddy and I are missing you terribly – though I haven't seen him for a few days. It turns out that renovating this house has been rather difficult, darling. So much noise. The incessant hammering interrupts my crystal healing meditation. And all that dust in the air is really playing havoc with my skin. Anyway, I've escaped to the Mountbattens' and I'm staying at their country estate for a few days while your father oversees the work. We were 'let go' from Escape to the Chateau, *my little sugar* bunny. Creative differences. The producer and I had totally different visions for our episode, so it was best we parted ways.

Have you thought about what you're doing for Christmas yet, my little pain au chocolat? The Mountbattens invited us here for Christmas, won't you please consider joining us? I know you're not the biggest fan of theirs, but you know I'm not either. However, their château really is fabulous, darling, well worth putting up with them and their bizarre ways to stay there. Please, my Bella, please join us. It'll be utterly unbearable without you. We can laugh at Clarice Mountbatten's new facelift. It's absolutely dreadful. Totally grotesque, a real botched job – even worse than the last one (if that's possible!).

Anyway, do let me know if you change your mind. Daddy and I will sort your flights. Speak soon, my love. Je t'aime x

From: Wilf@whittingtonfamily.co.uk

To: Arabella@whittingtonfamily.co.uk

Good morning my little lamb,

How are you doing?

Sorry about the hysterical voicemail your mother left for you last night. She accidentally cc'd the Mountbattens into her email to you. Something about a dodgy facelift?

Anyway, long story short. Your mother is back home now, and we're not invited there for Christmas any more. Shame, but I can't say I'm too disappointed. You know I could do *without that pretentious crowd, but Christmas won't be the same without you.*

We're just going to have a quiet one at the cottage now, it's coming along nicely. We'd love for you to come out and join us? Think about it, petal.

Love you, your papa xx

* * *

The December chill was in the air and the Christmas countdown just around the corner, but what a difference a year makes – it was unlike any festive period I'd known before. I felt shocked to my core every time I thought about what an impact my previous years' total festive expenditure for presents, decorations and general frivolities would've had if that amount had instead been donated to the community who used the services of the soup kitchen.

December was the busiest month at Dan's Kitchen. I was already working around the clock – dumpster diving with Dan and Susie by night, cleaning and cooking by day. I'd hardly had time to speak to my parents. Brief emails here and there, the odd Zoom session, broken up by dodgy signal.

I tried to stop my mind from wandering back to this time last year, when Francis and I had just returned from our skiing trip with the usual gang in Gstaad. We would be in full festive spirits, doing the social rounds with all our different groups of friends. One fabulous party after the other.

My Christmas list would usually involve a decadent check-list of my favourite designers. A new Hermès Birkin as the big present, as well as a classic Chanel. Something timeless from Tiffany & Co. Something trendy from Gucci. And perhaps some nice little stocking fillers from Fortnum & Mason, and some Fornasetti candles.

This year was a bit different. Dan, Susie, Elsie and I had set a challenge to buy each other a present for no more than £15, keeping our total Christmas present budget to less than £50. It was a sweet idea, but I'd be lying if I said I hadn't found myself longing for a Tiffany bag under our lacklustre tree, which we fished out of a skip during a supermarket bin haul.

My parents were no longer spending Christmas with the Mountbattens. I told them it was probably for the best – I could think of nothing worse than spending Christmas with Mr Mountbatten perving at my chest, while Mrs Mountbatten lectured her guests about the exact number of calories in a Christmas dinner. No, thank you. The best bit about a Christmas dinner *is* the calories.

Despite my parents' insistence that I spend Christmas with them in France, I knew I couldn't do that to Dan and Susie when they were so busy. And I wouldn't be able to sleep at night knowing I'd bailed on the guests of the soup kitchen – the warm-hearted and friendly people I'd grown close to, who looked to us to provide them with a delicious meal and cheerful company on Christmas Day of all days.

So instead, I lied to my parents and told them I couldn't get the time off work. I'd skirted around the details and said that in my new PR job, Christmas was the busiest period for our food clients. Luckily, they understood without asking too many questions. For years, Dad had dealt with manic Decembers at the Whittington Soup headquarters – even if he did spend more time doing 'festive networking' on the golf course.

I didn't want to admit to Dan and Susie why I wouldn't be spending Christmas with my family, for fear of questions about my past, but the festive season was getting me down. The fact that Dan and I had barely spent a day apart since our picnic in Festival Gardens made me feel even more guilty about lying to him. I couldn't deny or ignore my growing feelings. I'd never met anyone like Dan Rigby.

'Cheer up.' I felt him wrap his arms around my waist from behind as I worked my way through chopping a seemingly never-ending bag of wonky carrots for the evening's batch of soup.

One of the advantages of dumpster diving in December was that the chilly temperatures kept the majority of the food fresh. We'd also been busy stockpiling ingredients for the enormous Christmas Day community lunch at the soup kitchen. It meant that Dan, Susie and I had been doing more diving trips than ever before. I was starting to get used to trudging through the waste, identifying the best bags packed with unwanted food, and I'd finally started remembering not to wear my best jeans.

'Not a Christmas person?' Dan asked, delicately twirling a curly piece of my overgrown fringe around his finger and away from my eyeline. *All I want for Christmas is a haircut*, I wished, shuddering at the sight of my dead ends and faded highlights. Or at least a bottle of my beloved Olaplex No.3 Hair Perfector treatment.

'I am,' I replied, taking another carrot from the mountainous pile. 'It's just different this year.'

'Want to talk about it?' Dan asked, as he joined in my production line at the peeling and chopping station.

'Not really.' I shrugged.

'I know, you never do,' Dan said, throwing a carrot onto the freshly peeled pile and swiftly picking up another. 'But I get it. Everyone has a past. As soon as you do want to talk about it, I'm here.'

I smiled at him and how naturally understanding and compassionate he was as a person. I loved how his tough exterior was softening the more I got to know him. But those warm and fuzzy feelings were quickly replaced by my growing guilt. I knew I had to tell him and Susie the truth – and I made a silent vow to do it as soon as we got through Christmas at the soup kitchen.

Dan concentrated fiercely on juggling the vegetables we'd salvaged last night. We were working morning to night, cooking everything in batches and freezing as much as we could, ready to feed at least three hundred people on Christmas Day. The supermarkets had made things much easier, thanks to their excess festive waste. Seeing the amount of food being thrown away was depressing. The upside, however, was that we'd managed to scavenge enough packets of carrots, potatoes and sprouts to feed twice the number of people we were expecting. It was the vegan turkey alternative that was going to be the challenge. All we could do was hope that there would be a pile thrown away in the final few days leading up to Christmas.

Dan said it was unpredictable. It had been hit or miss in previous years, and sometimes they had to make do with only the trimmings as the main meal. Frustratingly, all the supermarkets had so far ignored Dan's pleas to donate the meat-free turkeys to the soup kitchen if they hadn't been sold by closing time on Christmas Eve.

'Have you looked into any more of those charity initiatives with local businesses I told you about?'

'Hmm?' Dan nibbled at a vegan mince pie.

'If you can't convince the supermarkets to donate some food to us for Christmas, why don't you get in touch with those food businesses I told you about? Like Whittington Soup?' I swallowed the lump in my throat as I said the name of my former family business.

'Pah,' Dan exclaimed, aiming the silver casing that had held the mince pie into the bin like a basketball player taking a shot. 'Don't talk to me about Whittington Soup.'

'Oh?' My carrot chopping slowed down at the tone of his voice. 'Why not?'

He looked at me, his eyes solemn. 'I think the question is where I should start...'

'What do you mean?' I asked surreptitiously, aware that my heart was starting to pound in my chest. 'I thought they were just a big soup company in Liverpool?' I could feel my cheeks flush pink with the guilt of the lie.

'It's soup for the rich, to start with, isn't it?' he snorted indignantly. 'And do you know how much they spend on "team-building holidays"?' he air-quoted.

I shook my head and tried to act normally, even though I felt my hands starting to tremble as I sliced through the carrot.

'The papers said it was about £800,000.' He laughed incredulously. It took me every ounce of willpower not to correct him that it was actually £750,000. But he had a point. That was a lot of money to spend on team-building, especially when it mostly involved drinking champagne and sunbathing, and not very much actual building of teams. 'Nearly a million pounds like, can you believe it?'

'Hmm,' I mumbled, non-committal.

'Their waste management is atrocious too. If you want to talk about food waste, talk to them first. It's a complete joke.' His face reddened as he rubbed the back of his neck.

The willpower came into play again. I wanted to correct him and tell him that things had changed. Last year, we'd signed a new contract pledging to reduce our food waste and move to a more sustainable model. Instead, I bit my lip and held my tongue.

'I used to write to them,' Dan continued. 'I'd ask – or beg, I guess – to consider whether they'd add the soup kitchen to their list of charities that they donated to – you know, the partnerships you mentioned.'

I nodded.

'But I wouldn't want to be involved with them now,' he said earnestly.

My stomach panged. He didn't want to be involved with them because everything was a mess there – a mess caused by yours truly. The soup world was smaller than I thought.

'Let's talk about something else,' I said, turning towards him. I desperately wanted to change the subject. 'What are our Christmas Day plans? Me, you, Susie, Elsie and Herbie, what are we going to do?'

'Apart from feeding three hundred people?' Dan replied.

'Apart from that.' I picked up the wooden chopping board which was covered in the vegetables I'd diced up, and poured them into the pan to lightly brown before adding the stock.

It was creamy Thai carrot, coconut and ginger soup on the menu tonight, with vegan carrot cake for dessert – a feast of the vegetable we found most frequently in our dumpster diving trips. The bags we found were always full of carrots that were absolutely fine, just a bit wonky or imperfect, and therefore shunned by shoppers.

'Depends if you lot are still standing by the end of the day.' Dan chuckled.

'Yeah, I guess all that cooking is going to be pretty tiring.'

'It is, but I meant if Suze brings her home-made mulled wine. Nobody's still standing after a day spent drinking that stuff.'

Dan made his way back towards me and leant on the counter of my efficient preparation line. He wore his everyday uniform of a band T-shirt and ripped jeans. They perfectly fitted his muscular physique – not gained from intense personal training sessions like Francis, but years of lugging heavy bags through industrial-sized skips. Who would've thought it? Somehow, I couldn't quite imagine it becoming the next big workout to hit my former members-only gym. Although goat yoga took off surprisingly well and nobody could've predicted that either.

'How about,' Dan said, midway through chomping on an apple, 'me and you do something tonight, just us two?'

My only way to reply was silently gesturing around the kitchen, which was filled to the brim with boxes and bags, each one fit to burst, and packed with hours' worth of food to prep and freeze.

'Don't worry, we're way ahead of schedule, we can afford a night off.'

'But according to my plan,' I said, as I consulted the stained spreadsheet on the counter, 'we're due another visit to the stationery shop tonight in case they've thrown away more decorations, wrapping paper and cards.'

The spreadsheet, or 'Bin Bible' I'd created referenced every single supermarket and decent-sized shop within a ten-mile radius of Toxteth. It listed which days offered the biggest amount of waste, when the bins were collected, which security guards could be persuaded to look the other way, and also the most weird and wonderful hauls from each shop (overall winners were a Phillip Schofield life-size cut-out and a perfectly intact 32-inch TV).

'Honestly, we'll be fine,' Dan reassured me. 'We have almost enough food already and there are still a few weeks to go until Christmas. They'll start to throw even more out as it gets closer.' He grabbed my hands. 'Go on, you know you want to.'

'OK,' I relented. I felt guilty for craving a night off, even just to give my hands a break from all the peeling and dicing. 'You're the boss.'

'Great!' Dan clapped his hands together, making me jump and Herbie bark. 'I know what we're doing – make sure you're ready for 7 p.m., your carriage awaits!' he shouted as he headed out the door.

'What carriage? Where are we going? What do I wear?' I yelled after him.

His floating head reappeared around the door. 'Something warm and festive,' he grinned.

TWENTY-THREE

The short length of the car ride hinted to me that we were somewhere in the city centre. But I couldn't be sure, as Dan had asked me to pull down my hat over my eyes halfway through the journey. Being chauffeur-driven was like living in a memory of my old life again. But instead of a sleek Mercedes, it was an old banger that rattled as it rolled through the streets. Dan had called in a favour with Fred, one of the Alcoholics Anonymous members he sponsored, to drive us to our surprise date.

'Watch your step,' Dan guided me from behind after we stepped out of the car. All I could feel was the sensation of his hole-ridden gloves rubbing against my eyelids – a combination of scratchy fabric and his rough hands. With my eyes closed, the rest of my heightened senses would've guessed that we'd travelled all the way to the North Pole. The overwhelming scents of pine needles, mulled wine, gingerbread, hot chocolate and roast chestnuts wafted under my nose. A festive megamix of 'All I Want For Christmas Is You' and 'Baby, It's Cold Outside' made its way to my ears, which were cosily nestled underneath the thick yarn of the multicoloured bobble hat that Elsie had knitted for me.

He gently manoeuvred me around what I guessed were crowds of people. 'OK,' he said, softly easing me into position. 'Now you can open your eyes.'

I squinted as my eyes struggled to focus on anything amid the fluorescent splashes of red and green, together with the soft glow of sparkling fairy lights.

'Winter Wonderland' the enormous wooden sign in front of me read, as my eyesight slowly returned to normal with each blink in the bright lights.

'Do you love it?' Dan asked, grinning like a six-year-old waking up at 5 a.m. on Christmas Day. His enthusiasm for Christmas was a complete contradiction to his occasional moodiness and his ruggedly handsome appearance.

'I do,' I stammered, taken aback as unexpected memories flashed by of the years spent at Winter Wonderland on the Albert Dock with my family, and with Francis.

Dan's smile faded as he shuffled uncomfortably in his big winter coat. 'Are you sure? We don't have to stay if you don't want to.' Again, he channelled his inner six-year-old, but if he had just been told to go back to bed by his parents. 'I thought it might cheer you up. I've never been here before.'

'No, it's fine,' I insisted. 'Honestly, I'm just surprised.'

'OK,' he said, his beaming grin once again illuminating his excited face.

My stomach unexpectedly flipped with a pang of guilt as Dan leant down to kiss me, even though he'd done it at least one hundred times before. It felt uncomfortable and surreal under the silhouette of the luxury apartment building that Francis and I had once called home. Luckily, I could see the soft lighting illuminating the windows of the penthouse flat, so I knew he must've been home and that we were safe from bumping into him.

Besides, how would anyone recognise me? I looked like a completely different person compared to my old self. My expensive hair colour had faded back to my natural mousy brown and the lack of styling had also revealed my natural curls, which now hung long and loose past my shoulders. A significant decrease in exotic holidays and last-minute sunshine getaways meant my skin was a completely different shade (therefore making my expensive make-up collection annoyingly redundant).

I hastily brushed away the thoughts of Francis, our life together and our Winter Wonderland date last Christmas. I reminded myself that although he spoilt me with as much Veuve Clicquot as I could manage (a lot) in the VIP package, he probably wouldn't have been able to name my favourite Christmas film.

Dan's ancient khaki gloves enveloped my bright pink mittens as he led me through the crowds of families buying popcorn, and the clusters of couples snuggling up to each other for pockets of warmth in the icy air. Chunks of polystyrene snow danced around us. The rising heat from steaming mugs of hot chocolate, held by bundles of people wearing Santa hats and reindeer ears, lined the path that he guided us down.

I knew from memory that following the path would eventually lead to the main sights of Winter Wonderland: a fairground, Santa's grotto and a food village. Winter Wonderland was as sickly sweet with my memories as the giant candy canes being sold on every corner. I was trying my best not to feel like I'd just binge-eaten sixty of them, which was the exact feeling in the pit of my stomach.

'This way,' Dan said, marching confidently along the path lined with miniature, bushy Christmas trees swaying gently in the December breeze.

I hadn't been this way before, I realised, though they did tend to introduce a new special feature each year. As we reached the end of the path, an enormous cinema screen occupied a section of the park, illuminating thirty Santa sleighs dotted around the snow-covered floor.

'*It's A Wonderful Life!*' Dan exclaimed to my puzzled expression. 'Susie told me it's your favourite Christmas film.' He cocked his head to one side.

His sweet gesture swiftly replaced any anxious feelings I had. I clapped my wool-clad hands together excitedly before pulling him in close to me, our cosy bobble hats pushing together. 'Thank you so much,' I whispered into his neck, sniffing in the scent of his aftershave, combined with the aromas of cinnamon and eggnog. It made a change from the bin juice that was our dominant scent after many nights spent dumpster diving.

Dan planted a warming kiss on my red nose. 'You grab a couple of blankets and I'll get us some hot chocolate, popcorn and chestnuts.' He pulled two tickets from his coat pocket. 'We're in sleigh six, I'll meet you over there,' he said, kissing my nose again, before disappearing towards the fairy light-speckled snack chalet.

Two giant Santa sleighs were positioned in front of the cinema screen, housing an assortment of red and white fluffy blankets and bouncy pillows. The sleighs were big, but similar to a skip, so I decided I would put the newly discovered agility I'd learnt through various dumpster diving trips to good use (who needed yoga, eh?).

Leaning my chest against the side of the red sleigh, I balanced precariously to try and reach a couple of the cleaner pillows and blankets further down. But the little mound of fake snow that I'd been using as my step quickly gave way, throwing me face down.

'Garghh, help!' I shrieked through a mouthful of fake fur and fluff. I kicked my legs, which were mid-air above my head, in an effort to try and balance my torso enough to push myself up and out of the sleigh. Thank God, or St Nick, that it hadn't happened to me in an actual rubbish-filled skip yet.

A couple of hands firmly gripped onto my legs and pulled them down over the side of the sleigh, helping me get enough balance to lift my body up and out. As soon as I found my feet, my bobble hat fell in front of my eyes. I lifted it up and my happy little festive heart fell to the pit of my stomach.

'Thank—' I only managed one word before I froze like the snowmen dotted around the park.

My heart felt like it was going to burst from my chest the second our eyes met. A rush of memories wrapped up in one giant Christmas present. Francis. It was Francis – all six foot four of him. He was clad head to toe in his usual chic winter wardrobe of Burberry and Barbour.

'Bloody hell, Bella,' he gasped, as his mouth fell open and he looked me up and down, his eyes bulging in shock.

We stood in silence for what felt like the period between Christmas and New Year, when nobody knows what to do with themselves.

Francis rocked backwards and forwards, his hands planted firmly in his cashmere-lined pockets. 'So,' he squirmed. I knew how much he hated awkward moments. This would be killing him. 'How are you doing?'

'I'm great,' I affirmed, running my fingers through my rough curls in an effort to comb them. I was suddenly feeling self-conscious of what I looked like after months of foregoing facials, eyebrow waxes, haircuts and manicures. 'I'm great,' I repeated. 'How are you?'

Francis avoided my eyes. 'Good. Yes, I'm good,' he stammered.

The hottest cask of mulled wine wouldn't have melted the ice between us. Both literally and figuratively, as there was a little ice wall conveniently placed in the middle of where we stood.

'Who are you here with?' The question rolled off my lips before I had a moment to register that I'd even asked it, never mind considering the answer.

'Oh, erm.' His face flushed with colour, the way it used to when he'd had too many espresso martinis on Boxing Day. 'Err,' he mumbled, as he continued shuffling from side to side, his hands fidgeting in his pockets.

My gut instinct told me to look behind me, in the direction where he'd glanced when I first asked the question. Behind the fur-clad arm holding up a phone to take a selfie in the warm, glowing winter light (#nofilter) was Tabby. My former best friend who had been in my bed with my fiancé when I last saw her. Before that day, she was one of my oldest, closest friends who hadn't so much as left me a voice note of apology, or returned any of my endless calls when I found out she'd been sleeping with my fiancé.

'Ah.' I pursed my lips together. 'Well, enjoy the film.' Francis winced as I stepped over the ice wall and shoved my way past him, cushions and blankets in tow.

I could feel his eyes burning the back of my head as I stomped past the sleighs, feeling the crush of the fake snow underneath every step I took in my well-worn wellies. I turned to face the opposite way when I passed Tabs, curled up cosily in her and Francis's sleigh, but not before noticing that she was still trying to get the perfect angle for her bloody selfie. No doubt hashtagging it #sleighfie.

Mine and Dan's sleigh, number six, was at the end of the front row – thankfully, a decent distance away from theirs. My whole body was shivering, and it wasn't from the cold any more. My ghost of Christmas past haunted me throughout my favourite film, as I repeatedly caught Francis staring at me and Dan.

Completely unaware of my ex-fiancé in the vicinity, Dan laughed, cheered and shed a little tear throughout the film. 'I can see why that's your favourite Christmas movie,' he said, pouring the final crumbs of popcorn directly into his mouth from the carton. I was usually the sort of person who finishes their popcorn before the film starts, but I couldn't bear to eat even one bite.

'I have to say, I was a little sceptical when Suze told me the name. Sounds cheesy as hell,' he said, brushing the tiny crumbs from his olive-coloured coat. 'But jeez, it's a journey all right. I'm going to be listening out for bells ringing all December now.' His smile quickly turned to a look of concern when he registered my expression. 'What's the matter?' he asked.

'What? Nothing,' I said.

Dan swivelled around, crunching the empty bags of popcorn and chestnuts in his hands.

'Why do you keep looking over there? You were doing it during the film too.'

'I don't, I didn't,' I stammered. 'I'm just enjoying the lovely festive atmosphere.'

Dan pulled me close. 'I hope you enjoyed it,' he said softly. 'Christmas is always a difficult time for me, but I really feel like—'

'Bella?'

My head was buried in Dan's coat, but I knew who that voice belonged to without having to look up.

'Hi, Francis,' I said, turning around. 'Tabby.' I nodded to the two of them. They were a sight in the snow. They both looked as though they'd just walked off the set of a seasonal photoshoot for a Chanel perfume. The deep tans hugging the pale space where their snow goggles would've been positioned told me they'd made it to Gstaad this year after all.

Tabs, subtle as ever, was unable to hide her shock.

'Fuck. Bella. Hi.'

I waved sheepishly, suddenly acutely aware of my mismatched, blatantly home-made mittens and hat, filthy wellies and scruffy coat. Although they were the ones who should've been embarrassed, after the compromising position they were in last time I saw them. At least they had clothes on this time.

Francis, ever the gentleman, didn't forget his Eton-educated manners. 'A pleasure to meet you,' he said, taking Dan's hand and shaking it in a firm grip.

'Hi, mate,' Dan replied, innocently naive and friendly. 'I'm Dan, and you are?'

'Francis,' he said, standing taller to emphasise his already statuesque frame. 'Francis Burton.'

'Bella, you look great,' Tabs lied through her snowy white veneers, as she leant in to double air-kiss me, while keeping her distance at the same time. Her familiar aroma of Penhaligon's perfume instantly took me back to those nights drinking champagne and dancing together in our favourite haunts.

'How lovely to meet your "man friend" too,' Tabs said patronisingly. She moved to air-kiss Dan, who almost planted one on her lips as he tiptoed into the unfamiliar etiquette.

Francis nodded at me. 'Bella.'

'Francis,' I said frostily.

The chill in the air was given a reprieve as we all jumped in unison at the loud bang of a firework above us.

'Oh yay, they're doing the firework display again this year!' Tabs enthused, clapping her leather gloves together. I was relieved that my hands were hidden by mittens as I thought about my non-existent nails and damaged cuticles from the relentless work I'd been doing at the soup kitchen.

'Great, well, we'll be seeing you then,' I said, as I linked my arm in Dan's and gently nudged him to understand our cue to leave.

'Bella,' Francis interrupted, while brushing off Tabs's attempts at wrapping her delicate hands around his.

'Bye, lovely to see you both!' I shouted, while pulling Dan

away, through the enormous crowd that was gathering to watch the fireworks.

'Bella!' I could hear Francis shout in the distance as we shuffled away, getting lost in the swarms of people that had suddenly descended on Liverpool's own Winter Wonderland.

TWENTY-FOUR

The silhouette of the soup kitchen stood in the middle of Toxteth high street, an imposing presence amid the occasional shooting star that ricocheted across the starlit December sky.

The humming engine of the car was the only sound in the eerily silent street.

'Always strange when it's this quiet,' Dan said, opening the car door and climbing out of the ancient Ford Escort. 'Ta again, Fred.' He motioned to the driver – Dan's friend from AA – whose face was almost entirely covered in a thick scarf and tweed flat cap.

'No worries, Dan mate, any time,' Fred whispered, his breathy voice hoarse from years of replacing drinking with smoking. Dan had called in a favour with Fred to chauffeur us to Winter Wonderland so we wouldn't have to worry about trying to squeeze into the extortionately priced car park.

'Why *is* it so quiet?' I asked as the car rolled away.

Every evening, the side of the soup kitchen doubled up as an unofficial dormitory for the homeless. It was the scene I'd accidentally stumbled upon during my first evening in my new hometown.

'The emergency shelter will have opened by now,' Dan replied. 'The council actually pulls its finger out of its arse in December.' He put his arm around me and kissed the point where my hat met my forehead. 'Pardon my crudeness.'

'That's a start, at least,' I said, as he rested his hand comfortably around my waist.

'It's a start,' he agreed, his expression turning stern. 'But it's where it ends as far as the powers that be are concerned. They don't give a shit.' He rubbed his glove-covered hands against his face, which was covered in month-old facial hair. 'I'm sorry, Bella. I just...'

'What?' I said, as I pulled his hands away from his face and held them in mine. The only light around us was a flickering bulb above the big wooden front door of the soup kitchen. The glass that once covered the bulb had been smashed, which meant the light was temperamental.

'Was that Francis guy your ex? I know you've mentioned him before...' Dan shuffled on the spot, leaning his back against the door and pulling his hands away from my grip. 'I'm not a jealous guy, honestly, I'm really not. I hate that I'm even asking you. I guess my insecurities got the better of me next to him.' He sighed and glanced around the scruffy surroundings. 'He just looked worlds away from' – he gestured to the smashed bottles on the floor and graffiti on the walls – 'all of this. He must be a model, right?'

'Not a model citizen, I can assure you,' I said, my words tinged with a bitterness I couldn't hide. Remembering my silent vow I'd made to myself – that I'd tell Dan and Susie everything after Christmas – I shut my eyes and took a deep inhale of the freezing December air. The only sound between us was the gentle hum of the broken CCTV camera above the door.

'I shouldn't have pushed,' Dan affirmed, sensing the tone. 'We'll talk when you're ready. Come on, let's get you home,' he said, sensing the discomfort I felt every time I considered coming clean about who I really was. 'It's Baltic out here.'

I hugged myself into his coat, which had seen at least a decade of winters but still kept the warmth in. We cuddled as we strolled along the dark pavements, lightly outlined by a delicate frosting of sleet, and headed towards my flat – the opposite direction to his. My mind was racing as I thought about my two different lives crashing into each other this evening, but I forced myself to calm down and concentrate on putting one foot in front of the other. Everything felt safe when I was with Dan.

'You made me so happy tonight.' I smiled, as I held Dan's glove-covered hand in my mittens. We walked around the corner, where his bright yellow van was parked outside my apartment building, shining fluorescently like a star at the top of a Christmas tree.

'Good, that was the aim,' he nodded. 'You've made me happy too. I've discovered my new favourite Christmas film.' He laughed as he leant down to kiss me mid-walk, his cold lips landing on mine just as we stopped in front of my building.

'So,' I whispered, while trying to fish out my keys from my brown leather handbag – a vintage Prada, which I hoped nobody would recognise from the subtle logo engraved into the hardware.

'So...' Dan repeated, his dark eyes taking in every inch of my freezing face. He knew what was coming and I did too.

'Do you want to come up?' I said, unwilling to wait a moment longer.

In the place of an answer, he kissed my neck softly. His breath sent chills down my spine as he planted delicate kisses where my scarf met my cold skin.

Our growing desire lingered in the cold air of the December night as we made our way into the building and up to my flat. Dan delicately teased at my jumper and the top button of my jeans before we'd even got halfway up the stairs through a blur of cold noses and warm kisses.

'Why are you so...' Susie paused, searching for the right word. 'Springy?'

'Springy?' I laughed as I shimmied between the peeling station and the chopping station in the soup kitchen, while avoiding Herbie who was sprawled out on the floor.

'Yes, springy!' she confirmed. 'You're like the Easter bloody bunny jumping around this kitchen.'

It was exactly two weeks until Christmas Day and precisely one week since Dan and I had started spending every night together. And every morning, afternoon and evening. And any moment that we could steal between our work responsibilities and festive preparations.

'I'm just happy.' I shrugged, noticing that I was, in fact, skipping between the different stations in my food production line.

'I need some happy.' Susie sighed, as she added raisins to the raw mixture that was to become her famous vegan Christmas tiffin.

'How long has it been?' I turned to her, pushing the bits of fringe that had fallen out of my hairband back with my elbow.

'Since?' Susie asked.

'Since, you know,' I hinted. 'Since you were last, *happy*?'

'Jesus,' Susie snorted. 'There was snow on the ground. And I'm not talking about this winter.'

'Ah,' I replied, turning back to tackle the mountain of sprouts that needed peeling.

'Ah indeed,' Susie confirmed. 'I have the worst luck with men. And women.'

I turned back to her in surprise. 'Oh? I didn't know you were that way...' I motioned, struggling to find the right word while feeling increasingly awkward. 'Inclined,' I added.

'I guess I am,' Susie said, panting slightly due to the level of energy that she was putting into stirring the mixture.

'You guess?' I said. 'What, don't you know?'

'I do and I don't.' She licked a drop of melted dairy-free chocolate that landed on her forearm. 'I genuinely do think I'm attracted to a person rather than a gender.' She continued mixing. 'Men, women... we're all the same at the end of the day. We're just people with feelings, and genitals.'

'Whatever tickles your pickle,' I affirmed. I'd love Susie no matter who she loved – man, woman, or both. I didn't care. I'd never had a friend like her.

'Who's tickling whose pickle?' Dan said cheekily as he pushed his way through the giant door to the kitchen, laden with bags.

'Well, someone's making Bella a rather happy little elf this Christmas,' Susie teased, as I concentrated on removing the green suit from each individual sprout.

'Good to know.' He smiled with a glint in his eye.

I blushed as I remembered exactly what we'd been doing just a few hours earlier.

'So,' I exclaimed, willing the subject to change. I grabbed the spreadsheet that set out the exact plan for Christmas Day, including cooking timings, as well as cards and presents for the guests that were still to be written and wrapped. Even though we had two weeks to go, we were stockpiling, preparing and freezing as much as we could, just in case supplies were limited closer to Christmas.

'We're almost all good for the food.' I ran my highlighter down the colour-coded lists. I've always loved a spreadsheet. 'Except the vegan turkeys.'

'This was so much easier before every man and his dog decided to go vegan,' Susie moaned. 'I blame the YouTubers.'

A knock at the door interrupted Susie's impending rant about how YouTubers, influencers and social media as a whole was to blame for everything that's wrong with society – a topic she was particularly impassioned about after a drink or two.

'Excuse me,' a timid voice at the door said. We all turned to look at the woman with long, multicoloured hair who was standing in the doorway.

'Jemma!' Dan exclaimed, sprinting over and encasing her diminutive body in a big hug. 'This is Jemma,' Dan announced when he eventually let her go.

'Hi,' I said, while Susie waved.

The woman looked familiar to me, but I couldn't place her. Perhaps she was somebody I served during the soup kitchen mealtimes. We could serve more than a hundred people a night sometimes, so it wasn't always easy to keep track of everyone, unless they were regulars.

'I'm in a bit of a rush, Dan,' Jemma said nervously, as she fidgeted with the straps of her big backpack and shifted awkwardly from one foot to the other.

'Of course, of course,' Dan said. 'Come this way, we can go in the office.' He gestured towards the door as Jemma walked out.

Dan turned back to Susie and me. 'Sorry, I'm not sure how long I'll be with this. I'll go out after to see if there are any vegan turkey developments.' He grabbed a stash of bin liners and a couple of cool bags.

'Want me to come with you?' I asked.

'No, it's fine,' Dan said. 'It won't be much effort if we don't need to get anything else. I'll come to yours afterwards, as long as you don't make me watch *Elf* again.' He rolled his eyes jokingly. He loved it really.

Dan quickly planted a kiss on my forehead. 'I'll see you later,' he shouted over his shoulder, as he pulled the door closed and headed to the office with Jemma.

'Who's Jemma?' I asked Susie.

'No idea,' Susie replied. 'Probably somebody to do with the drug and alcohol support groups.'

'Ah yes,' I nodded, but I still couldn't shake the feeling that I recognised her face, and her distinct colourful hair, from somewhere.

TWENTY-FIVE

'Mum, what on earth are you wearing on your head? Is it a crown?' I leant in closer to get a better look. Mum and Dad's internet was erratic, and they couldn't get their heads around Zoom, but for once they weren't upside down or speaking to me through cat filters, so things were definitely improving.

'Don't be silly, my little sugar bunny, of course it isn't a crown,' Mum said as I squinted at the screen. 'It's my Christmas tiara,' she winked and lifted her champagne glass up in a toast.

'Christmas *tiara*?'

'Yes, my little blueberry muffin. I don't wear it *every* year, I only keep it for *special* occasions. But I thought my beautiful daughter might appreciate my effort if our contact is confined to a computer screen this Christmas.' She prodded the camera angrily. They were already on their third iPad after Mum had thrown two out of the window in a rage.

'Where did you get it?' I asked.

'Funny story, darling. I must've told you, *non*?' She took a sip from her glass. 'It was a present from the princess of Azerbaijan.'

'The who?' I sipped my drink – I was going to need it to get through one of Mum's infamous tales.

'The princess of Azerbaijan.' Mum nodded. 'She gave it to me when I lost my seventh attempt at the Miss World finals.' Her eyes widened. 'It was a total shambles, that competition. Totally corrupt. Pfft!' she snorted. 'I think she felt sorry for me, so she nicked it from her great-great-great-great-grandmother's collection one night after we'd been clubbing with Prince and Bowie. But anyway, I digress!' She clapped her hands together to my frozen, flabbergasted expression.

'Are we still playing Zoom charades?' I asked, glancing at the clock. I loved catching up with my parents, but I needed to wrap up the conversation before Dan got back from dumpster diving. 'Is Dad joining us?'

Luckily, Mum didn't catch on to mine and Dad's secret sub-charades – our Christmas tradition that we played every year. We'd innocently pretend we couldn't figure out what Mum was acting, so she'd be forced to do it for ages. The longest round so far was Mum's thoroughly entertaining re-enactment of *Game of Thrones* that lasted around forty-five minutes, as we watched her comically act out brutal murders and insinuations of incest while donning her best Prada jumpsuit and six-inch Jimmy Choos.

'Your father is pottering,' Mum said, with a flick of her red lacquered nails. 'Pottering, pottering, pottering. That's all he does these days.'

'Don't worry, we'll do charades another time,' I interrupted, not wanting to encourage one of Mum's long rants about Dad completing all the DIY chores she would set for him. If he did them too quickly, he wasn't taking enough care. If he did them too slowly, he was being inefficient. Poor Dad couldn't win.

I checked the time again, feeling twitchy. It was 9 p.m., which meant Dan would be making his rounds at the shops that shut their doors early during the festive season. He'd be knee-deep in discarded food, wading through the rubbish in the hope of finding those prized meat-free turkeys that we could freeze for Christmas dinner.

'I think that was the most I've ever scavenged,' Dan told me later that evening, as he stripped off his bin-smelling clothes.

'Why do you seem so sad about it then?' I asked, while Herbie rolled around on my bed.

'Don't get me wrong, I'm happy. Of course I am,' he said. 'But doesn't it show how much food goes to waste? Perfect food that's just left to rot while so many people go hungry.' I watched his body tense, as it always did when he talked about the subject so close to his heart. 'I'll never understand it, I guess. I don't get how some people can have so much when others have so little. I can't comprehend how big soup corporations like the one I won't name because I'll just get angry, refuse to donate food to us at Christmas.' He shook his head. 'But we don't need their help, or want their help, anyway.'

I felt a pang of guilt. I wished I could've done something to help Dan and the soup kitchen through my family business – the business that Dan seemed to hate so much. And another pang hit me as I remembered my previous buying, and more importantly, throwing out habits. The minute the food was a day past its best I'd bin it, even if it looked perfectly fine. And the sad thing was, I'd do it without a second thought. It was easily replaceable, after all.

'But on to happier notes...' Dan said, as he pressed himself against me, his bare chest against my jumper, his strong arms wrapped protectively around my waist. 'What are our plans this evening?'

'I think our original plans have been scuppered by the enthusiastic pooch making himself at home.' I nodded towards the bed where Herbie lay, staring innocently at us and wagging his tail.

'Always geggin' in, aren't you, Herb lad?' Dan grinned, before turning back towards me and gently brushing my hair away from my neck. 'I want you so bad,' he whispered into my ear, making every single hair on my body tingle with anticipation.

'We'll just have to watch *Elf* again until he falls asleep,' I teased.

Dan rolled his eyes before shifting his attention to the fridge. 'What do you fancy for tea?' he asked. I'd been so busy at the soup kitchen that my fridge was practically empty. Apart from wine and chocolate – the essentials, obviously.

The light flakes blowing in the wind outside the window momentarily distracted me from our clingy-dog and lack-of-food problems.

'Oh look, it's snowing!' I announced with childlike glee. The flakes were coming down quickly and seemingly getting heavier by the minute.

But as Dan and I moved closer to the window, we could see they weren't snowflakes. They were burning cinders dancing around the night sky – the wind was blowing them along the street. The ashy lumps were quickly followed by a thick, grey fog that fell like a blanket.

I moved to the next window along and could see a faint outline of orange flames in the distance amid the smoke. My hand shot to my mouth before any words could come out. Dan and I knew where the smoke was coming from. We knew which building the flames were ripping through. It was Elsie's flat, and it was the soup kitchen.

TWENTY-SIX

Dan and I battled against the shower of ashes and through the thick grey fog as we bolted down the streets of Toxteth. The area from my apartment block to the soup kitchen felt twice the distance, as we held scarves around our mouths and shielded our eyes from the dense smoke and soot whirling in the wind.

The cold December night was more like a scorching summer's evening, as we dashed towards the burning building. The towering flames glowing amber and red grew bigger and brighter with every step we took, filling the streets with a hot breeze.

We turned the corner and were immediately hit with the full sight of the soup kitchen in the clutches of the blazing inferno.

'Oh my God,' I cried, to Dan's stunned silence. Bricks fell to the ground as the flames engulfed the walls and the distant sound of sirens moved closer, their flashing lights illuminating the sky.

'Elsie!' Dan broke from his shock and bellowed over the roar and crackle of the fire.

I gasped, breathing in the smoke, at the sight of the blazing building that was home to Elsie's flat. My heart thundered behind my pyjama top as I stared at the scene in front of me. 'Where's Elsie?'

Before I could stop him, Dan charged forwards. 'Dan, stop!' I croaked. He ran down the side of the building, where piles of bricks were falling as the flames took over. His shadowy figure darted towards the entrance to her flat at the back, and he disappeared in the darkness of the night.

My shoulders trembled as I stood there, my body stiff with fear. Time stood still, until the sudden flurry of firefighters, police officers and paramedics pulled up outside the burning building. I begged them for help, pointing to Dan's last location and explaining there was an elderly woman inside. I couldn't take my eyes off the route Dan had taken – the route he'd emerge from if he and Elsie got out. *If.* That possibility felt as heavy as the dark clouds of smoke in the sky.

A group of firefighters followed where Dan ran from my side, and all I could do was wait to see if they could find him. But the front of the building was completely covered by the raging flames.

I held my scarf-covered throat with my shaking hands and tried to swallow the anxious lump that sat in it as every minute passed by. My body was rigid with worry as images of Dan and Elsie inside the building, and the worst-case scenario, dominated my mind.

Then, in the middle of the chaos, a figure wrapped in an ash-covered purple dressing gown was carried out in the arms of a firefighter.

'Elsie,' I sobbed into my sleeve, as the smoky figures came into view, illuminated by the blue flashing lights of the waiting ambulance behind me.

I held Elsie's hand, which was hot to the touch, as the firefighter lowered her onto the stretcher and a paramedic rushed to position an oxygen mask onto her ashen face. 'I'm OK,' Elsie croaked, gripping my hand tightly.

She was quickly wheeled away from me and manoeuvred onto the moving platform attached to the back of the ambulance. 'Where's Dan?' I cried, as the doors closed and I couldn't fight back the tears any longer.

The fluorescent glow of the yellow ambulance broke up the dark waves of smoke that fell densely in the air as it tore down the road, the high-pitched sound of its sirens remaining long after it drove away.

I sobbed, as I looked up at the crumbling building that was being destroyed by ferocious flames.

I blinked the wet tears into my dry eyes and shielded them from the heat of the air before watching as shadowy figures emerged from the devastation. I held my hands to my open mouth. It was Dan. He was being propped up between two firefighters. I ran towards him and wrapped my arms around his neck. His body was limp as he mumbled something inaudible.

'Excuse me, miss, I'm sorry. We need to get him to the hospital.' One of the firefighters gently nudged me away and the paramedics gathered around.

'Is he OK?' I begged, horrified at the image of the strong man I knew being carried along like a rag doll.

They didn't say a word and a sudden chill hit me, encasing my body, which had been sweltering from the heat of the fire. 'Is he OK?' I asked again as I shivered. He had to be OK. He couldn't not be OK.

I wiped my stinging eyes from the smoke in the air. My body was drenched in sweat from the scorching heat of the fire, but now, as the worry took over, my skin tingled with goosebumps.

'Can I go with you?' I trailed alongside the stretcher as they lifted Dan into the ambulance. His skin was covered with ash and his eyes were closed, but my heart leapt when he squeezed my hand in his. I didn't let go as the paramedic placed an oxygen mask over his face.

The fire roared wildly behind the doors of the ambulance, tearing through the blackened bricks that remained. I watched the chilling finality of the devastating scene through the windows. The sheets of water from the fire engines' deluge guns gradually calmed the raging flames until they simmered down to a gentle crackle.

Within minutes, all that was left was a hollow shell. A ghostly silhouette. It wasn't the soup kitchen any more. It wasn't Elsie's home any more. All that was left was a blackened ruin of rubble.

Footsteps stomped down the hospital corridor and I stood from my seat outside Dan's room. I knew who that panicked stride belonged to.

Susie rounded the corner and crashed into me, wrapping me in a bear hug. 'Fucking hell,' she cried, snivelling into my shoulder, her tears dampening the fur of my dressing gown. 'Are they OK?'

'They're all right.' I sighed with relief and held her tightly. 'They think it's smoke inhalation, but they're keeping them in for observation and tests.'

'But they're both OK? Dan and Elsie, they're both OK?' Susie asked, with such relief that she was hardly able to string the words together. 'Thank God,' she stammered. 'I thought that was it, Bella. I thought...'

'I know,' I said. 'I know.'

Susie nodded; we didn't need to say any more. She rubbed her face, which was blotchy and stained with tears. Her eyes were black and smudged with the final remnants of mascara that clung stubbornly to her eyelashes.

'The soup kitchen is a big pile of ash,' she whispered, as we sat down on the chairs in the corridor. 'This will break Dan. This is everything he has, it's his world. And it's gone up in flames. *Actual* flames.'

'It'll be OK,' I answered, not knowing what else to say and trying to convince myself as much as her. 'Everything will be OK,' I repeated, unable to meet her eye as I stared at the white wall in front of me.

A group of doctors and nurses passed along the corridor, pointing at clipboards and speaking softly in hushed voices.

'You know Elsie,' I said, watching as they walked away. 'She's made of strong stuff.' My attempt at trying to reassure Susie didn't work. Her body was both stiff and shaking at the same time.

'Excuse me?' A police officer stood in front of us, breaking up the dreadful atmosphere. 'Are you with Dan Rigby?'

'We are,' I replied, rubbing my eyes and standing up.

He nodded. 'Can I ask who owns the building where the fire took place?' he asked gently, sensing how distraught we were.

Susie broke out of her trance temporarily. 'It's Dan. He owns it. Well, him and his grandmother own it together.'

'Is she the lady they pulled from the flat?' he asked.

'Elsie? Yes.' I rubbed my fingers nervously.

'How's she doing?' he asked.

'The paramedics think she'll be OK,' I said.

'Good, I'm glad to hear it.' He rubbed his chin with one hand. 'Look, I'm sorry to bother you with this. I know it's the last thing you need right now, but I need to ask the owner some questions about the fire for our investigation.'

'Now?' Susie questioned.

'Yeah, I do apologise, but it's standard procedure' – he placed his hands in his pockets – 'when it's likely arson.'

'Arson?' I did a double-take, and Susie and I looked at each other.

'What makes you think it's arson?' Susie said, her voice shaky. 'Why the hell would someone set fire to a soup kitchen?'

His uniform moved slightly upwards as he shrugged his wide shoulders. His expression was as puzzled as ours. 'Who knows why people do what they do. Boredom, revenge, gang initiations, off their head on drink or drugs... We always see an increase in crimes like this around Christmas.'

Susie and I shook our heads in shock.

'I'm really sorry, but the sooner I get some answers to these questions, the sooner we can leave you to it.' He nodded towards Dan's room.

'Let me go and ask him, I haven't seen him yet. I need to give him a hug and see if he's up for it,' Susie said. She opened the door, leaving the two of us alone together outside.

'I can't believe somebody would do that,' I said, numb. I couldn't find the words; I couldn't think straight. Susie was right. This was going to break Dan.

The door opened again and Susie gestured for the police officer to go in. 'He's a bit groggy, but he's happy to talk. Said he'll do anything to help you find the scumbags who did this.'

The police officer thanked us for our time and walked into Dan's room, closing the door behind him.

Susie looked at me, her face broken with devastation. 'Thank God Herbie was at your place. He's usually with Elsie on Mondays.'

'It doesn't even bear thinking about.' I shook my head.

'Oh shit!' Susie exclaimed suddenly. 'What about all the food? The food we have for Christmas dinner?'

We all knew the burnt-out remains of the building meant our Christmas dinner for the soup kitchen community was now nothing more than ash.

'They'll understand,' I tried to reassure a teary-eyed Susie. 'Everyone will understand.'

'They will,' she sniffed, 'but that's not the point.'

I knew it was testament to Susie's character that at a time like this, she was still thinking about how we could save Christmas for the soup kitchen guests. Susie and Dan were unlike anyone I'd ever met in my life. I couldn't imagine Francis and Tabs ever acting this selflessly in their whole lives.

'What are we going to do?' I said to Susie, trying to stay strong while battling the tears that were forcing their way from the backs of my eyes. My numbness quickly turned from shock to despair. 'What if Dan isn't all right? What if Elsie isn't? What about the soup kitchen? What about all those people looking forward to spending their Christmas Day there?'

'We'll figure it out,' Susie replied, taking a deep breath. It was her turn to think rationally now that my mind was blank with panic. 'Let's just take it one step at a time.' She squeezed my hand between hers, then pulled her spare set of keys for Dan's van from her pocket, the huge bundle of keyrings jingling as she did so.

'I'll take the food Dan found this evening out of the van and try to store it somewhere,' Susie said. 'At least there are cool bags in the van – we can store some stuff in there – but... well, we'll just have to see what we can do,' she stammered. 'I feel like if I don't do something useful I'm going to explode. I need a distraction, and that's what Dan and Elsie would want us to do. Elsie especially, she'd lose her mind if we wasted perfectly good food.'

'She'd probably chase us out of the hospital.'

'She would. She'd probably outrun us too – she's surprisingly sprightly, thanks to all that Zumba.' Susie gave me a final squeeze. 'I'll be back soon, keep an eye on them for me.' She managed a half-smile before rushing down the corridor.

TWENTY-SEVEN

Dan made us promise we'd visit Elsie first during the hospital's visiting hours. Elsie was in her usual high spirits as Susie and I took it in turns to hold her delicate hand and reassure her that she'd make it to bingo soon (while tactfully breaking it to her that it might be a little while longer until she could go back to Zumba).

I was alone for today's visit, while Susie dealt with the aftermath of the fire, and the community clubbed together to round up a team of volunteers who could temporarily carry on the amazing work of the soup kitchen. We'd had a quote for the refurbishments, and even at a reduced rate, we were looking at £20,000 minimum to get Dan's Kitchen back on its feet again. The insurance small print stated that fire caused by arson was not included in the basic policy Dan had taken out. None of us had any idea how we would find that money, but the most important thing was getting Dan and Elsie back to full health first.

Clutching my polystyrene cup filled with lukewarm, bitter coffee, I followed the loop around the ward, from Elsie's room to

Dan's. Ambulance sirens rang in the air as I trailed through the endless corridors that smelt like lemons and bleach. I passed exhausted-looking doctors and nurses moving from room to room, patients being pushed along in wheelchairs, and I walked alongside some families carrying balloons and flowers, while others wept desperately into crumpled tissues.

The door to Dan's room was shut, but I could see he was awake as I peeped through the small window and pumped the hand sanitiser outside.

I burst through, excited to see him. 'Hey, stranger,' I said. 'How are you doing?'

Dan ignored my happy greeting as he lay completely still. His eyes had lost their sparkle; in the dull light of the room, they looked darker than the blackened bricks that remained where the soup kitchen once stood.

He stared vacantly at the ceiling, the thin, pastel-green sheets tucked tightly around his body. The only movement was the blink of his thick eyelashes, while his gaze didn't move from the same spot above his bed.

'I've just seen Elsie. She's in great spirits, as ever.' I smiled in an attempt to lighten the frosty atmosphere; it was reminding me of when Dan and I first met. 'Typical Elsie, she refused to listen to the hospital radio and had her headphones on. The main thing she wanted to talk about was bingo and what she'd missed on *Coronation Street*. After asking about you, of course.' But the only response Dan could offer was a slight nod.

I lowered myself into the chair next to his bed; the wipeable fabric squeaking as my jeans slipped along it. I traced my finger gently over the tattoos on Dan's exposed arm. The other was wrapped in bandages that covered the burns he'd suffered while rescuing Elsie.

'The doctors said you saved her life,' I said gently, to Dan's silence.

His only answer was the steady rhythm of his chest moving up and down underneath the sheets. My heart filled with gratitude that he still had that – his breath, his beating heart, his life. Thank God, or whoever was up there, that the firefighters had got him and Elsie out alive, and they were both being kept in hospital as a careful precaution. But Dan didn't share my optimism.

'I've lost everything,' Dan said, his voice raspy from inhaling the fumes.

'You haven't…' I squeezed his forearm.

'I have, Bella. You don't understand.' His eyes were guarded. He swallowed hard and his Adam's apple bobbed beneath the tattooed skin of his throat.

'Of course I understand. The soup kitchen was your life.'

'It was,' he agreed, then hesitated, his eyes bottomless with grief. 'But it wasn't just the soup kitchen. It's the arson attack. I know why we were targeted.'

'You do?' I said, puzzled. 'Have you told the police? The detective Susie and I spoke to seemed to think it was a random attack.'

'Money means you can get away with anything, doesn't it? They'll never be held to account.' He ground his teeth, his voice thick and loaded with anger.

'What do you mean? Who? I thought it was just some yobs causing trouble.'

'There was evidence in there,' Dan snapped, his jaw clenched.

'Evidence of what?' My eyes narrowed as I looked at him.

'Evidence of a massive cover-up. A huge corporation profiting off misery and abuse.' Dan shook his head, before wincing at the pain. 'But now, the evidence I had to actually *prove* it is gone forever. And they'll win. Again.' His glossy eyes blinked away the beginnings of tears.

'Who will win? Dan, what on earth are you talking about?'

'Jonathan Burton,' Dan said, his face flushing with anger.

'Jonathan? How do you know him?' I quickly remembered that *I* shouldn't necessarily know who he was – that he was my dad's previous business partner and my former future father-in-law. 'I mean, isn't he the soup guy?'

'Yeah,' Dan snorted. '*The soup guy*. The man in charge of Whittington *fucking* Soup.'

I flinched at the fury behind his words. 'I don't understand...'

'This is everything I've been working for,' Dan said. 'Jonathan knew I had evidence that showed what was going on with their meat suppliers – the superfarms in Europe. I had evidence that couldn't be replaced. Evidence that we'll never get again.'

'What do you mean, Dan? What evidence?' My heart started to thud and my skin prickled.

'The animal welfare campaigning group I'm part of. There's a woman there called Jemma, she—'

'The one with the multicoloured hair?' I interrupted. 'The one who was at the soup kitchen yesterday?'

Dan nodded.

And then it hit me – where I'd seen her before. She was outside the Soup Convention. She was the protestor holding up the placard, chanting and showing it to the guests inside the queue of cars.

'Jemma infiltrated the superfarms that supply Whittington Soup. She risked everything to find evidence of the *real* story – animal cruelty, the exploitation of refugees as workers, illegal working conditions... you name it. It's modern day slavery – of animals *and* humans. You don't need to be a vegetarian or a vegan to know that what they're doing is wrong.'

Dan's voice was seething with rage. 'Jemma's been working on it for months. She'd finally been able to access the paper files that linked the farms with Whittington Soup. She'd managed to persuade the terrified workers to sign documents that outlined their testimonies of what was going on there, and she'd filmed the abuse of the animals.'

His voice sounded strangled and strained. 'The arson attack is my fault because I told Jonathan that we knew what was happening, that we were going to go public with what we'd found. Jemma trusted me with it, she trusted me to do the right thing. And now it's gone.'

Nothing made sense. It couldn't be true. Whittington Soup would never do that. *Never.*

'But I don't understand,' I stammered. 'If it's true—'

'What do you mean, *if* it's true,' Dan said angrily. 'Of course it's true, I've seen it all with my own eyes.'

'Well, if it is,' I said, to Dan's exasperated breath, 'then can't Jemma just get the files again? And the footage?'

'Bella, it took her *so* long to get into a position of trust at the farm where she could access the files. You wouldn't believe what she had to do, what she had to see.' Dan pinched his lips together. 'The files are closely guarded, they're a paper trail, they're not just available for anyone to find. And she had to gain the trust of the traumatised workers. As soon as she did, she had to leave before anyone suspected anything. She'll never be able to set foot near those farms again. We lost our chance. And we'll never get it again.' Dan looked away from me, signalling a silent end to the conversation.

I couldn't believe what Dan was saying. They must've got it wrong. I knew that company inside out. It was my family business. It was started by my own great-grandfather! Though of course I didn't, and couldn't, tell Dan that. Animal welfare was something Whittington Soup prided themselves on; they only ever worked with high-quality suppliers and well-respected British farmers.

'I need some air,' I mumbled. Dan's hatred of the business,

and the reasons why, started to piece together – now I knew why he felt so intensely about it. 'I'll be back in a minute.'

I was unsure Dan even heard me. He turned away and curled up in the hospital bed, staring straight ahead at the white wall next to him.

How was this happening? Could Jonathan really be behind this – behind everything Dan said? Why would he work with unethical, illegal suppliers like that? And would he really turn to arson? Jonathan had his faults, but I couldn't believe he was a man capable of something so horrific, and even worse, risking the life of an elderly woman and those who fought to save her, including Dan.

I paced up and down outside the hospital, next to the smokers blowing clouds of cigarette smoke in front of me. Did my dad know about the suppliers? Of course he didn't. My dad would never allow that... Then it dawned on me, as a puff of smoke slowly evaporated in the fresh winter air. Did Jonathan plan all of this? Even throwing my dad out of the business? No, he couldn't have done. I shook my head again and was suddenly aware of the strange looks I was attracting from the gathering of smokers. But *could* he have done it? I asked myself the question again, the thought of it weighing heavily on my shoulders as I rolled them up and down, the tension aching in every inch of my skin.

I needed answers. I needed to know whether what Dan said was true and I needed to know what happened in that board-room behind closed doors. I sprinted through the hospital, feeling frustrated by the inefficiency of the sluggish automatic doors as I followed the winding route back up to Dan's room.

'Dan, I need to go—' I swung the door open but was taken aback to see a figure sitting in the seat next to Dan's bed. It was a figure I recognised.

'Pippa?' I said, my mouth hanging open in shock. It was Pippa Grant from *Soup Story* – the journalist who'd spearheaded the horrendous smear campaign against me and my family, and furiously grilled me at the humiliating Soup Convention presentation.

'Bella...' She stood up to face me. Her cherry-red lips grew into a wide smile, animated by a glint in her eyes.

'What's she doing here?' I asked Dan, who was sitting up in his bed and looking less like the broken man that he was just twenty minutes earlier.

'You two know each other?' Dan asked.

'We certainly do,' Pippa smirked, her back to him.

'Pippa's going to run a story about the arson attack,' Dan said. I could tell he had his fight back. 'Hopefully it'll help find the culprit.' He pursed his lips together; he clearly hadn't told Pippa his theory about who it was. She'd think he was crazy, making an allegation against someone like Jonathan Burton with absolutely no evidence. 'And it might help raise the £20,000 refurbishment costs to get the soup kitchen on its feet again.'

'I see,' I said, trying to mask my suspicion of Pippa. She'd have an ulterior motive, I knew it. She was much too underhanded to be here out of the goodness of her heart.

Pippa cocked her head to the side and looked at me. 'But surely Bella could just pay for the refurbishment?' she said slowly.

'Sure,' Dan managed a gentle laugh. 'How much do you think I'm paying her, like? I know her soup is great and everything but—'

'Oh, you're *working* at the soup kitchen?' Pippa smirked.

'Can we talk outside, please?' I begged.

She nodded and picked up her handbag, though I knew she was relishing her moment. I smiled at Dan as I held the door open for her. I shut it carefully as soon as we were both behind it, triple-checking it was definitely closed so that Dan couldn't hear our conversation.

'Please don't tell him who I really am,' I said, my desperate words jumbling out of my mouth. 'Please, Pippa, I'm begging you.'

Pippa eyed me up and down, her steely blue eyes cutting in a cool stare. 'I'm writing a story about this, whether you like it or not,' she said unsympathetically. 'Dan is going to find out who you are sooner or later, why don't you just tell him now?'

'Because!' I threw my arms up before regaining my composure. 'Because I've kept my real identity a secret from him for a while now, OK? I know it's wrong, but it's done now,' I rambled. 'I didn't want him to know who I really was because I knew he wouldn't like me. He'd see me as an over-privileged, spoilt brat – which I guess I was, really. And then there's just the teeny tiny fact that he *hates* Whittington Soup and considers anyone associated with it as his enemy. Perhaps for good reason...' I blabbered before stopping myself.

'Did you really think he'd *never* find out who you are?' Pippa asked incredulously.

'Of course not!' I shrieked, and Pippa shuddered at how high-pitched I was getting the more I started to panic. 'My plan was to tell him after Christmas. I was always going to tell him after Christmas.' I shuffled desperately from foot to foot. 'And I can't exactly tell him right now, can I? Not while his whole world has gone up in flames.' I bit my lip as I felt a tear sting my eyes.

'Look.' Pippa rolled her eyes impatiently. 'It isn't totally random that I'm here, OK? My editor recognised you in the pictures our photographer took of the fire. He had me ask around a bit. He wanted me to see if it was true, if it was really you – if the soup dynasty heiress, Arabella Whittington, was *really* working in a soup kitchen. And trust me, he'll want to run the story with or without any input from you, so at least you'll get your say if you talk to me.'

'I haven't forgotten what you did to my family,' I interrupted. 'You humiliated us.'

'I'm sorry about that,' Pippa said, coldly and unapologetically. 'The tip-offs we got were too good to ignore.'

'That doesn't make it right, or fair.' I wrapped my arms around my chest.

'Anyway.' Pippa rolled her eyes again and pushed her dark hair over her shoulder. 'I promise you're better off speaking to me about all this directly. We'll do a quick interview now, and then you can tell Dan who you really are before it's published. I just want your side of the story. Nothing bad – no scandal or anything like that. But if anything, having your input will make the story about the soup kitchen bigger and better. Which, of course, means it's more likely to raise lots of money for the refurbishment.'

I leant against the wall and breathed deeply, weighing up the options in my head. This was it, the moment I could take what I'd been through and use it for something good – to help the soup kitchen get back on its feet. I just had to make sure it was *my* story. And I had to tell Dan and Susie first.

'OK,' I whispered. 'But can you definitely hold off from publishing it for a couple of days?'

'Yeah, that shouldn't be a problem.' I could sense the excitement in her voice. 'So, you'll do it?'

'One more condition,' I added.

'Go on...'

'I really don't want the article to be all about me. I get that it's an interesting angle and I understand why you want to include my story, but the focus should be on the soup kitchen and the fundraising. We *need* to hit the £20,000 target, otherwise it's gone forever.'

'Of course.' She nodded. 'As I said to Dan, the story might

help uncover who was behind the arson attack too. We already have a quote from the police asking for witnesses or anyone who might've seen anything suspicious on the night to come forward.'

I knew who might've been behind it, but I wasn't going to tell *her* that. I needed to know for myself first.

Pippa guided me towards two chairs further along the corridor. We sat down and she pulled out a notebook and pen from her bag.

I bit my lip and pasted on a fake, quivering smile, while clutching my hands together.

'So, *Arabella Whittington*,' she emphasised, smug in the knowledge that she was privy to my real identity. 'Going from life as a millionaire soup heiress to working at a soup kitchen is pretty interesting.'

I nodded in dazed agreement, forgetting that it was, in fact, my life she was talking about.

Pippa didn't hold back in her questions about every single aspect of my life. She and her editor had clearly done their research. They'd trawled through my old social media, and seemingly studied all past interviews that I'd naively assumed were hidden in the dark depths of Google.

'Tell me about you and Dan. Obviously you're very fond of each other...'

'Yes, we're... close,' I said, not wanting to give anything away as Dan and I still weren't 'officially' together.

'A little different from your ex-fiancé, Francis Burton, right?'

'The less said about him the better,' I snapped, then inhaled and tried to calm myself. 'Sorry,' I said. The first rule of good PR is not pissing off the journalist. 'Sore subject.'

'I understand,' she nodded. 'I mean, I *totally* get what you'd see in Dan. He's got a real moody and mysterious kind of vibe going on – ooh, like the Dreamboat Duke in *Bridgerton*!' She clapped her hands together excitedly.

'Yeah, I guess so,' I agreed, trying to stifle a giggle at the thought of Dan's face with that description of him. Though she had a point.

'But he has a social conscience too, like the way he champions important causes and stands up for what he believes in. Ooh, just like Marcus Rashford!'

I nodded. I wasn't a football fan (much to Elsie's dismay), but he was my favourite footballer if I had to pick one.

'He's kind of rugged, in a brooding, sexy, manly kind of way.' Pippa shimmied her shoulders in delight.

'Are you writing a news article or the next *Fifty Shades of Grey*?'

'Creative licence, part of the job,' she replied, scribbling my words down in shorthand. 'And what about... Susie?' She flipped the pages over and scanned her notes. 'Dan mentioned her when we were chatting earlier.'

'Oh, Susie's great. She's kind and hilarious, totally bonkers though – mad as a box of frogs,' I chuckled.

'A little different from your usual circle of glamorous Scousewives and Sloane Rangers?' Pippa raised an eyebrow.

'Just a tad.' I had a silent laugh as I imagined any of my old friends' disdain if they were ever witness to Susie's penchant for DIY everything – clothes-making, hair dyeing, even bikini waxing. 'They're worlds apart. But Susie's the best friend I've ever had.'

'Thanks, Arabella, I think I have everything I need for now.' Pippa closed the notebook, nestled the pen into the wire binding and placed it in her handbag.

'OK,' I said cautiously. 'And *please* can you make sure the piece isn't published for at least a couple of days? I have a lot of explaining to do.'

'Sure.' She followed my gaze towards the closed door of Dan's room. 'Good luck with it all,' she said, her frosty exterior thawing a little. 'Dan seems like a great guy, I'm sure he'll understand.'

I traipsed back to the room, explained to Dan that he should rest and that I'd taken care of the interview. I hoped Pippa's intuition about Dan's level of understanding was correct.

TWENTY-EIGHT

Missed calls: 128. WhatsApp messages: 346. That was the last count before I turned my phone off and hid it in the fridge.

It turned out Pippa's intuition of whether Dan would understand was yet to be revealed. But her intuition as a journalist was perfect – she (and her editor) could certainly sniff out a good story.

It was the day after the interview and everything had gone horribly, horribly wrong. My plan had been to tell both Susie and Dan who I really was at the hospital this morning, before the article was published. But Dan had called to stay he was stuck in a queue waiting for the consultant, and that he was going to be released by midday anyway, so we could talk then. Stupidly, I agreed, assuming I had plenty of time because the story wasn't set to be published for another couple of days. But that wasn't the case.

My 'fall from grace', as the papers deemed it, had exploded. The story had been syndicated to the national media, and my words were twisted and sensationalised more and more with every article. Uncharacteristically, Pippa had apologetically explained during my frantic phone call to her that they'd edited her work and she had no say in any editorial decisions once it was sold to other papers.

I felt sick with worry because the story had broken so much sooner than she'd promised (another pointless apology from her), and I still hadn't had the chance to explain everything to Dan and Susie. It was already online everywhere, and Pippa had given me a heads up that the tabloids were running the story too.

It felt like the walls of my flat were closing in on me. I'd forced myself to hide my laptop out of reach, and it was stuffed underneath my bed. I was tearing my hair out reading the online comments about the story – the keyboard warriors telling me how ugly I looked compared to old photos, and what a downgrade 'Hobo Dan' was next to Francis Burton. As well as Dan's awful nickname, Susie was referred to as 'Mad Susie' after I stupidly said she was 'mad as a box of frogs'. I'd obviously meant it in an endearing way, but that was lost in translation when it came to embellishing a story.

The phone calls and messages I'd received so far were mostly from my worried parents. The papers had made the judgement that nothing would stand in the way of their dramatic story about me – the multimillionaire soup heiress who was scrubbing floors in a soup kitchen – and they'd painted Toxteth and Dan's Kitchen in the most awful light possible.

Mum was concerned that I'd joined some sort of hippy cult, like the one she and Stevie Nicks had to dramatically escape from, back in the eighties ('We thought when it was described as *dry*, they meant the weather, not no alcohol!'). She'd also convinced herself that the fire was part of a gang attack and that I must board the first flight to France immediately. 'Even,' she'd whispered, 'if it means flying economy.'

Dad reassured me that Mum had been watching far too many true crime documentaries on Netflix, and they just wanted to know that I was OK and safe, whether I did want to escape to France and if they could do anything to help. It was killing me not telling them what Dan had said about Whittington Soup and Jonathan, but still, I had absolutely no evidence that it was even true.

As a distraction, I tried to calm my rattled thoughts by watching the *Real Housewives of Beverly Hills* episode I'd seen at least twelve times. But there was something else playing on my mind – something the papers had insinuated about Dan and Susie.

Through the noise of the scene on my television, I heard heavy footsteps outside. They were bounding up the communal staircase. The door to Susie's flat swung open and slammed shut with such vigour that the cushions on my couch vibrated. I heard Dan's VW van screeching down the road before I had a chance to look out of the window. So, they'd seen the story. I was desperate to speak to Dan, but reasoned that it might be easier to get through to Susie at first, and she only lived approximately six feet away from me.

I pulled the belt on my fluffy dressing gown tightly and shuffled out of my flat. Heavy metal music boomed from the gaps in Susie's front door. I knew from experience of Susie's music choices that this meant she was not feeling particularly cheery. I tapped on the door. Nothing. I lied to myself that it was probably because she couldn't hear me over the music. I knocked again, a little louder. 'I'm sorry,' I muttered, leaning my forehead against the bright turquoise door.

A piece of neon yellow paper landed on my slippers from the gap underneath.

Go away Bella/Arabella or whatever your bloody name really is. We saw the stack of newspapers in the hospital waiting room. To quote the headlines and online comments, 'Mad Susie' is currently otherwise engaged. 'Hobo Dan' has gone home. Why don't you run back to Mummy and Daddy – and Whittington Soup (WTF?!) – and leave us alone?

I scrunched the note up in my hands and sulked back to my flat which felt, impossibly, smaller than ever. Perching on the end of the sofa, I held my head in my hands. What had I done? More importantly, what could I do to fix it? If Susie's reaction was that bad, I could only imagine how upset Dan was feeling. But what did I have to lose? I had to tell him. I had to explain everything.

Totally forgetting the fact that I was wearing fluorescent pink flamingo pyjamas with a matching dressing gown and slippers (complete with glittery horns), I marched out of my flat.

Rain flooded the streets of Toxteth, as shop signs flapped in the wind. Every raindrop weighed down the fluff of my dressing gown until I arrived at Dan's. I was panting and struggling for breath from the increasing weight of the soggy outfit and the speed that I'd sprinted.

'Jesus, Bella,' he cried as he opened the door. 'What the hell are you thinking? It's torrential out there.' He gently pulled me with his unbandaged arm into the warmth of his home. Herbie greeted me by licking the rain from my soaked pyjamas.

'I...' My lip quivered, and I shook with the cold that drowned my body like an ice bath. 'I don't know where to start.'

After kindly passing a warm and fluffy towel to me, Dan ran a hand over his freshly washed hair. I knew he would've been desperate to wash the hospital smell from himself. He sat tentatively on the arm of the sofa, which was covered in thick blankets expertly knitted by Elsie, who was still in hospital for observation. His silence felt like it would never end as he stared at the floor in front of him.

'I just don't understand,' he said eventually. 'Why would you lie?' He fiddled with the towel wrapped around his waist, before awkwardly folding his arms across his tattooed chest. 'To me? To Susie? Even to Elsie?'

'I didn't *technically* lie,' I murmured guiltily, knowing I'd lied about my name. 'I just didn't offer the information. But I promise I was going to tell you, right after Christmas.'

'Oh well, that makes everything OK then,' Dan said, still avoiding my desperate gaze. 'What was it? Were you spying on me for Whittington Soup? For Jonathan?'

'What? Of course not!' I pulled the dressing gown hood down and dragged my drenched hair out from underneath the soaking wet fluff.

'How could you not tell me that Whittington Soup is your family's business?' He shook his head in disgust, the water droplets from his hair brushing against his skin. 'I can't believe it, Bella. You know how I feel about that company.'

'But it's not a bad business, Dan. Those things you said about the suppliers and the cruelty can't be true. I should know, it was my great-grandfather who started the company and built it from nothing. And the reason why he started cooking soup in the first place was to help people in need.'

'You haven't seen what I've seen.' Dan ignored my explanation. 'You clearly have no idea what goes on there.'

I wrapped my arms around myself and tried to stop my body from trembling. 'Maybe I don't. Not now, anyway,' I admitted. 'But I know it wasn't like that when my dad was in charge.'

'You know I was there, don't you?' Dan said. 'Protesting at the Soup Convention with Jemma?'

'You were?' I remembered the angry crowd outside, the signs displaying graphic photos of animal cruelty, the passionate chanting.

'Yep,' Dan said firmly. 'I'm sorry, Bella, I just don't understand how you didn't know what was going on.'

'I... I just... I assumed the protests were about another

company at the convention. I had no idea it was anything to do with Whittington Soup.'

'So was it some sort of experiment, you living here, hey?' Dan huffed, ignoring my pleas of innocence. 'A fun story you could tell your friends about when you went back home? I've seen those programmes, when someone rich goes to live with someone poor.' He rubbed his exhausted eyes. 'They say, "Oh, look how they live, how quaint. Bless them, they can't afford their food shopping," then they go back home and pity them from the comfort of their mansions.'

'Dan, it's not like that. You have to believe me.'

'What then? A little project to show your daddy you can stand on your own two feet, then you'll run back home and enjoy your trust fund?' Dan laughed to himself. 'I can't believe I've been so stupid. I thought I knew you, Bella, I thought I was fall—' He stopped himself. All I wanted in that moment was for him to finish that sentence, to say those words.

'Please,' I begged after a long silence. 'That's really not what this is. You don't understand.'

He paced up and down in front of me. 'I *knew* you looked familiar when I first saw you. I should've known you were the socialite daughter of the Whittington Soup dynasty. Bella *Whitson*,' he scoffed. 'And that guy, Francis? The Ryan Gosling lookalike at Winter Wonderland, he's your *fiancé*? He's Jonathan Burton's *son*?'

'Ex-fiancé,' I clarified.

'No wonder the papers are mocking me.'

'He's an awful person,' I said. I felt my soaking wet pyjamas stick to my skin as I sat timidly on the corner of the sofa next to him. 'We were engaged, yes, but I broke it off because he did something unforgivable. And I was going to tell you everything, I swear I was. Things have been so crazy lately. I wanted to celebrate Christmas with you first, but then I promise I was going to—'

'It's a bit late for that now,' Dan interrupted my rambling. 'And to think, I was going to ask you to be my girlfriend.' He shook his head.

My sadness turned from tears to anger as I remembered what I also saw in the papers.

'You're not exactly the picture of innocence in all this,' I said. 'You didn't tell me that you and Susie were together once. What about all those photos of you both, standing hand-in-hand outside the soup kitchen. Don't you think I would've liked to have known that the two of you have history?'

Dan laughed in shock. 'Are you messin'?'

'The pictures said it all,' I sulked stubbornly. I knew there was probably nothing to it really, and that I was just trying to deflect my own guilt.

'Right. Sure. Because that's the same level of betrayal as yours.' Dan stood up and tightened the white towel around his waist again. 'I think you should leave,' he said, his stubble-covered jaw clenched. 'You need to just let it be for a bit, Bella. I need some space.'

I pushed myself to my feet. 'Fine,' I said, feeling the tears starting to burn my eyes. 'Maybe I need space too,' I lied.

'We're obviously from different worlds,' he said. 'I appreciate what you tried to do with the interview, Bella, Arabella. Whatever your name is. I'm sure you meant well. But you *lied* to me. Not just about who you are, but your connection – your family connection – to the thing that I hate the most, something I've been fighting against for years.'

He walked towards the door, his head bowed, with Herbie at his heels. 'I can't do this any more, I need time to think.'

'OK,' I whispered. I didn't have the energy to fight, to convince him that this – what we had – was worth fighting for.

Dan nodded, before passing an umbrella to me – he was still a gentleman, despite everything – and opening the door.

I stepped out into the rain and turned around to tell him I

was sorry again. But before I could, the door shut in my face. I walked slowly in the torrential downpour, letting it soak through my nightwear.

Susie's music was still blaring from her flat when I reached my front door. Peeling my drenched clothes off and wrapping a towel around myself, I lay on the bed and felt my blinks getting longer and longer before I couldn't stop them from taking over any more. My dreams were a haze of burning fires and supermarket bins, Chanel dresses and stained wellies. A blur of my new life – Dan, Susie, Elsie and Herbie – and my old life – Mum, Dad, Francis, Jonathan, Tabs and Polly.

A knock at the door woke me from my dreams. The clock informed me it was 8 a.m. the following morning. I'd slept through the night. *It must be Dan*, I thought, my stomach doing a flip. He must've slept on it and now wanted to talk. I stumbled from the couch and swung the door open with glee.

'Hey.' Francis leant against the door frame. 'Can I come in?'

TWENTY-NINE

'What the hell are you doing here?'

Francis propped his long arms against either side of the door frame. 'I saw the papers,' he said. 'I just wanted to make sure you're OK.'

'How did you find me?' I glared. After the exhaustion of last night, I'd fallen asleep in my towel and was suddenly aware of how naked I was. I tightened it around myself.

Francis smirked. 'I've seen it all before, Bella.' He gently moved me out of the way and marched into my flat, pushing the door closed behind him. 'One of the gossip blogs did a comparison of where you used to live – where *we* used to live,' he corrected himself. 'And where you live now.'

He touched the ceiling with his fingertips before stretching his arms to the opposite walls. 'A mate of mine helped me track you down, but gosh, I didn't think it'd be this... cosy.' He wrinkled his nose. 'I have to say, it's not quite how I imagined you living. You wouldn't even stay in a four-star hotel when we were together. "Darling, it's five stars or I shan't set foot in it,"' he mocked.

'Well, I probably wouldn't be here if it wasn't for you, would I?' *Or your father*, I added silently.

I eyed him up and down. He was still sporting his unchanged preppy combination of cream chinos and pale shirt, with a jumper tied around his shoulders. Only this time, the outfit was paired with his Burberry trench coat to shield him from the storm outside.

'Please, Bella.' He turned to face me. 'You need to let that go now.'

'Let it go? Are you kidding me? I walked in on you *shagging* my *best friend*. How can I let...' I pinched the bridge of my nose between my fingers. 'I'm not getting into this now. Why are you here, Francis?'

'I told you,' he said impatiently. 'I want to make sure you're OK.'

'Well, you've seen me.' I held one arm out, conscious of the other one clinging to the towel. 'I'm OK. Now you can bugger off.'

'I know you, Bell.' One step forward with his long legs meant he was right in front of me before I had a chance to move away. He studied my face. 'You're not OK. But I'm here to help you.'

'I don't need you.' I stepped back, stumbling into a chair.

'Fine, you might not need me, but I do think you need a break.'

I snorted. 'Yes, I probably do need a break, but nowhere near you.'

'OK,' he sighed. 'Nowhere near me, I get that. But I want to make things up to you. I want to be friends. I want you to forgive me. Can't you just trust me?'

'Ha!' I cried dramatically. 'Trust you? Where did that get me last time? And anyway, aren't you with Tabs?'

'Tabs?' He stroked the stubble lining his jaw. 'Jesus, no. I couldn't deal with her taking two hundred selfies before we left the house.' He rolled his eyes. 'We broke up.'

'You seemed pretty cosy when I saw you both at Winter Wonderland.' The words bumbled out of my mouth. I didn't know why I said it, I didn't know why I cared. Dan was a million times the man Francis was.

Francis rolled his eyes. 'I only went there to watch your favourite film. *Our* favourite film.' He put his hand out to stroke my shoulder. I pulled back.

'Netflix would've been easier,' I scowled.

'Look, I know you've moved on with that Hobo Henry guy.' He waved his hand dismissively.

'His name is Dan, he isn't a hobo. And yes, I have,' I said, unconvincingly. I didn't know where Dan and I stood, given our conversation last night. I couldn't hide my sadness at the mention of his name. The mascara stains all over my towel and cushions didn't do a very good of hiding it either.

Francis clocked the obvious tear stains. 'I see, trouble in' – he glanced around the cramped flat again – 'paradise?' He raised an eyebrow. 'This is all the more reason why I'm here. I know you don't have your parents around. Please, just let me get you out of here for a while.'

I opened my mouth to protest, but before I could say a word, he knelt down so that we were eye to eye from my place on the chair. 'You don't need to stay with me, you've made your feelings clear. I'll put you up in a hotel and you can just relax for a little bit, have a break from all this.'

'But why do you want to help me? What do you get out of it?' I asked suspiciously.

'Nothing,' he said firmly. 'I'm trying this new thing out where I'm not an awful person. And I still feel terrible about what I did to you. It made me realise what I'd done – what I'd lost – when I saw you at Winter Wonderland with that *guy*.' He dismissed Dan with a wave again. 'Let's just say this is my way of apologising, OK?' He put his hands into the pockets of his trench coat. 'I mean it, I'm really sorry, Bella. I've been an idiot, and I'll never forgive myself if I don't make it up to you somehow.'

I weighed up the options in my head. I could continue wallowing in this tiny studio flat that was already starting to give me cabin fever without the soup kitchen to escape to. I could envisage the coming days – listening to Susie's relentless metal music playing through the paper-thin walls and driving myself insane wondering whether Dan would ever forgive me.

Or, I could take a couple of days out, have some space away from Toxteth, clear my head and think of a new plan to salvage everything. Plus, I might be able to get some information from Francis about Jonathan and what he did – whether he was behind the arson and the plot to kick my family out of the business. I was essentially using Francis for his wallet and his potential inside information, but I figured it was the least he could do after how much pain he'd caused me.

'Fine,' I relented. 'I have literally nothing to lose at this point.'

Francis didn't attempt to hide his delight. 'Excellent!' he said. 'You go and pack a bag, I'll get the hotel booked.'

'Where am I staying?'

'It's a surprise,' he answered, tapping on his phone.

I grabbed my laptop from under the bed and my phone from the fridge, and chucked them in a bag with some fresh pyjamas, clean underwear, T-shirts, my toothbrush and toiletries. I threw on a pair of jeans, a jumper and my boots, and ran some curling mousse through my hair, which was still wild and frizzy after yesterday's impromptu power walk in the rain.

'Ready?' Francis said.

'Yep.'

Francis opened the door at the exact moment that Susie

went to knock on it. She had a plate of my favourite white chocolate chip cookies in her hand.

A wave of recognition flooded her face as she clocked Francis and glared at me. 'I see,' she said. 'I made you some sorry cookies.' She shoved the plate into me.

'Susie, it's not what you—'

She stormed back into her flat and slammed the door before I could finish. On went the music. On continued the angry painting and angry baking.

'Argh!' I cried. My weekend bag thudded as it hit the floor. 'Why is this happening to me?'

'Come on.' Francis put the cookies in my kitchen and pulled me out. He picked up my bag and shut the door behind me. 'You can text her from the car. Put her in the picture.'

Too exhausted and emotionally drained to argue, I followed Francis down the stairwell. His new custom-built Overfinch Range Rover had already attracted a crowd of admiring teenagers.

I caught Susie's eye from the window as I opened the door to the passenger's side. I shook my head and mouthed, 'It's not what you think,' but she quickly shut the curtains after giving me the finger.

I let myself sink into the buttery leather as I texted her, already knowing that her phone would be switched off or my number blocked.

'Hello, Francis, where would you like to go?' the husky satnav voice asked.

'Titanic Hotel,' Francis commanded. He clicked his seat belt and turned to me. 'Let's get you back where you belong, hey, Bell?'

THIRTY

Bubbles fizzed around my skin and danced inside the crystal glass in my hand. The chunks of ice clinked together as I propped the chilled bottle of Bollinger back inside the ice bucket.

I let myself sink back into the warm bathwater and held the champagne flute to the side. The scent of freshly cut flowers was overpowering as I used my free hand to pour more Jo Malone bath oil into the free-standing tub.

Floor-to-ceiling views of Liverpool provided the backdrop to the panoramic windows on the left and right side of the enormous roll-top bath. Looking to the right, the roof terrace of mine and Francis's old apartment building stood out amidst the hustle and bustle of the Albert Dock's glamorous restaurants and swanky cocktail bars. Through the window on the left side of the Carrara marble en-suite, Toxteth was just about visible in the distance.

The chilled bubbles tingled my lips as I took a sip and counted the spotlights dotted around the high ceiling. This felt so familiar, yet so alien. Staying at the Titanic Hotel was a

regular pastime. I had a longstanding weekly day spa appointment and I'd even spent a month living here while mine and
Francis's apartment was being refurbished. The hotel was a
second home to me, and my luxury suite couldn't have been
more different from my studio flat back in Toxteth – I calculated that the bathroom was the same size as my entire flat. Plus,
I couldn't actually use my bath there, thanks to the enormous
crack in it.

A buzz echoed around the room. I stretched to reach my
phone from the side of the sink.

Let me take you for dinner tonight? x F

Francis had been true to his word and given me space to
think. Three days of it, to be precise. Those blissful seventy-two
hours had been spent in a lazy, hazy daze of bubble baths,
pamper appointments and room service binges. I'd been
massaged, scrubbed and exfoliated to within an inch of my life.
It was heaven. Extravagant, indulgent heaven. Any feelings of
guilt about the cost were quickly wiped away with the reminder
that it was Francis footing the bill, and he deserved to pay for
every penny of it. Plus, I was waiting for my chance to interro-
gate him (subtly, of course) about Jonathan.

Getting lost in the decadence of it all felt good, but no
matter how many trashy reality TV shows I distracted myself
with (an impressive number), or heaped plates of truffle fries I
ate (an equally impressive number), I was devastated at the
thought that I might've lost everything I had with Dan, as well
as my friendship with Susie.

Francis had tried to assure me what I'd done wasn't that bad
and that they were being incredibly dramatic. It might've been
the champagne hitting me, but I was beginning to wonder
whether he was right. *Yes*, I should've told them earlier who I

was and about my past. But I didn't *lie*, I just didn't explicitly offer the information. Although, I guess I did lie about my name. But the intention to tell them was there – I'd promised myself I was going to do it right after Christmas. It wasn't a betrayal per se – more of an oversight. The newspaper article was completely misquoted, so surely they couldn't blame me for that.

I only hoped Susie hadn't told Dan that she saw me leaving with Francis, but I knew it was unlikely she'd have kept it to herself, considering how close she and Dan were. Plus, she hadn't even read my messages of explanation – the little blue ticks on WhatsApp hadn't yet appeared.

My phone buzzed again.

Please? Keeping me company tonight is the least you can do after maxing out my credit card on 24-carat gold facials and uncountable bottles of Bolly. x F

I took another sip from the glass. I supposed he had a point, despite owing me a lifetime of 24-carat gold facials after catching him in bed with Tabs.

I typed on the keypad, my fingers moist from the bubbles.

Sounds just like old times. Fine, but I don't have anything to wear. Unless we're going somewhere that deems ripped jeans and baggy old t-shirts acceptable?

My phone pinged again approximately fifteen seconds later.

That attire is never acceptable. I'll have something sent to you. The car will pick you up at 8 p.m. x F

This wasn't a terrible idea, I reassured myself. As he said, going for dinner with him was the least I could do, given he'd bankrolled this jolly of mine. I wasn't stupid and I wouldn't be taken in by his wining and dining. I knew his game. Francis had said he simply wanted to help me out in my time of need, but I knew him well. He wanted to be the heroic prince, saving the princess from the castle (or the tiny studio flat). As long as I kept my wits about me and didn't get sucked in by his charm (or more champagne; I'd forgotten how much I missed it), then I could easily keep him at arm's length.

I dropped my phone onto the furry bathmat, placed the glass onto the side and let my entire body sink into the deep bath. If only my heart wasn't shattered into tiny pieces at every thought of Dan Rigby that constantly popped into my head, I could've really enjoyed the warm and luxurious, rose-scented water.

'This way please, Miss Whittington.' The maître d' guided me through the intimate restaurant, lit only by fairy lights decorating the walls and the scattered candlelight. 'It's lovely to see you again, have you been away?' He beamed a welcoming smile.

'I have,' I replied. The silk of the ruby-red dress that the concierge had delivered to my hotel room whispered against my legs with every step I took closer to Francis. His face was gently outlined by the soft light of flickering candles dotted around the tables.

'It's always nice to come home, isn't it?' The maître d' pulled out a chair from the cosy table in the corner where Francis was sitting.

'It is,' Francis said to him. 'Thanks, Pierre.'

Pierre nodded and straightened the black bow tie sitting at the top of his whiter-than-white shirt. 'Can I get you something to start? Some champagne, perhaps?'

'Yes, please. Dom Pérignon. Oldest vintage you have,' Francis said without hesitation.

I smoothed my dress as Pierre placed the napkin over my lap with the elegant swish of a white glove-covered hand. 'Right away,' he said.

'You like the dress?' Francis gestured to me.

'I do,' I nodded. 'Although had I known I'd be wearing it, I probably wouldn't have eaten as much chocolate or ice cream over the last few days.'

The glint of Francis's eye glistened in the light of the candle. 'You're perfect as you are,' he said softly.

'I should've known you'd book a table here.' I hastily changed the subject and glanced over my shoulder at the restaurant.

'Of course I'd choose your favourite,' Francis replied.

Pierre swiftly presented us with two crystal flutes and a bottle of vintage Dom Pérignon, which he carefully placed in an ice bucket after pouring.

'Well, *our* favourite,' Francis said. 'Can you believe how many memories we have here? Our first date, Valentine's Day...' He trailed off, shaking his head at the memory of us together before he shacked up with my former bestie. 'Sorry,' he mumbled.

The reminder of him and Tabs in bed together only fed my strength to keep my wits about me. I wouldn't be sucked into reminiscing about our life together. Even if he kept the vintage Dom coming.

'So, has the time away helped?' Francis tore a piece of bread and dipped it in the porcelain plate filled with pools of olive oil and balsamic vinegar.

'Kind of.' I shrugged. The truth was, while it was nice to relax and live in a bubble of luxury, I was still no clearer on my next move. I still hadn't heard from Dan or Susie, and I couldn't go to the destroyed soup kitchen even if I wanted to – if the soup kitchen ever opened its doors again.

'At least the stories in the press have calmed down now,' Francis said, looking the menu up and down. 'You haven't had much luck with them lately, have you?'

'You could say that,' I replied, remembering my former work BFF Polly and her unceremonious firing from Whittington Soup by Jonathan for leaking stories to journalists.

'How's your dad?' I asked casually. I traced the stem of the glass on the table and admired my newly manicured nails.

'Yeah, fine.' Francis rolled his eyes. 'Same old, obsessed with work.'

'Speaking of which, did he ever mention anything to you about switching meat suppliers at Whittington Soup?' I said, as nonchalantly as I could manage. I tore a piece of bread in half and dipped it in the black circle of balsamic inside the pale yellow olive oil.

'No, why on earth would he bore me with details like that? He knows I don't give two hoots about his work. As long as the money keeps going to my trust fund, obviously.' He winked. 'Anyway, I'm sure if he changed something like that it was for the best.'

'Mmm,' I mumbled through my mouthful of warm focaccia. 'And I don't suppose he ever talked to you about what happened in the boardroom? When my dad was voted out?'

'Not really,' Francis said, browsing the menu intently. 'Just said that he tried to convince them to keep Wilf on, but they were having none of it. They were concerned about those leaked stories, I think, and the reputation of the business.' Francis looked up at me. 'Why? Hasn't your dad moved on now? Isn't he living it up in France?'

'Yes, of course.' I shook my head. 'I was just wondering if he ever mentioned it, that's all.'

'That reminds me,' Francis said. 'Whittington Soup sent the belongings you left at the office to our apartment. I've been meaning to get in touch to tell you. They're with the concierge.'

'Oh gosh, of course.' I'd forgotten all about anything I'd left on my desk in the mist of confusion that descended when my dad and I were unceremoniously turfed out of the company headquarters. 'I'll pick those up, not that there will be anything interesting.'

'Shall I order for us?' Francis smiled.

'Sure,' I said. I knew Francis well enough to know I wouldn't get anywhere by pushing on with the subject matter of Jonathan. It was unlikely he knew anything anyway. As Francis said, all he cared about was his trust fund.

Francis gestured at Pierre, who rushed over with his notebook in hand.

'Winter truffle soup to start with.' Francis smiled at me. 'Chateaubriand, cooked rare, with all the trimmings for main. And we'll have two glasses of the 2016 Parussi Barolo with the steak, please, Pierre.' He thumped the leather menu shut.

'Absolutely. Excellent choices, Mr Burton,' Pierre said, taking the menus from him.

'This will be the first time I've had steak in months,' I admitted. 'I've kind of been...' I covered my mouth and whispered, 'Vegan' – it was a French restaurant, after all.

'Gosh,' Francis said. 'Don't say it too loud, they'll throw you out of here.'

Pierre brought us complimentary dishes from the head chef between courses. It almost felt like old times as we sipped the vintage champagne and worked our way through our favourite choices from the menu.

'How's the steak?' Francis asked.

Perfectly pink on the inside, our shared chateaubriand was cooked just the way I liked it. The surprise came when I felt a wave of nausea after a few bites. 'Probably just my body getting used to eating meat again,' I reassured a concerned Francis. I washed the sickly feeling down with the velvety Barolo and munched through the triple-cooked chips and seasonal greens instead.

'Heard from your parents lately?' Francis said. His ability to drink red wine and eat a dark-coloured dinner without spilling a speck on his crisp white shirt never failed to amaze me.

'Yeah, a little,' I said, as I fiddled with the stained napkin on my lap. 'I haven't exactly updated them about everything – I just told them I'm staying with a friend for a bit of headspace.'

'Probably for the best,' Francis nodded.

A gentle buzz tickled my leg. I picked up my new YSL clutch bag – another gift from Francis – and looked at the notification on my phone. It was a calendar reminder of a date that Dan and I had made; we were planning to check out a jazz club that had just opened its doors.

It reminded me of where I should be.

'What's that?' Francis said, wiping his mouth delicately.

'It's a reminder, something Dan and I were going to do. Something I hope we're *still* going to do.' My stomach churned with both worry and hope. All I wanted was to be in a tiny jazz bar, cosied up in Dan's strong arms.

'I see.' Francis lifted the glass to his lips.

'You were right, perhaps this time out did us both good,' I said, optimistic that there was still hope for us – that he could forgive me, that we could work it out.

'Mm-hmm,' Francis mumbled, his body turning stiff in the chair.

Pierre arrived to clear the table, balancing the plates and dishes expertly across his arm. 'Can I get you any dessert? More wine?'

'No, I think we're finished here,' Francis said sharply.

'What is the matter with you?' I hissed as Pierre walked away. 'You know this is what I want. I want to be with Dan.'

'Are you really that naive, Bella?' Francis raised his voice, before clocking the looks from the diners around us and quietening to a whisper, despite the anger fizzing behind his words. 'Do you *really* think that you and some homeless kitchen worker can go off and live a happy little life together?'

I pulled away from the table, leaning into the back of my chair. 'Dan isn't a homeless kitchen worker...'

'Do you actually think you'll be happy without all your designer handbags and expensive shoes?' Francis hissed. 'In that dingy little flat, working in a soup kitchen of all places, cleaning your own bathroom, buying your clothes second-hand, going on *staycations?*' His expression was one of sheer horror.

I sat quietly, stroking the stem of the crystal champagne flute. He thought he knew me so well, but he didn't know me at all.

Francis swiftly readjusted his rage and sat back in his seat, his chest puffed out and hands resting on the back of his head. 'I don't think so, Bella. You know you'll never meet anyone else like me and have what we had. Yes, I fucked up. I fucked up in a fucking *gargantuan* way. I've admitted that and I'll regret it forever, OK? But you and I both know what we had together was special.'

Then, the arrogance in his eyes turned to sadness. 'I'll do anything, Bella. I'll do anything to have you back with me.' He reached for my hand across the table. 'I don't care what it takes, I'll do it. I'll make it work. Just please don't go back there. Come back to me. Come *home.*'

We sat in silence as his eyes stared intensely into mine, and under the table, I stroked the spot on my finger where my engagement ring once sat.

'Sorry to interrupt.' Pierre appeared from the side. 'Your bill, Mr Burton.'

'I need some fresh air,' Francis said, his long legs almost knocking the table over as he stood. 'I'll be back in a minute.'

The familiar scent of his intense Creed Aventus aftershave wafted through the restaurant as he stormed away. His appearance attracted the admiring glances of the glamorous women sipping cocktails at the bar, as it always did, wherever Francis went.

I sipped the final dregs of champagne that bubbled at the bottom of the tall flute and traced the outline of the black leather pouch that the bill was neatly tucked into.

Here I was, sitting in 'our' restaurant. Nothing had changed, but everything had changed. I hated to admit that the last few days of decadence and the evening filled with fine food and fine wine had clouded my judgement somewhat. After all, if Francis hadn't done what he'd done, we'd still be having dinner here together. Perhaps even as a married couple by now.

But everything was different. It wasn't just the fact that what he'd done to me was utterly unforgivable – and a vision I'd *never* be able to wipe from my memory, no matter how much bubbly he plied me with, or how many designer gifts he bought for me.

It was the realisation that I didn't *like* my old life of endless spending any more. I hadn't given the handbags and shoes in my cupboard a second thought while I was busy preparing food in the soup kitchen. I didn't hanker for overpriced cocktails in a pretentious bar whenever Susie and I had our movie nights with dodgy pizza and cheap wine. I wasn't missing Francis's top-of-the-range car or unlimited credit card for a single minute when I was with Dan.

I'd hoped Francis was going to reappear again soon so I could let him down gently. Despite all the seriously questionable decisions he'd made, I truly believed he wasn't a bad person deep down.

The leather pouch in front of me was stamped with the

restaurant logo. I opened it and ran my fingers over the bill. Francis always paid before I had a chance to look.

Bottle of Dom Pérignon Vintage, £520
2x glasses Massolino Parussi Barolo, £80
2x winter truffle soup, £44
Chateaubriand including sides, £95
Total (not including suggested 25% gratuity)
= £739

I spat out my mouthful of champagne and it landed all over the delicate silk of my dress; my rare accomplishment of not spilling anything was sadly short-lived. I was too busy dabbing myself and the table with my napkin to notice Francis sliding back into his chair opposite me.

'What's the matter?' he snapped.

'The bill,' I squeaked.

He picked it up and scanned it. 'What? Is it wrong?' He studied the room, looking for Pierre. 'It looks right to me.' He calculated the total in his head and looked at me, perplexed.

'It's seven hundred and thirty-nine *English pounds*!' I cried.

'Yes.' Francis eyed me. 'And?'

'That's over eight hundred pounds with a tip! For one meal! Is that how much we'd usually spend?' I asked.

'No.' Francis shook his head.

I felt my shoulders relax as I breathed a sigh of relief.

'It'd usually be more,' he said nonchalantly. 'They didn't have the year of the vintage Dom I had my eye on. And we only had two glasses of Barolo, usually we'd go for the whole bottle. Plus, we didn't have dessert,' he said, pleased as punch as he placed his black credit card over the bill.

'Oh my God,' I said, 'I have to go.' I grabbed my clutch bag from the floor.

'What on earth is the matter with you? If you're freaking

out over the dinner total, it's just as well you don't know how much that suite you're staying in costs, and how much the new dress, bag and shoes set me back.'

'How much?' I asked nervously.

'All in all' – Francis leant back in his chair casually – 'probably the best part of ten k.'

'Ten k? Ten *thousand* pounds?' I shrieked. People were starting to look at us again.

'Yeah.' Francis's expression was still completely bewildered. 'Why?'

'That's *half* the money the soup kitchen needs to raise.'

Francis rolled his eyes. 'Oh, that again.'

'Yes, *that* again! If you knew how some people live their lives, the struggles they have to go through, what they experience on a day-to-day basis, maybe you'd feel terrible about blowing that sort of money so flippantly too.' I sighed and rubbed my temples before leaning forward and meeting his eyes. 'Francis, I don't think you're a terrible person, despite everything you've done. But you and me... it's never going to work, too much has happened. You think you know me, but I've changed, and I don't want to go back to my old life. I like my new life.' I smiled. 'I like it a lot.'

Francis's fringe flopped over his eyes as he dipped his gaze to the table. 'I just wanted to make it up to you,' he said quietly.

'You have, in a way,' I said. 'You've made me realise something really, really important. And I couldn't have done it without you, without all this.' I gestured around the Michelin-starred restaurant. 'Keep the bag,' I said, placing it in between us. 'I'll have the dress dry-cleaned and I'll send it back to you, and the shoes too – I don't fancy walking back to the hotel barefoot.' I looked down at them and their overpriced beauty under the table.

'Don't be ridiculous, Bella,' Francis said. 'Keep everything. Think of the outfit as an apology present. You can wear it when the soup kitchen branches out into fine dining.' He half smiled, defeated.

'I do appreciate everything you've done.' I rested my hand on his arm, before standing up from the table. 'And for being there when you knew I needed someone. I really do accept your apology, Francis, but I have to go. I have somewhere I need to be.'

THIRTY-ONE

A sea of fabric surrounded me as I sat cross-legged on the floor of my Toxteth flat. The torrential rain and forceful wind outside battered the small window next to me. My flat was tiny, a bit cold and a little damp, but there was nowhere else I'd rather be. After leaving Francis at the dinner table, I checked out of the hotel (after hugging the amazing roll-top bath goodbye). Then, I jumped on the bus back to Toxteth and collected my belongings that were still in storage. Since getting home, I'd spent hours unpacking the boxes and pulling my clothes, handbags and shoes from the cramped cupboard in my flat.

It was like every birthday or Christmas I'd known – surrounded by expensive clothing and accessories that had been gifted to me by family, friends and my fiancé. But this time, I wasn't looking forward to showing off my new outfits at a party or on holiday, I was preparing to sell them.

I remembered Susie telling me about a website where you could sell your clothes. When I'd checked it out, I discovered a premium section for designer clothes and accessories. You could sell everything second-hand and you could charge even more if they were unworn, unused or still had the label on, like most of mine did.

Piles of printed spreadsheets covered my feet. After using up all my remaining printing credit at the local internet café, I'd trawled through the website and made notes of prices to list my clothes, handbags and shoes. There was another section on the website for jewellery and watches, so I'd rescued my beloved Cartier watch from its hiding place in the loose bathroom ceiling panel. Then, I carefully wrapped everything up in tissue paper, before packaging them in pristine gift bags.

I calculated that if I sold everything I listed, it would take me to approximately £15,000 – and the sale of the watch would nudge the total over the £20,000 fundraising target for the soup kitchen. The bulk of the money would pay for all the refurbishments needed to fix the damage from the fire, including Elsie's flat. Any extra would help Dan get back on his feet with the running costs and supplies. I snapped the lid of the watch box down, leaving all my emotions and memories of my previous life inside.

Stunning Cartier watch, hardly worn, professionally cleaned, all certificates included. Selling for £6,000 or next best offer.

I scanned through all the photos I'd uploaded to my laptop – the pictures hardly did justice to its beauty. Through my research, I'd discovered that jewellers often bought unwanted jewellery from the site, so I hoped it might catch somebody's eye. The pre-worn discount made it a reasonable price for such a beautiful watch, gifted to me by my parents for my twenty-first birthday (hopefully the inscription, *To our belle petit chou*, wouldn't put anybody off – and that they wouldn't google it and find out it means 'To our beautiful little cabbage').

I took a sip of red wine and scrolled through my account. Hermès, Louis Vuitton, Chanel, Prada, Gucci, Balenciaga... all those names I'd cherished so much. The clothes, shoes and handbags that held so many memories from a past life – they'd soon be a distant dream. I clicked publish on my listings and closed my laptop.

The coffee froth lining the top of my mug threatened to overspill onto my pyjamas. My head pounded as I felt the effects of a restless night's sleep. Why would anyone want my second-hand clothes? This was supposed to be the plan that saved the soup kitchen, but what if it saved nothing? Was I being utterly naive? After Francis revealed the total cost of my staycation and designer gifts, I realised that the answer was to sell my old life – sell everything to the highest bidder. Then, I'd use the money to do something meaningful, for once in my life.

I logged into my email account and glanced at my inbox folder. I rubbed my eyes as I clocked the four-figure number in bold beside it. The sleep deprivation was clearly messing with my head. I took a gulp of the coffee, extra strong with three shots of espresso, in my mug.

Enquiries: 1,682 and counting. I scrolled through them. The messages were flooded with desperation from buyers eager to get their hands on my Hermès Birkins, Celine sunglasses, Manolo Blahnik heels, Chanel pearl necklace and every other piece that was listed. Private messages asked if I'd accept a higher offer. Some asked for same day postage and others begged for a discount. I pulled my hair up into a messy bun and polished off the rest of the coffee. This was going to take a while.

THIRTY-TWO

The next morning, after packing up almost everything I owned, I logged into the Whittington Soup email account, which I finally had access to again, after being reunited with my old work laptop that was in the box of belongings I'd left behind.

Somebody must've forgotten to delete my email account after I left, and I scrolled through the inbox before tapping on the junk folder. Nope, didn't need a penis enlarging drug. Didn't want to join a dating group to find a Sugar Daddy either. Or did I? No, I shook my head. I didn't want to recreate my shoe and handbag collection *that* badly. Or... did I? No, I shook my head decidedly again.

But as I clicked off the junk folder, an email caught my eye. And my mouth dropped open when I realised who it was from.

Later that morning, I rounded the corner of Bold Street in the city centre, under the watchful eye of St Luke's – affection-ately known as 'the bombed-out church'. The bustling street was alive with the promise of the day. It had become one of my favourite spots in Liverpool, and I appreciated its bohemian charm more than ever as the December sun shone down on it.

Animated groups laden with bags finished their Christmas shopping by scouring the area's amazing vintage shops, while hungry mouths headed for brunch, and troops of glamorous girls were already getting ready for the night, as they walked around with rollers in their hair and their faces painted with perfect make-up.

My phone bleeped with a message – it was from the person who'd written the email I'd found, plus a letter that had been shoved in the box after it was delivered to mine and Francis's apartment when I'd moved out. They were confirming our meeting, saying they were on their way.

I headed towards Leaf, the venue that my coffee date and I had agreed on – the place that used to be where we once ate and drank together, during an era that already felt like a lifetime ago. I pushed open the glass door and the blue-haired waitress gestured towards a table next to the window. Watching the world go by on Bold Street was the ideal activity to calm my nerves, the pit in the bottom of my stomach clenching tighter every time the door opened.

I checked the time on my phone. They'd be here soon.

Staring out of the window, I was entranced by the normality of life in the city centre when the shadow of a figure emerged from the other side of the table. I looked up, recognising the golden cat necklace first. It was hanging on the neck of the person I'd sat opposite for a year at Whittington Soup. It was Polly.

'Hi,' she said timidly. She wrapped her furry coat around herself tightly, in a nod to the unfamiliar atmosphere that had dawned between us, in a place that was so familiar.

'Hi,' I replied awkwardly.

'Shall I sit?' She motioned to the wooden chair opposite.

'Of course,' I said. She nodded and silently sat down.

Until I'd read her email and her letter, I was still hurt by what she'd done to me and my family. She was my work BFF until she betrayed me – the one who was always there for me, until she leaked the horrendous stories to the press about me and my family. Allegedly.

'How have you been?' she asked quietly.

'Fine,' I said evasively.

The conversation stalled, and we were both grateful to the waitress for taking our drinks order. I tapped my nails on the wooden table.

Neither of us knew where to start, until Polly took an audible, deep breath. 'I swear to you, Bella, it wasn't me who tipped off the journalists about those stories.' The words tumbled from her mouth as if she couldn't hold them in for a second longer.

'I know you said that in your email and your letter, but the tip-offs to the journalists came from your email address,' I explained.

'They did.' She nodded. 'But I promise I didn't send them. Someone else must've used my email account or my computer.' She shuffled in her seat.

I sighed and considered how everything was beginning to add up. 'To be honest, I had a nagging feeling something wasn't right when I found out it was you.' I nibbled my nail nervously. 'But when I didn't hear from you after you left, I thought maybe it was true,' I added quietly, ashamed of how naive I'd been, and what an awful friend I was for believing Jonathan over Polly.

The waitress brought our coffees over, placing them in front of us.

'I couldn't get in touch with you,' Polly said. 'Jonathan told me you were so furious and hurt by my actions that you didn't want to ever speak to me again – even though I tried to convince him it wasn't me. I left my phone on my desk, they didn't even give me a chance to pack up properly.' She shook her head at the memory. I remembered how her phone went to voicemail every time I called, and I assumed she was avoiding me out of guilt. 'I tried to find you on social media,' Polly said. 'But it was like you'd disappeared. I guessed you'd deleted your channels after everything happened.'

'I think I blocked you.' I winced, feeling petty. 'When I thought you were guilty because you were ignoring my calls. I'm sorry.'

'It's OK,' Polly said, nodding in sympathy. 'I emailed your work address and sent a letter to your apartment. I hoped they'd reach you and you'd get in touch with me.'

'That explains why I didn't,' I said. 'I didn't have access to my Whittington Soup email after I left. And I moved out of the apartment Francis and I shared when I walked in on him in a rather compromising position with Tabs.'

Polly's mouth fell open. 'No way! With Tabs?'

'Mm-hmm.' I nodded, before sipping my Americano.

'Wow.' Polly raised her eyebrows. 'You've really been through it, Bella. I hope you know that I'd never do anything to hurt you or your family. I loved every minute of working with you.'

'I did too, that's why I was so upset about it.'

'But there's something you should know,' Polly half interrupted, unable to keep her words in her mouth any longer. She leant forward, her hands clutched together on the table.

'Go on...'

'Jonathan isn't who you think he is,' she went on, her eyes pleading behind her glasses. 'Jonathan is behind *everything*, Bella, including those tip-offs from my computer. I'm sure of it. He's the reason your family lost everything.'

I sighed. 'I know. Well, I think I do.'

'Really?' Polly straightened back into the chair. Clearly, she thought it was going to be more of a battle to convince me that my dad's business partner was behind the leaked stories about my family and the boardroom vote. And possibly, something much more sinister, if what Dan had said about the suppliers and Jonathan's role in the fire was true.

'I found something on his computer,' Polly said.

My heart leapt in my chest. 'What?'

Polly leant in closer to me, over the table. 'I was working late one night, and Jonathan asked me to sort out some files on his computer. While I was organising them, I found documents that weren't on the shared cloud server. I didn't get a chance to look at them properly, but they were contracts, and you could tell he was trying to hide them.'

She pushed her glasses up her nose. 'I recognised the names of the farms on the documents because I'd been sorting out the supplier contracts and filing them in date order. But the next time I tried to look at them properly, when he left work early one night, they'd disappeared, and I couldn't find them again. I assumed he was suspicious that I'd seen them. And the next day he fired me. At first, I thought it was because I'd found what I found, but he fired me in front of everyone and said it was me who was leaking the stories about you and your family.'

'So he framed you?'

Polly nodded and brought the mug to her lips before lowering it again. 'I suppose getting rid of me was two birds, one stone. I think *he* was the person who leaked the awful stories to the press about your family, so he needed someone to take the fall for that. But he also thought I was getting too close to uncovering something I shouldn't know about. What it was exactly, I'm not entirely sure, but I think it had something to do with those contracts.'

I nodded at every word. Each piece of the puzzle was slowly coming together. But there was still one big problem. Without the evidence about the suppliers that was destroyed in the soup kitchen fire, and without the evidence of the contracts that Polly had found on Jonathan's computer, there was no way of linking the two together – there was no way of finding out the truth and exposing him.

'It's really important that we find what was on that computer,' I said. 'Something bigger is going on.' I hesitated at my instinctual mistrust of Polly, before shaking myself to sense. She was framed, she'd done nothing wrong. She was as much a victim of Jonathan as my family was. I knew I could trust her.

'What is it?' she asked.

'I think Jonathan might've planned an arson attack on a soup kitchen to get rid of evidence, and I think it's linked to those files you found.'

'Was it Dan's Kitchen in Toxteth? I read about that in the paper,' Polly said sadly. 'How awful, why on earth would Jonathan do that?' She sat back in her seat.

'We need to expose him. We need to get access to his files. If we can find the evidence, then we can use it against him.'

'Anything that leads to that awful man's comeuppance is something I'm happy to help with,' Polly said firmly. 'He never did pay me my three months' salary after firing me. And I'm still mortified after being hauled out by security guards in front of my colleagues. Plus, I never got my Fleetwood Cat mug back.'

'Aha!' I held a finger out on one hand and reached down, delving into my handbag with the other.

Polly's face lit up when I placed her beloved mug on the table – the one I'd saved from our shared workspace on my last day in the office. 'Oh my God, thank you, Bella!' She grinned while hugging the mug to her face and stroking it as if it was the fluffy cat on the front.

'Don't worry, Polly. We'll fix all this. We'll make sure Jonathan is punished for what he's done to the soup kitchen. We'll clear your name, and we'll clear my family's name. Are you in?'

'I'm in.' She nodded with vigour.

I clinked my mug against her favourite mug across the table.

THIRTY-THREE

I'd never imagined that Susie's wacky wardrobe would come in useful, but that day had arrived. Over time, she'd lent me boxes of clothes that were supposed to be 'work appropriate', but were bursting with possibilities for disguises. Much to Polly's disappointment, I'd already moved her swiftly away from the random tiaras and feather boas at the bottom of one box, reminding her that the point was to look inconspicuous.

We each chose hats that we could tuck our hair into, in our effort to go incognito. Polly teamed her fedora with a long black dress and necktie, while I was wearing a suit that Susie had previously worn to a fancy-dress party when she went as Elton John. I'd convinced Polly that the matching glasses and red wig were one step too far if the idea was for us to blend in. Instead, I opted for a beret and chunky tortoiseshell glasses with clear lenses (not the star-shaped, diamanté-encrusted ones that officially went with the outfit).

Disguises complete, we picked up our props and jumped in the Uber that would take us to the Whittington Soup headquarters in the commercial district. The busy launch that they'd been promoting on social media was the perfect setting for our plan. Flocks of people were already gathering outside, so we sat around the corner and waited for the crowds to quieten down, until we could slip inside while casually flashing our home-made press passes to the staff with clipboards.

Walking into that place again was surreal, like being in a dream. Everything was so familiar – it was my family business, somewhere I'd grown up visiting my dad, before working there myself. But the happy memories were tainted with the bitter and scheming betrayal of Jonathan.

Jonathan persuading me to join the company as PR manager made sense now. It was all part of his plan to get me and my family out. He knew he could make me look as though I couldn't handle the job if he manipulated all the leaked media stories to damage the reputation of the business, and the family behind it. Part of his plan was sabotaging my presentation at the Soup Convention too. It explained the broken USB stick and media grilling which contributed to my flustered, disastrous performance.

Most importantly, he knew that if his plan worked, then he could convince the board my family's reputation was so bad that they should vote my dad out in order to save the company. And thanks to the new by-laws that Jonathan had sneakily implemented – and my dad signed off without looking too closely because he had no reason not to trust Jonathan – all Jonathan needed was a confidential majority vote from the board, and my dad could be dismissed without a fight.

I clenched my fists as I walked past the boardroom where it had all happened. Polly and I, the bizarre-looking double act that we were, weren't going to let him get away with it. Armed with our weapons (notebook and Dictaphone) and the insider spy knowledge you can only get from binge-watching James Bond movies the night before, we'd successfully sneaked into the press conference, which was buzzing with journalists.

We knew from past soup launches that Jonathan would be

busy with the marketing team downstairs, who would hold the audience's attention with a presentation about the new launch, before a question and answer session with the media. So, Polly and I crept through the corridors that we knew so well. We were probably being a bit dramatic; we were breaking into a soup company's headquarters, not MI6. But we sneaked around carefully all the same – peeking our heads around doors before venturing in, giving each other hand signals to stop when we heard the slightest noise, and continuing when the coast was clear.

Jonathan's office was empty and locked, as we expected, but Polly knew he kept his spare key in the plant pot beside the boardroom. My hands trembled with anticipation when I turned the key in the lock, and I beamed at Polly as the door opened.

Jonathan's signature scent – expensive cigars and expensive Scotch – hit me as we walked into his office; the far wall was filled with leather-bound books and the other, a huge window that looked out onto the glorious sights of Liverpool. Polly and I clapped our hands together quietly with glee. Our plan was working! That was until she confidently typed Jonathan's password into the computer and 'incorrect' flashed over the screen in angry red letters.

'What?' Polly's eyebrows knitted together. 'He's changed it!'

My heart sank. I knew it was all going too smoothly.

'He must've done it after I left.' She sat back in the soft leather seat.

'That just shows you we're onto something,' I said to her. 'Why was he so paranoid if not?'

'True. How many guesses do you think we have?'

'Usually five,' I replied, trying hard to conceal my disappointment. This was our *only* chance to do this. To expose Jonathan. To uncover evidence about his part in the destruction of the soup kitchen and to get justice for my dad, and our family business – to restore the Whittington name and my great-grand-father's legacy.

'Try "Francis".' It was an obvious guess, but you never know.

The tone of the error alert blasted through the silence of the airy office.

I looked around the room. There was a box of his favourite cigars on the table in front of the cushy leather sofa.

'Cohiba Behike,' I said, holding the box up to her so she could see the spelling.

Another high-pitched ping.

'Two attempts left,' Polly groaned. 'We're never going to get it.'

I pinched the bridge of my nose. *Think. Think about Jonathan.* What did he love more than anything? Money, yes, but the password wasn't likely to be that. His son, of course, but obviously not enough to use his name as his password. Unless it wasn't just his name...

'Try "Francis02071990",' I said, my body practically vibrating with excitement. 'Second of July 1990; it's his birthday.'

That familiar tone pinged again – the barrier to our mission.

I walked around the room, racking my brain and trying to think about what it could possibly be. I knew we had time, but not all the time in the world. The presentation would only last an hour. Leaning against the window, I looked out across the city. The green space sat in harmony with the office blocks and luxury flats surrounding us. Below us was the staff car park; I scanned it until my eyes landed on something.

Never mind Francis, *this* was Jonathan's baby. A sparkling clean, bright red Ferrari 458 Spider parked across two parking spaces.

One space had an engraved sign reading 'Jonathan Burton, Managing Director', and the second, which used to say 'Wilfred

Whittington, Chairman', was now covered up. I dug my nails into the fleshy part of my hand as I remembered why we were here. It was our last chance.

I read the personalised licence plate out loud to Polly.

I turned around, away from the window, and Polly looked from the computer to me, her eyes shining triumphantly. 'We're in.'

'Settle down please,' Dave's voice bellowed. 'We know it's all very exciting, but we must get through the questions we're sure you're all desperate to ask!'

I hadn't missed Dave's patronising voice at all. It boomed through the microphone as the room pulsed with anticipation. Polly and I sat in our seats at the back of the auditorium. We'd missed the exciting news of the presentation, but we were sure that the news we had was going to excite the journalists in the room even more.

The chatter subsided as every head in the crowd turned their focus towards Jonathan and Dave, who were sitting behind a desk on the raised stage. The new Whittington Soup logo was emblazoned on an enormous cinema screen behind them, above a new tagline that read: 'The UK's leading luxury soup brand you can trust'. *Hmm*, I smirked. He was going to regret changing that tagline soon.

'Yes, Paul, your question please.' Dave gestured to the man in front of them.

'The news of the expansion to Europe is very exciting,' the journalist said, lifting his Dictaphone closer to the stage. 'Can you talk about the finances behind the plans? Do you have any new investors on board?'

Expanding to Europe? How the hell had Jonathan managed that? The European market was something we'd been trying to crack for years, but unless our profits quadrupled (at least) and our competitors somehow went bust, it was never something we could realistically achieve.

'We won't be dissecting the details,' Jonathan said confidently into the microphone. 'But what we can say is that Whittington Soup has never been more streamlined, and our finances – and profits – are looking better than ever.'

'Your question please, George.' Dave pointed into the crowd.

'It's been a few months since Wilfred Whittington's exit, and you took over the position as chairman. Do you have any plans to replace him?'

'None,' Jonathan said firmly. 'No plans. We're doing just fine as we are, without him.'

I pursed my lips together.

'Yes please, John.' Dave pointed to another journalist.

The man stood up. 'What do you say to the animal rights protestors who are calling for greater transparency when it comes to farming practices?'

'We'd welcome it,' Jonathan nodded earnestly. 'Of course we would. Nobody wants an animal to suffer unnecessarily. But there should be greater punishments for these people who break into farms, or infiltrate them by posing as staff members and taking photos or videos – they're radicals, they're extremists.'

'That's a strong message you're sending,' the journalist said.

'It's becoming more and more frequent.' Jonathan clasped his hands together. 'And I think it's wrong.'

Another raised hand in the audience. 'I'm assuming we can take that as confirmation that you won't be branching out into plant-based offerings any time soon.' They sniggered.

'Absolutely not.' Jonathan chortled. 'But I'd like to reaffirm that no animal will suffer unnecessarily if we have anything to do with it.'

Now was my chance. I knew it, and Polly knew it.

I stood up. 'Are you sure about that?' I said, my voice shaking.

The sea of faces turned towards me. Jonathan and Dave squinted against the bright lights of the room.

'Sorry,' Dave said, holding his hand up above his eyes to shield himself from the bright glare. 'I didn't catch your name...'

'Can you say, with absolute certainty, that Whittington Soup is an ethical company using ethical meat suppliers?'

Jonathan looked towards Dave before leaning in closer to his microphone. 'Of course,' he said confidently. 'I must direct you towards the heritage of our business, it's all in the media pack we've put together for you today. At Whittington Soup we've always prided ourselves on working with suppliers that have been approved by the appropriate ethical bodies.'

'I'm aware of your heritage.' I nodded my head, pushing my glasses further up my nose, which felt damp with the sweat of adrenaline. 'But can you confirm that is still the case? Can you confirm the contracts you have with your existing suppliers? Name them for us, perhaps?'

'I don't know about that,' Jonathan said dismissively, shuffling in his seat. 'That's private company business.'

'Is it?' I asked. 'What about, hypothetically, if the farms you work with are not in the UK? If they're superfarms in Europe? And they're proven to be unethical? What about if there was concrete evidence that showed the horrific abuse of animals and the workers being cruelly taken advantage of, with terrible conditions and an illegal pay packet that's a quarter of what they should be earning?'

'I don't see how this is relevant,' Dave stated, stony-faced, while looking over the crowds of journalists who had turned to face me in their seats. 'You said it's hypothetical. We don't work with suppliers like that. It's totally irrelevant.'

'Well, I'd say it is relevant, because it's true.' I raised the printed contracts in my hand. I wished there was an audible gasp from the audience, as if we were in a movie and this was when the bad guy got his comeuppance, but there wasn't. However, many eyes peered in my direction and looked closer at me. 'I have the contracts with those exact suppliers here.' I shook the papers, holding them up higher and showing them to the room.

Then someone stood from their seat. 'That's Arabella Whittington!' they shouted, pointing at me. 'That's Wilfred Whittington's daughter!'

Feeling like I was in a film, I dramatically removed the thick glasses from my eyes and pulled off my hat, letting my hair fall to my shoulders. Yay! *Now* there were gasps from the audience!

Jonathan pushed his seat back and it tipped over, falling to the floor with a thud. 'This is ridiculous,' he bellowed, his beady eyes peering at me. 'She's bitter because the board voted her father out of the company. She's just a silly, spoilt little girl.'

'Am I?' I locked eyes with him. 'If I'm so "silly" then how did I find these too?' I picked up the other pile of papers on my seat. 'Boardroom minutes,' I confirmed. 'Amazing what the board will do when they're manipulated, isn't it? When malicious stories about my family are leaked to the press and my father is made out to be a – and I quote – "threat to the survival of the company, thanks to the reputation of his family and his overspending".'

'He *was* a threat to the company,' Jonathan spat, aggressively pointing his fingers at me. 'And he *did* spend too much. The man was like a kid in a candy shop,' he roared. 'Why else do you think I had to change suppliers and balance the books again? Besides, those contracts don't prove anything. There's no evidence of abuse at those farms.' He chortled. 'Go back to shopping with Daddy's credit card, Arabella Whittington. Let the grown-ups get on with business.' He rolled his eyes at the audience before pulling the chair from the floor and throwing himself down on it.

I was seething, fizzing with indignation. 'There is evidence,' I said slowly, through gritted teeth. 'There's a whole load of evidence at Dan's Kitchen – the soup kitchen in Toxteth that's run by the campaigner Dan Rigby. Ring any bells?'

Jonathan glared at me, his eyes cold. 'Isn't that the soup kitchen that burnt down recently?'

'Yes,' I said, taking in his arrogant stance, sitting on the chair. He looked as though he was sunning himself on a beach in Barbados. 'Sadly, it is. The soup kitchen *did* burn down. Almost killing Dan Rigby when he tried to rescue his eighty-five-year-old grandmother who lived there.'

There were murmurs and shaking heads around the room.

'But some things weren't destroyed.'

Jonathan's relaxed rocking on the chair came to an abrupt halt and his face froze.

'Like the hundreds of hours of shocking animal abuse caught on video, and the interview testimonies of the people who work there, confirming the appalling conditions and wages. And, funnily enough, the CCTV footage that picked up your car driving past the soup kitchen on the night of the fire.'

Jonathan's face was flushed pink. 'That doesn't prove anything. The video footage was probably doctored. You know what those animal campaigners are like.' He forced a laugh and looked to the crowd desperately for backup. 'And what, so it's a crime to drive around now?'

'Of course not.' I smiled. '*Of course* it isn't a crime to drive around,' I emphasised. I felt like a lawyer in one of those high-brow American legal dramas. Or like Elle Woods in *Legally Blonde*. 'But it *is* a crime to pay two yobs to set fire to a soup kitchen.'

Jonathan's face paled from pink to white.

'Did you even consider the elderly woman who called the soup kitchen her home, who lived in the flat behind it?' This wasn't just about justice for Dan and my dad; Jonathan had to pay for what he did to Elsie too.

Jonathan's nostrils flared as his chest heaved up and down. 'Enough of this rubbish,' he exclaimed. 'This is slander. This is defamation of character...' he stammered. 'This press conference is over.' He pushed his chair back and stood up. 'Come on, Dave,' he said.

Dave sat with his hands firmly on the table, looking towards me and not meeting Jonathan's panicked eyes.

'I said, come on, Dave,' he hissed at his right-hand man.

Jonathan stormed off the stage, mumbling expletives, when Dave didn't move an inch.

The journalists turned to me with a barrage of questions and desperate pleas for an exclusive interview. Of course, the evidence *had* been destroyed in the fire and the soup kitchen couldn't afford to replace their broken CCTV system, but Jonathan didn't know that. He didn't know that Polly and I had also printed out his bank statement with payments to two shifty teenagers we'd looked up on Facebook, the day after the arson attack.

Polly and I looked at each other and grinned. We didn't have time to answer the media's questions; our next stop was the police station.

THIRTY-FOUR

An overflowing skip marked the entrance to the shell of the soup kitchen, which could be easily missed due to the destruction of the building. Despite its abandoned appearance, the sounds of people chatting and hammers hitting bricks got louder with every step I took towards it.

I carefully manoeuvred the piece of plywood that had assumed the role of a door and stepped inside. The place that held so many happy memories was still a wreck of rubble and mountains of charred bricks, but the bustle of people made it feel less eerie than its first impression from the street.

'Hey, Fred.' I clocked Dan's loyal friend piling up mounds of rubbish to be thrown in the skip. 'Is Dan here?'

'He's back there, in the kitchen.' Fred pointed behind him. 'What *was* the kitchen, I mean.'

'Looks like you're making good progress though.' I looked around the ruined space that was once the entrance hall and the children's play area.

'They've finally given us the green light to start work now that the building won't collapse any time soon,' Fred said. 'We're stripping everything out while we raise the rest of the

money to fix it up. God only knows how long that'll take, like,'
he said sadly, popping a pencil behind his ear.

I smiled, feeling the delicate crinkle of the cheque in my
pocket. I knew nobody used cheques any more; it was more
for dramatic effect when I broke the news to Dan. I didn't
think a note of a bank transfer would have quite the same
impact.

I tiptoed between the piles of debris and the ruined flooring
which had been yanked up, leaving holes that would swallow
my feet with a wrong step. The imposing door to the kitchen
was still mostly intact. Pushing it open, I heard Dan before I
saw him. The unmistakeable riffs of the Red Hot Chili Peppers
boomed from the speakers, and he looked as though he was in
one of those smash rooms where you take a hammer and destroy
everything.

'Hey,' I shouted over the music. He continued taking out his
frustration on a burnt-out cupboard.

'Hey!' I yelled louder.

He heard my voice over the music and turned to face me.
Goggles hid his eyes, while heavy layers of dust and dirt covered
his T-shirt and jeans.

'Bella?' He pulled the goggles up and wiped his sweaty forehead with his arm. 'What are you doing here?'

'I'm back,' I said. 'I'm home.'

He placed his tools of destruction on the table in front of
him. 'Oh,' he said, pulling the rubber gloves off. There was a
line of dirt that marked where they'd covered his arms.

I dragged my finger along the rough outline of what used to
be a kitchen counter, feeling suddenly nervous. 'I didn't get the
chance to explain...'

'I read your messages,' he said, 'eventually.'

I tried to hold back my optimistic smile.

'But what about Francis, your ex?' He stumbled over his
words. 'Susie said she saw you pack up and leave with him?' He

tried to act casual and brushed a gathering of dust off his T-shirt.

'It's over with him,' I said. 'It always has been,' I added quickly. 'He was just trying to help out, to give me some space away from everything. To make up for what he did, I guess...' I took a couple of tentative steps closer to Dan. 'And it did help, if I'm honest. The time away completely opened my eyes to something that's been right in front of me all along.'

Dan fiddled with the hammer on the table, stubbornly refusing to meet my desperate gaze.

'Honestly, I swear to you on Herbie's life, there's nothing going on between me and Francis.'

'You're using my dog to make me believe you?'

'You know how much I love Herbie.'

Dan folded his arms but couldn't hide the smile slowly creeping across his face. 'Bella, I have to tell you, those photos of me and Suze in the paper, of us holding hands outside the soup kitchen—'

'It doesn't matter,' I said firmly. If Dan could accept my past, then I could accept his. If he and Susie had a history, it was none of my business.

'Listen to me,' he said. 'It was a very, very short-lived thing, and we quickly realised we were better off as friends. It's something we don't even talk about now, apart from laughing about it occasionally, because it's so unimportant. It meant nothing to either of us. I just assumed you knew about it.'

'Oh,' I replied. 'That explains it then.' I breathed a sigh of relief, thankful that there wasn't some big, romantic love story, and that they would eventually realise they belonged together.

'There's something else...' I pulled the cheque from my pocket and placed it on the wooden worktop. 'Look.' I pushed it closer to Dan.

'What is this?' Dan said, his brow furrowed. 'Forty thousand pounds? Made out to the soup kitchen?'

'I raised it.' My attempts to calm my excitement at raising twice the amount needed for the refurbishment were not subtle. 'I sold all my stuff from my old life – all my designer clothes, shoes and handbags.'

I felt like I was going to burst with happiness. 'It's for you, for the soup kitchen. It's twice as much as the target, so it's enough for the building refurbishment and to fund food, supplies and staff for a while. It'll get it up and running again, and it'll cover Elsie's flat too,' I beamed.

Dan stared at the thin piece of paper in his hands. The piece of paper that was worth so much to both of us.

'I can't.' He shook his head, dust delicately falling onto his shoulders from his hair. 'This is too much.'

'You have to,' I said.

'It's charity. I'm not accepting charity,' he replied firmly.

'It isn't that at all,' I insisted. 'This place has changed my life for the better. This is my way of helping, of giving back. It's a thank you.'

He shook his head again and placed the cheque onto the makeshift table. He put his hands either side of it and leant his body over the top of it, his head dropping between his shoulders. I watched as he stood there in complete silence, the only movement was the flecks of dust still falling from his dark hair with every gentle shake of his head.

'Bella,' he finally mumbled.

'Shh,' I said. I stepped over the old toolboxes and pulled him back up from the table, so he stood over me. I balanced on my tiptoes in my hole-ridden Converse and kissed him on the lips. His kiss matched mine, softly at first, until his hands worked their way from my waist up to my neck and hair, and he kissed me hard.

'Thank you,' he whispered in my ear.

I struggled to pull myself away from him as the relief of our reunion flooded my body. 'Come on.' I wrapped my hand around his. 'Let's go and find Susie. I need to beg for her forgiveness too.'

'So, you didn't abandon us forever?' Susie sat cross-legged on her sofa, a rainbow of bright colours thanks to the various blankets and cushions strewn across it.

'Of course not,' I said. 'Do you really think I'd do that? Honestly?'

Susie shrugged stubbornly. She'd been playing hardball for the best part of an hour and I was starting to feel seriously concerned that at any moment she was going to make me get on my hands and knees and beg for her forgiveness.

'You know me, Susie. At least, I hope you do,' I said. Dan and I were planted on the oversized neon beanbags opposite her.

'But that article...'

'Absolute nonsense,' I said. 'All they wanted was a good, juicy story. They totally twisted my words.'

'They called me "Mad Susie",' she air-quoted, wrinkling her nose.

'That's because I said you're "mad as a box of frogs", which you are – you've said it yourself!'

Susie pouted at me and crossed her arms sulkily in response.

I sighed. 'I gave the interview on the promise that they'd make sure the focus of the article was the fundraising for the soup kitchen. Instead, they took my words and ran with the most salacious angle they could find. And they published it early, before I had the chance to explain to you both about my past.'

Susie fiddled with the tassels on her tie-dye T-shirt. 'Are you really an heiress? To a soup empire?'

'Was,' I corrected her. 'I *was* an heiress. I recently came to the realisation that I don't want that life – my old life. I want the life that we have' – I gestured to Dan and Susie – 'the three of us. And Elsie and Herbie, obviously.'

'You mean you're happy here in Toxteth?' Susie asked.

'I am.' I smiled, clocking the same area of damp in Susie's ceiling that was in my flat. 'I genuinely am.' I held Dan's hand next to me.

'Well,' Susie said, putting down the cushion she'd been hugging. 'It does explain a lot. We did think you were a bit of an alien when we first met you, but we just put it down to you being a Wool.'

'A Wool?' I asked.

'You know,' Susie said. 'A Wool. A Woolyback – you live near Liverpool, but not *in* Liverpool. You don't have a purple wheelie bin.'

'They're a badge of honour, let's be honest.' Dan nodded in agreement. 'Our first day together was pretty memorable anyway, who could forget your first attempt at making soup?' He laughed.

'And who doesn't know how to use a washing machine?' Susie giggled. 'Or cleans their carpet with a mop? And puts Fairy Liquid in the loo?'

'Or has never got public transport?' Dan added.

'I know.' I could hardly believe it myself. 'Quite ridiculous really.'

'A smidge,' Susie said, before looking at me happily. 'But we wouldn't have you any other way.' She stood up and held her hands outstretched; I hoisted myself up and joined her for a hug. 'Would we, Dan?'

'I don't know, I still wouldn't mind if she cleaned things properly in the first place, then I wouldn't have to go over everything afterwards.' He laughed as I playfully slapped him on the arm.

'I'm just relieved you're back, to be honest,' Susie said. 'I've been doing so much angry baking. I've eaten my bodyweight in biscuits since you've been gone.' She gestured to her kitchen. It was piled high with packed containers and plates lined with cling film, securing stacks of vegan brownies, biscuits, cakes and cookies.

'I'll happily take one for the team and help you out with these,' Dan said, peeling the cling film away from the plate filled with chocolate-covered flapjacks.

'Me too, just to help you out.' I nodded.

'You guys are too good to me.' Susie smiled, her braided hair hitting me clean in the face as she pulled me in for another warm hug.

THIRTY-FIVE

The date on my phone said it was Christmas Eve. The news on TV informed me it was Christmas Eve. My Facebook memories reminisced about it being Christmas Eve. But it didn't feel like any Christmas countdown I'd ever experienced before.

My sleep deprivation didn't stem from an evening of champagne and dancing at Alma de Cuba's Christmas party. Instead, I'd spent the night finding storage space for forty-five vegan turkeys, which felt like a task on *The Apprentice: Festive Special*. Susie and I had been hard at work, using all our charm, hustle and bribery (casks of Susie's special mulled wine worked a treat) – coupled with creative packing techniques – and the meat-free turkeys were sufficiently stored. Without any praise from Sir Alan Sugar, sadly.

A vibration from the pocket of my jeans shook me from my thoughts. It was a message from Dad. I clicked it and saw a photo of me as a young girl, dressed in a crimson velvet dress with a Santa hat on my head. I was tucking into a bowl of something delicious.

Merry Christmas Eve, my little lamb, he texted. *Your mother and I are just reminiscing about our favourite Christmases.*

Merry Christmas Eve, Dad, I replied, with lots of smiley emojis. *I think I vaguely remember that one! What am I eating though? Doesn't look like our usual Christmas Eve food. Where are the pigs in blankets? Where's the cheeseboard?*

Hang on... he typed.

The next minute, a small square lit up the screen. It was a vibrant bowl of soup.

Ernie Whittington's traditional Christmas soup, Dad said. *The best soup! Do you remember it? We always tried to replicate it the way your great-grandparents made it, but we never quite got there.*

He waited a few moments before sending his next message. *Who needs pigs in blankets or a cheeseboard when you can have soup, hey?*

It dawned on me at that moment – the temporary answer to the soup kitchen's problems.

Absolutely! I replied to Dad, with a row of soup and heart emojis.

'I thought it was December? It's bloody roasting in here!' Susie made her presence known as she prised open the door to my flat amid the chaos of vegetables packed onto every surface the tiny space would allow.

'What the...' Dan said, squeezing in behind her. They'd headed straight over after picking Elsie up from the hospital and settling her into her temporary home in Dan's flat. Thankfully, her tests had given her the all-clear and she was back just in time for Christmas.

'I know, I know. It's a little "chaotic",' I shouted above the exceptionally loud and ancient kitchen fan. I clocked Susie and Dan sharing a knowing glance with each other from the corner of my eye. 'But trust me, I have a plan.'

'Does it happen to involve seasonal veg, by any chance?'

Susie asked, pushing a giant bag of potatoes to one side and making herself comfortable on the sofa.

'Woah, woah, woah,' I cried. I turned the bubbling pan down and wiped my hands on my stained apron. 'No time for sitting,' I insisted as I marched over to her and Dan.

'Blimey, Bella,' Susie said, squinting at me. 'You look bloody awful.'

I bent down and checked my reflection in a shiny pot. I had seen better days, yes. I used my elbow to brush a stray hair away from my eye, which was swollen and red due to a lack of sleep and a diet consisting solely of advent calendar chocolate from a supermarket bin.

'Susie's right,' Dan said. 'Not about looking awful!' he quickly added, sensing the glares from the two women in the room. 'I mean, you look beautiful, of course, but maybe you should just sit down for a minute, have a cup of tea?'

'No,' I said firmly.

'Or coffee?' Susie said, staring at my knackered eyes with concern.

'No!' I insisted. 'There's no time. Can you both just stop and listen to me for a minute?'

They stared at me in complete silence, with a hint of fear etched on their tired faces.

I adjusted my apron and straightened my posture, my stomach fluttering with anticipation. 'We're going to save Christmas at the soup kitchen, and this is how we're going to do it...'

THIRTY-SIX

Rows of twinkling fairy lights, potted fir trees and makeshift Christmas artwork lined the burnt exterior walls of the soup kitchen on Christmas Day. While the fire had destroyed the front of the building, the back had just about survived and stood as an empty shell. The garden, though still covered in the evidence of the fire and the efforts to stop it, was mostly intact.

We needed to save the money I'd raised for the refurbishments, so Dan had begged and borrowed everything we needed to create the outdoor dining room I'd envisaged.

With the strict deadline of lunchtime on Christmas Day, everything had been constructed in less than twenty-four hours. Every member of the community helped in one way or another. The children of regular guests created festive paintings and drawings that decorated the blackened exterior walls and the interior of the giant gazebo that Dan had tracked down. Locals dropped off their spare chairs and the school gave us their desks so that we had enough table space. Toxteth Garden Centre even donated their ex-display furniture for more seating, and patio heaters for warmth.

Dan ransacked the soup kitchen's shed and found the

summer supplies that had been salvaged from the DIY store bins last year. There was a small fire pit we'd use to roast chestnuts and afterwards toast marshmallows on (after our debate that it might be too soon for a fire, we came to the conclusion that nothing worse could really happen).

Tinsel, wreaths and fairy lights decorated the inside of the gazebo, which was starting to take shape as a Christmas grotto. Dan had even found an abandoned Christmas tree on the roadside, which now held pride of place.

The weather forecast promised the perfect December day – dry and crisp, with fresh winter air and the hope of a light snow sprinkle. The guests simply had to bring along a bowl, a spoon and a mug, if they could, as almost all the crockery and cutlery had been ruined in the blaze. If they were able to, they could also bring a small present that would be placed in a big Santa sack and given out to everyone after dinner.

Although Elsie had only been released from hospital the day before, her clean bill of health meant she'd elbowed her way in to get involved with the efforts. Despite our pleas that she should take it easy and rest, she took it upon herself to create handmade Christmas cards for every single one of the guests.

Meanwhile, Susie split her time between helping Dan with the garden construction and me with the mammoth task of making enough food to feed three hundred people, having lost all of the frozen ingredients and prepped food to the fire.

Susie's eyelashes fluttered in the outline of glittery red and green eyeliner as she took another sniff from one of the giant pots that lined every surface in my cramped flat.

'Bella, this soup is just... I have no words,' she stated, putting the lid down.

'Wow, that's a first!' I teased as we finished packing up the soup, ready to take to the newly constructed, temporary soup kitchen.

'Seriously,' Susie said, tightening the bobbles that held her long hair up into bunches. 'How do you make soup taste *that* good? It's like Christmas in a bowl.'

I shrugged, trying to look cool and calm about the marathon effort it had taken to not only make enough soup, and on time, but also to replicate my great-grandfather's traditional Christmas soup recipe as closely as possible.

'It's cinnamon, isn't it?' Susie eyed me with a knowing look. The goggling eyes of the giant Santa face emblazoned across her jumper shifted from side to side with every slight movement she made.

I kept schtum.

'Cloves?' she questioned.

'Come on,' I said. 'Let's get a move on. It's 11 a.m. already, we're serving up soon.'

'I *will* figure it out,' Susie said, piling the pots carefully on top of each other and into the set of shopping trollies that Elsie's Knit and Natter group (or as Elsie called it, 'Stitch and Bitch') had kindly let us borrow.

After what felt like fifty trips up and down the stairs bringing all the borrowed pots, pans and containers loaded with Christmas soup down from my flat, Susie and I headed over to the soup kitchen.

Our original, pre-fire plan that the five of us (me, Dan, Susie, Elsie and Herbie, of course) would toast Christmas morning with Buck's Fizz and presents before officially opening the soup kitchen with Susie's legendary mulled wine went out the window when it became all hands on deck to save the day for the guests and volunteers who had nowhere else to go. So, I was living off adrenaline, caffeine and what could only be described as Christmas spirit.

The cold chill of the December morning tickled my nose as we walked the short distance from my flat to the soup kitchen. It was the same road that Dan and I had sprinted down when we'd followed the roaring flames that were destroying the building that meant so much to us.

'Can you believe it's Christmas Day?' Susie sighed.

'I know,' I replied. 'It feels a bit surreal, given everything that's happened. I didn't know I could function on so little sleep.'

'You've been amazing,' Susie said. 'Not just amazing. Incredible. Actually, words can't do justice to what you've done.'

'Oh, stop,' I said, shuffling along in my UGG boots, which had changed from tan to a completely different colour thanks to the various stains and splashes from my cooking marathon. 'Look at you getting all soppy, you haven't even had a mulled wine yet!'

'How do you know I haven't?' Susie turned to me and grinned cheekily, while carefully dragging the trolleys behind and in front of her. 'Seriously though,' she continued, as we turned another corner with the precariously packed trolleys. 'You came into our lives so quickly – in such a random, strange haze – but Dan and I, we adore you, Bella.'

She came to a halt and gestured for me to stop too. 'Come here, I want to hold your hand.' She pulled my red mittens into her Rudolph mittens and faced me. 'We really do. You've changed all our lives for the better. Especially Dan's. He's usually such a closed book, so guarded, but it's like he has a new lease of life since he met you. I've never, ever seen him this happy.'

I felt the butterflies in my stomach flutter.

'You have no idea how much that means to me.' I pulled Susie in for a hug. The gentle bristles of our faux fur hoods tickled each other's noses as we hugged tightly, surrounded by the soup-filled trolleys.

'MERRY CRIMBO, LESBOS!' a kid wearing a Santa hat shouted as he cycled past us.

'Can always rely on the neighbourhood toerags to ruin the mood.' Susie giggled.

'At least it's festive-themed verbal abuse today.' I grinned.

'Hey!' Dan jogged along the road with Herbie at his side. Dan's Santa hat bobbed up and down, and Herbie's tail wagged with every step he took towards us.

'Merry Christmas,' Dan said, before kissing me gently on the lips. 'Two of my favourite ladies in the world.'

'Where's the third?' I asked as he hugged Susie.

'She's at my flat, busy making her 250th Christmas card.' His full lips curled into a smile. 'She is quite possibly the most stubborn woman I've ever known in my life, although I do have a few to choose from now.'

Dan's standard uniform of an obscure band T-shirt paired with an old pair of hole-ridden jeans and knackered hoodie had been replaced with smart chinos and a garish Christmas jumper that looked like it might've even featured a button to play a tune.

Susie stood up from her cuddles with Herbie, who was wearing an equally festive red and green collar, with bells that jingled every time he moved. 'What's with the festive get-up?' Susie asked, clocking Dan's outfit and eyeing him suspiciously.

'I'm just getting into the festive spirit!' Dan announced, taking four heavy trolleys in his hands and pulling them along with ease, his muscles bulging under the snug, multicoloured jumper.

'Who is this imposter and what have you done with Dan Rigby?' Susie snorted.

'It gives you a new perspective on life when you nearly lose everything you love.' He looked up at the blackened remains of the soup kitchen building, before turning to me with a smile. 'I feel like I've lived through my own version of *It's A Wonderful Life* these last few weeks,' he said. 'Which reminds me, Bella, can I grab you for a minute?'

'Sure,' I said. 'Let's just get these pots on the heat first. I can't have my sleepless night of soup-making go to waste.'

We turned into the back gate of the soup kitchen. From the second we set foot inside the previously neglected yard, Susie and I couldn't believe what was in front of us. We'd witnessed Dan running around all day yesterday but hadn't seen the finished transformation for ourselves. Between the sparkling lights, shabby-chic decor and the rustic jumble of donated furniture, blankets and cushions, it resembled a trendy hipster bar more than a decrepit garden in a burnt-out soup kitchen.

'Wow,' I breathed, almost dropping the heavy pot in my hands.

'Bloody. Hell,' Susie added.

'Boss, ey?' Dan asked, outstretched arms showcasing his pride at his accomplishment.

'Boss?' I said. 'Dan, this is unbelievable!'

'It looks better than the actual soup kitchen would've done.' Susie managed to get her words out, despite her mouth hanging wide open.

Dan ran his fingers along the silver and gold tinsel that adorned the makeshift fences. 'Everything is donated,' he said. 'Every single person we know in the community has given us something to use today.' He turned away abruptly, just as I caught sight of the wetness in his eyes.

'It really is a Christmas miracle!' Susie chimed in, clapping her hands together.

Dan laughed as he unloaded the vats of soup onto the makeshift kitchen counter and borrowed heat-plates.

'Shall I go and get Elsie from your place, Dan?' Susie suggested. 'The guests will be arriving soon, and she'll probably want to greet everyone.'

'That'd be great, cheers, Suze.' Dan threw his keys to her. 'Please remind her to wear something warm and comfortable, not her "disco dress".' He shook his head. 'She thinks she's invincible. I have to keep reminding her that she was in a hospital bed yesterday.'

'Will do, though I can't promise that *I* won't come back wearing a "disco dress",' Susie giggled, and slipped through the little wooden gate that Dan had fixed between the crumbled walls.

'Gosh, is it hot out here or is it just me?' I pinched my jumper and moved it backwards and forwards from my chest, matching the rhythm of my racing heart.

'It definitely isn't hot,' Dan replied, 'given that it's December, in Liverpool.' He gently wrapped the ringlet that had fallen out of my messy bun around his finger and began planting kisses along the line of my exposed neck.

'Stop it,' I teased, only half serious. 'I need to get the soup warm before everyone arrives.'

'Fine,' he whispered softly in my ear, his warm breath making the hairs on the back of my neck stand up. 'But I do want to talk to you later.'

Herbie started barking at the fence as the faint sound of Slade's 'Merry Christmas Everybody' caught our attention, gradually getting louder and louder. Dan and I exchanged puzzled looks.

The gate opened and Fred wandered into the garden. His thick white hair and bushy beard meant he bore an uncanny resemblance to St Nick at the best of times, but he'd dressed for the occasion in a full Father Christmas outfit, with an old-school boombox on his shoulder.

'Merry Christmas, Dan!' he sang. 'Merry Christmas, Bella!' He held his arms out to a confused, barking Herbie. 'It's me, Herb, ya soft lad. See?' Herbie switched from terrified into excitement mode when Fred lifted his Santa hat, helping the adorable pooch to recognise him.

Dan's expression was halfway between disbelief and

delight. 'Wow,' he said, 'that's quite an entrance. You definitely look the part.'

'Well, y'know,' Fred said nonchalantly, as if he was wearing a normal work suit. 'Thought it might be nice for the kids.' He put the boombox down next to the dining table. 'Brought this so we can have some festive tunes. It's probably older than the two of you put together, but it does the job.'

'It's perfect,' I said. 'We can't have Christmas without Christmas music!'

'Fred picked up a lid and smelt the bubbling soup inside the pot. 'Bloody 'ell, Bella,' he said. 'That soup is something else, like.'

I playfully slapped his hand away and grabbed the spoon before he could dip it in for a taste. 'You'll just have to wait until everyone arrives.'

'Fine.' He sighed, and sulked back to the chair. ''Ave to say though, I was devoed when I heard we weren't gonna get a proper Crimbo dinner. Best scran of the year!'

'Erm, Fred?' Dan gestured at the ruined shell of the soup kitchen and the charred bricks.

'I know, I know, soft lad.' He waved his hand in the air. 'I just mean that for some of us round 'ere, Crimbo at Dan's is the only time of the year we get a decent roast.' Fred quickly took the hint that he wasn't going to get much sympathy from Dan, whose bloodshot eyes served as a reminder that he was still recovering from the stress of recent events. 'Anyway. My point is that Bella's soup smells like a roast in a bowl!' He gleefully slapped the table.

'Why, thank you,' I said to his cheerful smile.

'Well, now that the Christmas music has officially arrived, and Susie's getting Elsie, are we all good to go?' Dan asked, taking my hand and squeezing gently.

'We are!' I beamed, admiring our handiwork – a Christmas miracle indeed.

. . .

Small presents were exchanged, Elsie's handmade cards were gratefully received, crackers were pulled, bad jokes were told, and my special Christmas soup went down a storm. It might've been unlike any 25 December I'd ever known, and of course I missed my parents, but it was by far one of the best, if not *the best* Christmas Day I'd ever had.

After feeding three hundred hungry members of the community, the mass clean-up operation was in full swing. Everyone fiercely insisted that I wasn't allowed to lift a finger – Susie even chased me out of the kitchen while throwing sprouts at me (they're sturdier than they look!).

So, after running on an impossibly small amount of sleep over the last few days, I was beginning to doze off in a cosy spot underneath a mound of blankets next to the patio heater. But my post-Christmas-lunch nap (always the best nap of the year) was interrupted by a cold, wet nose and slobbering, enthusiastic kisses that could only belong to a mixed-breed, greedy but gorgeous, grey-eyebrowed dog called Herbie. I tapped the space next to me so he could curl up beside my legs, which he did, happily.

I stroked his fur as I looked up at the silver winter sky. There had been no snow – of course, there never was. I didn't know why I got so excited about the possibility of it every year.

'Here you both are,' Dan said, plonking himself down on the chair next to us. 'What a day.' He put two steaming mugs down on the table.

'I know, I'm exhausted.' I yawned, and Herbie copied me.

'I'm not surprised, it's been non-stop.' Dan grinned. 'But you did it, Bella. You saved Christmas at the soup kitchen. Not just that – you *saved* the soup kitchen.'

'I wouldn't go that far,' I said, feeling my cheeks flushing, a stark contrast to the cold air.

'You did.' Dan sipped his drink. Hot chocolate for him,

mulled wine for me. 'Things have been so busy, I haven't been able to ask you what I wanted to.'

'Oh gosh, yes,' I said, sipping the piping hot wine, the warmth of it lovely and soothing around my cold hands. 'Sorry, it completely slipped my mind.'

'It's fine,' he said. 'I wanted to ask you... well actually, it was Herbie's idea.' Dan gestured to him, and Herbie looked at me with his big brown eyes, trying to communicate that, yes, this was all his doing.

'Who's humanising Herbie now, hey?' I teased.

Dan took another gulp, giving himself an adorable chocolate moustache. 'You see, he's rather fond of you, our Herbs...'

I nodded.

'And he'd like you to stick around.'

I nodded again.

'Herbie would like to know if you'd consider sticking around, for good, with the two of us – and maybe calling his dad your boyfriend?'

I looked from Dan's warm eyes to Herbie's cocked head and back to Dan again. How could I say no?

THIRTY-SEVEN

Two and a half years later

I hand the box to the postman and take the receipt stating proof of postage. That's it – it's gone – my final tie to Francis Burton. Unfortunately for Francis, he's about to have a taste of a different life, just like I did. He's been sacked after being caught having an affair with his boss's wife, and has also discovered that Jonathan drained his trust fund.

Half of the money went towards Jonathan's legal fees for his trial; he'd admitted his part in the arson attack (in return for a more lenient sentence), but insisted he didn't know Elsie lived at the soup kitchen. Jonathan had been using the other half of Francis's trust fund to silently finance an 'ag-gag' campaign group which was lobbying to introduce legislation that could already be found in some states in America and areas of Australia. It criminalised the act of photographing or recording abuse in farms, therefore helping farms with unethical practices continue under a blanket of darkness and silencing any potential whistleblowers. However, their campaigning didn't get very far in the UK, and the group had disbanded after Jonathan's funding stopped.

Luckily, enough evidence eventually came to light to shut down the unethical farms in Europe that Jonathan had awarded the Whittington Soup contracts to. The farm workers were given new jobs with fair payment, and decent living and working conditions. The abused animals were roaming free and happy in the rolling hills of the charity that saved them after reading about their plight in the news.

A few months ago, I received a sheepish email from Francis, apologising for what his dad had done to me and my family. He asked if I would consider sending my engagement ring back to him. He said if he could sell the three-carat ring, it would help him start again in his new life in Scotland. I have no use for the ring, so I didn't hesitate in boxing it up and sending it away, wishing him luck for the future. Despite what he – and his dad – did, I don't bear Francis any ill will. If anything, I pity him. I know he'll have a hard time adjusting to a different lifestyle than the one he's accustomed to.

'Sorry, Bella, I almost forgot.' The postman reaches into his satchel. 'This is for you.' He hands me a magazine wrapped in paper packaging.

'Oh my God!' I shriek and clap my hands together as I realise what it is.

The postman looks at me with an amused, quizzical smile. He gives Herbie a chin tickle, offers me a friendly wave, and heads down the driveway.

Barely able to contain my excitement, I pull my phone from my pocket and dial Dan's number as I shut the front door. 'It's here!' I squeal down the phone before Dan even has a chance to say hello. 'It's here, it's here!'

'OK, calm down.' Dan laughs, and Herbie barks in excitement at my heels.

'Can you believe it?' I say.

'I can, given they told us it was coming out in June and it's now June.'

'I want to open it.'

'No!' Dan protests. 'You can't do that, we have to see it together.'

'Fine,' I sulk.

'I have a few bits to tie up here and then I'm all yours. Meet me at the soup kitchen at six? It'll still be warm thanks to this heatwave, we can sit out in the garden.'

'It's a date,' I say. 'I'll bring it with me, you get the alcohol-free prosecco chilled.'

'Deal,' Dan agrees.

I grin down the phone. Good job I'm not on FaceTime; this excitement combined with a balmy summer morning, and I can hardly wipe the sweat from my face before another layer appears.

'But, Bella, no peeking.'

'I know, I know,' I say, pulling at the sides of the brown paper packaging wrapped snugly around *Soup Story* – the bible of the soup industry.

'See you later, love you,' Dan says.

'Love you too.' I smile.

By the time 6 p.m. rolls around, I've cleaned our house from top to bottom, batch-cooked eight tubs of vegetable soup for the soup kitchen and mowed the lawn, despite having never felt the slightest inclination to so much as glance at a lawnmower in my entire life. This represents the effort required to distract myself from *Soup Story*, which I'd quickly hidden in my favourite hiding place, the fridge.

I hold the chilled package to my forehead as if it's an ice pack while Herbie and I walk the short distance from our new home in Toxteth to the soup kitchen. We're in the final stages of renovating a ground-floor flat in an old Georgian townhouse with a garden that backs onto Princes Park, much to Herbie's delight. The building has as many years of history as it does years of neglect. Every moment that we aren't at the soup kitchen (and that isn't many, as it's practically our second home) we're knocking down walls and ripping up floors. But the mammoth effort is worth it, and it's almost restored to its former glory.

I push open the wooden fence into the garden of the soup kitchen – the same spot where we held our haphazard Christmas after the fire.

'Here comes the sun,' Dan says to me, as the sunlight slowly works its way into the garden, and what was once covered by shade is lit up by the warm, dappled sunshine. 'You can't beat Liverpool this time of year.'

Dan picks up two champagne flutes from the makeshift tiki bar and places them on the table in front of us, before popping two ice cubes into Herbie's bowl to cool the water down from the stifling warmth. The pop of the zero per cent alcohol bubbly fills the air, adding to the quintessential summer soundtrack of splashing paddling pools, families laughing and mellow music in the distance.

'Where's Susie? We can't look at the magazine without her,' I say as Dan fills my glass.

'She said to go ahead, she's got something to do and she'll pop over later.'

'Ooh, is she with Jemma?'

'I think so.' Dan smiles as he sits down opposite me. Susie's met her match in the feisty stakes when it comes to her relationship with Dan's activist friend, Jemma. They're a match made in stubborn heaven.

'I love them together,' I say.

'Me too.'

'Cheers!' We clink our glasses together and I feel the warmth of the early evening sun on my face.

'OK, *please* can we open it now?' I beg, as I stop fanning myself with the paper-wrapped magazine and put it down on the table, stroking it excitedly from top to bottom. 'I've been waiting all day. I even mowed the lawn to distract myself.'

'Y'what?!' Dan cries. 'Do we have any grass left?'

'It's a little patchy.' I shrug.

Dan picks up the magazine and passes it to me. 'You open it.'

'No, you should.'

'Absolutely not,' he insists. 'You did everything to organise it, you open it.'

'OK,' I squeal, tearing off the packaging as though it's wrapping paper on a Christmas present.

'Oh wow,' Dan whispers as the paper falls away.

'Oh my God!' I cover my mouth with my hands.

'We're on the cover,' Dan says. 'The actual front cover of an actual magazine.'

'We're like soup royalty. We're the Kate and Will of the soup world!' I jump up and hug the magazine to my chest. 'I can't believe it! We're cover stars of *Soup Story*. Do you know how long I've dreamt of this moment?'

Dan stifles a laugh. I can tell it's taking every inch of his willpower to remind me that it isn't exactly *Vogue*. 'How long?' he humours me.

'Only forever!' I say with glee. 'I've had a subscription since I could read!' I sit back down. 'I wish Mum and Dad could see it.'

'We can send them a copy.' Dan shuffles his chair around the table so it's next to mine.

'An eight-page spread inside too?' Dan smiles as he runs his hands over the glossy pages. The focus of the story is how we've gone full circle – from my great-grandfather cooking in his tiny kitchen and helping people make the most of their wartime rations, to the soup kitchen branches that Dan and I have opened – twenty-one around the UK when the story went to press. And they're not just soup kitchens. We have a library and a creche in each branch, and we host adult learning classes, after-school clubs, and every community group from slimmers to swingers (dancing, not the adult activity, as Dan likes to joke at every opportunity).

'Pippa did owe us a favour though, didn't she?' I grin. 'It's nice to have her on our side, at last. Especially now that she's the editor.' I prop my sunglasses onto the top of my head as I shield my eyes from the bright sun. 'I'm so happy, Dan. I'm just so, so happy. I honestly don't think life can get much better. Is that ridiculous?'

'Well, where do you go from here, when you're a *Soup Story* cover star?' Dan teases. 'You'd better check our diary, make sure we're free for the Met Gala and the Oscars.'

'Ha ha,' I mock, taking a sip of the chilled drink. 'Very funny.'

Dan leans back into the chair next to me and I stroke his arm. The scars where his skin was burnt by the flames of the soup kitchen fire are starting to fade, as is the memory of what happened.

We don't need to say anything. We sit for a moment and enjoy the scents of warming barbecue coals being carried along in the balmy breeze.

'Bella.' Dan taps me on my arm as I begin to doze off.

I open my hazy eyes and Dan has one knee on the ground, the other bent in front of him. He takes a black box from the pocket of his ripped shorts. My heart throbs against my white vest top. As he opens the box, the sparkle of a ring I immediately recognise catches the light of the sun.

'Will you marry me?' he asks.

The vintage ring is the one I fell in love with down a back-street in Siena on our round-the-world backpacking trip.

'Yes,' I say, quietly at first. 'Yes!' I shout, as I realise what just happened – Dan proposed!

I pull his T-shirt towards me and kiss him hard on the lips. Herbie props his front paws onto my knee and tries to join in, as he always does whenever Dan and I show any affection in front of him.

'You've made me so happy, ever since you stumbled into my life.' Dan grins at me. He ruffles Herbie's fur with one hand, before taking my hand in his. 'You've changed everything for the better.' His lips touch mine again.

Dan takes the ring out of the box and gently pushes it onto my finger until the sapphire is settled into position. It caught my eye that day in Italy as the most elegant ring I'd ever seen, but it's even more beautiful up close as the sunlight reflects off the deep blue gemstone.

'We're engaged! We're actually engaged!' I clap my hands together, while Herbie wags his tail and rolls around in front of us. Such a clever boy – definitely fluent in English. 'We need to call my parents!' I shout.

Dan hit it off with my parents when we spent a week with them in France as a stop on our globe-trotting adventure – a reward to ourselves when we cut the green ribbon on our twelfth Dan's Kitchen in the UK.

I've missed Whittington Soup, but I've finally found my calling – both in life and my career – with Dan's Kitchen. And the Whittington family name has been restored after Jonathan's comeuppance. When everything came to light, the members of the Whittington Soup board begged and pleaded with my dad to return to his post as chairman. He finally agreed to go back part-time, but under the condition that he could have a better 'work-life balance' – in his words – which means he and Mum can split their time between France and Liverpool. Mum has been busy too – she's relaunched her modelling career, advertising a series of non-invasive anti-ageing solutions. She's a huge star in Ukraine, apparently.

Dad has promised his protégé, Polly, that he'll spend less time on the golf course and more time showing her the ropes at Whittington Soup, as she settles into her new role as the head of marketing and PR, where she's already flourishing. In her role, she's spearheaded Whittington Soup's new vegan range, in which they've partnered with a pioneering Swedish firm creating plant-based meats. Kudos to them, it's difficult to tell the difference. Polly has also ensured that a percentage of the profits are given to the Dan's Kitchen branches and donated to homeless shelters around the UK.

Whittington Soup has reappointed the British farmers they worked with for years, before Jonathan secretly plotted to change the suppliers. There was a flurry of amazing publicity when the company was awarded the prestigious 'From Farm to Fork' award of special recognition to its farm animal welfare work, and its commitment to source 100 per cent of its raw agricultural materials sustainably and ethically.

In short, everything is exactly as it should be.

'Fizz top-up?' Dan asks to my nod, and he dashes to the open patio doors of the kitchen.

I sit admiring my ring as it glistens with every slight movement of my hand. I hold it over the *Soup Story* front cover and fight the urge to pinch myself to see if this is really happening and isn't a dream.

'My little lamb.' I hear my dad's voice and presume Dan has phoned my parents while he's in the kitchen.

But I turn around and there he is – my dad is standing next to Mum, Susie and Elsie.

'What on earth…' Before I have the chance to process what's happening, they're all crowded around me, hugging me tightly.

'Congratulations, *mon petit chou!*' Mum plants lipstick-stained kisses all over my cheek. Susie and Elsie hug Dan closely from either side.

'I can't believe you're all here.' I throw my sunglasses onto the table and wipe my eyes. The sweat has already started to melt my eye make-up and adding tears into the mix means my mascara stands no chance.

'*We* can't believe you're engaged!' Mum says. 'This man is a hero. He deserves a medal for putting up with you,' she jokes.

'Bella deserves a medal for putting up with *him*,' Elsie says.

'The man doesn't even own a decent pair of shorts,' Susie adds.

'What's wrong with these? I've had them since I was eighteen.' Dan pulls the khaki, hole-ridden shorts at each side. 'They've served me well.'

Susie and Elsie roll their eyes and smile at my family.

'Wilf, let me show you the new barbecue.' Dan pats my dad on the back, and they wander towards the end of the garden.

'I'll get us girls some drinks,' Susie says. She heads inside the kitchen to the industrial-sized fridge, shouting over her shoulder, 'Who fancies some bubbly?'

'Woof!' Herbie barks.

'Always, darling,' Mum replies.

'I'll never say no to bubbly,' Elsie agrees.

'I'm going to stick to the Nosecco for now, thanks, Suze,' I say.

I follow Susie inside to track down more bottles of the non-alcoholic fizz, but before I can reach the newly constructed walk-in pantry, she pulls me to one side.

'Excuse me, but what's with the booze-free fizz?' she asks, nodding towards the stacked bottles suspiciously. 'Don't tell me you're teetotal now – who will I have my wine and pizza nights with?'

My natural reaction is too fast to hide, and she clocks my glance downwards.

'Oh. My. God!' Susie holds her cheekbones between her hands. 'How many weeks?'

'Shhh,' I say, looking around to make sure nobody can hear us. 'We have our twelve-week scan next week, hence the secrecy.' I rub my growing tummy. It's just about big enough that I can use the 'bloated from lunch' excuse. 'We were planning on telling everyone the minute we got back from the scan. Fingers crossed, if everything's OK.' I smile.

'It will be, I'm sure it will be.' Susie looks around to make sure nobody's near before gently placing a hand on my stomach, her big eyes wet with tears. 'Oh, Bell.'

'I know,' I say, 'I know.' I've been counting my lucky stars every single day.

In the background, our old record player plays a crackly rendition of 'All You Need Is Love' by The Beatles. And do you know what? I think they could be right.

Time passes by during a perfect evening at the soup kitchen, as we toast to new adventures and good health in the hazy Liverpool sunshine – my old life with my new life, and the life we'll soon meet.

A LETTER FROM DANIELLE

Dear reader,

I want to say a huge, heartfelt thank you for choosing to read *Stone Broke Heiress*. Readers are the people who genuinely make authors' dreams of telling stories come true. So, thank you for reading mine, and I really hope you enjoyed it.

If you would like to be the first to know about any of my book news, just sign up at the following link. Your email address will never be shared, and you can unsubscribe at any time.

www.bookouture.com/danielle-owen-jones

If you did enjoy this Liverpool love story, I would be incredibly grateful if you could write a review on Amazon or Goodreads. I'd love to hear what you think, and as a debut author, it makes an enormous difference in helping new readers to discover one of my books for the first time.

Please keep an eye out for my next book, which is out in summer 2022. It's about two strangers who buy a house together. They say opposites attract, but laid-back yoga teacher, Zack, and highly strung workaholic, Lucy, can't stand each other. What could possibly go wrong?

I love hearing from my readers – you can get in touch through Facebook, Twitter, Instagram, Goodreads or my website.

Love,

Danielle x

www.danielleowenjones.com

ACKNOWLEDGEMENTS

Firstly, thank you to you, dear reader, for taking the time to read my book! I've loved books all my life, and being a published author truly is a dream come true for me. I do hope you enjoyed my 'riches to rags' love story set in the glorious city of Liverpool.

I owe so much to my wonderful agent, Clare Coombes. Thank you for having faith in me and for giving me confidence in my writing. This book wouldn't be what it is today without your incredible input – you've transformed it in so many ways. I wanted this book to represent Liverpool in the right way, and you've been integral to that. Thank you for championing me and my writing.

Emily Gowers, my amazing editor. Thank you for taking a chance on me as a debut author. Your initial enthusiasm for the book blew me away, and I'm so grateful to have your expertise and brilliant ideas. You've shaped this book and made it the best it can be. A huge thank you to the Bookouture team too – from contracts to publicity, you're an unstoppable force, and I'm so proud to be a Bookouture author. Thanks also to the fellow authors for the warm welcome to the Bookouture family!

I can't write these acknowledgements without saying a huge thank you to an integral part of this story – the people of Liverpool. My great-grandmother grew up in Old Swan before moving to New York, but she bid farewell to Manhattan after just a few years because she missed Liverpool so much. That's Liverpool loyalty for you! I'm incredibly proud of my Scouse roots – there's nowhere like Liverpool.

I'm very lucky to have immensely supportive family and friends. We might be spread around the UK (and the globe), but as our song goes, 'We Are Family.' Thanks for always having so much faith in me: Owen-Jones's (and Nain!), Howards, Gilberts, Scurrahs and Coackleys. The family members who aren't here anymore, but always told me to follow my dreams and who would love that this book is set in Liverpool – my nana, Mary (she also made a legendary pan of Scouse!). And my grandad, David.

Of course, my oldest friends, Loren and Hannah, who especially know how much this means to me. A special shout-out to my writing cheerleader, Becky, for the excellent pep-talk-walks during lockdown, and for being an early reader when I was terrified of anyone reading my first drafts. Thanks to all my wonderful Kirkby Lonsdale pals, The Besties, Lazzle & Sazzle, The Welshies, The Journo Girls and Book Club.

The online writing community has been incredibly supportive and welcoming. Thanks for helping me to navigate the world of publishing as a debut author. Especially Meera, I'll never forget going through submission anxiety with you. Thanks for keeping me sane (as sane as you can be during submission, anyway!).

Finally, for my mum, Colette, and my husband, Tom. My two incredible cheerleaders. I honestly don't think this book would ever have been finished without you two. It would forever be confined to a hidden laptop file and my annual New Year resolutions list, where it lived for TEN years before this publication date. Thank you for giving me the confidence to do it. You've both had more faith in me than I've had in myself at times. I'm so lucky, and I'm so grateful for you both.

Finally, *finally*! Thanks to Poppy for her constantly wagging tail and unwavering general enthusiasm for life. Whenever I struggled with a plot problem while writing, it was usually solved with some time out and a cuddle from the world's happiest cockapoo.